FRIGHT FEST

THESE THREE CREEPY STORIES ARE ALSO AVAILABLE AS SEPARATE EDITIONS:

NIGHT OF THE LIVING DUMMY

DEEP TROUBLE

MONSTER BLOOD

LOOKING FOR MORE THRILLS AND CHILLS? CHECK OUT THESE OTHER FREAKY Goosebumps BOOKS:

THE HAUNTED MASK

ONE DAY AT HORRORLAND

THE CURSE OF THE MUMMY'S TOMB

BE CAREFUL WHAT YOU WISH FOR

SAY CHEESE AND DIE!

THE HORROR AT CAMP JELLYJAM

HOW I GOT MY SHRUNKEN HEAD

Goosebumps®

FRIGHT FEST

R.L. STINE

SCHOLASTIC

Scholastic Children's Books
A division of Scholastic Ltd
Euston House, 24 Eversholt Street
London, NW1 1DB, UK
Registered office: Westfield Road, Southam, Warwickshire, CV47 0RA
SCHOLASTIC, GOOSEBUMPS, and associated logos are trademarks
and/or registered trademarks of Scholastic Inc.

Goosebumps: Night of the Living Dummy
First published in the US by Scholastic Inc, 1993
Copyright © Scholastic Inc, 1993

Goosebumps: Deep Trouble
First published in the US by Scholastic Inc, 1994
Copyright © Scholastic Inc, 1994

Goosebumps: Monster Blood
First published in the US by Scholastic Inc, 1992
Copyright © Scholastic Inc, 1992

This edition published in the UK by Scholastic Ltd, 2010

Goosebumps series created by Parachute Press, Inc.
"Behind the Screams" bonus material by Matthew D. Payne and Joshua Gee

The right of R.L. Stine to be identified as the author of this work
has been asserted by him.

ISBN 978 1407 11642 6

British Library Cataloguing-in-Publication Data.
A CIP catalogue record for this book is available from the British Library.

Printed in the UK by CPI Bookmarque, Croydon
Papers used by Scholastic Children's Books are made from wood grown in
sustainable forests.

1 3 5 7 9 10 8 6 4 2

www.scholastic.co.uk/zone

3 SCARY BOOKS IN 1!

NIGHT of the LIVING DUMMY

1

DEEP TROUBLE

143

MONSTER BLOOD

271

Goosebumps®

NIGHT of the LIVING DUMMY

"Mmmmm! Mmmm! Mmmmm!"

Kris Powell struggled to get her twin sister's attention.

Lindy Powell glanced up from the book she was reading to see what the problem was. Instead of her sister's pretty face, Lindy saw a round pink bubble nearly the size of Kris's head.

"Nice one," Lindy said without much enthusiasm. With a sudden move, she poked the bubble and popped it.

"Hey!" Kris cried as the pink bubble gum exploded on to her cheeks and chin.

Lindy laughed. "Gotcha."

Kris angrily grabbed Lindy's paperback and slammed it shut. "Whoops – lost your place!" she exclaimed. She knew her sister hated to lose her place in a book.

Lindy grabbed the book back with a scowl. Kris struggled to pull the pink gum off her face.

"That was the biggest bubble I ever blew," she said angrily. The gum wasn't coming off her chin.

"I've blown much bigger than that," Lindy said with a superior sneer.

"I don't *believe* you two," their mother muttered, making her way into their bedroom and dropping a neatly folded pile of laundry at the foot of Kris's bed. "You even compete over bubble gum?"

"We're not competing," Lindy muttered. She tossed back her blonde ponytail and returned her eyes to her book.

Both girls had straight blonde hair. But Lindy kept hers long, usually tying it behind her head or on one side in a ponytail. And Kris had hers cut very short.

It was a way for people to tell the twins apart, for they were nearly identical in every other way. Both had broad foreheads and round blue eyes. Both had dimples in their cheeks when they smiled. Both blushed easily, large pink circles forming on their pale cheeks.

Both thought their noses were a little too wide. Both wished they were a little taller. Lindy's best friend, Alice, was nearly seven centimetres taller, even though she hadn't turned twelve yet.

"Did I get it all off?" Kris asked, rubbing her chin, which was red and sticky.

4

"Not all," Lindy told her, glancing up. "There's some in your hair."

"Oh, great," Kris muttered. She grabbed at her hair but couldn't find any bubble gum.

"Gotcha again," Lindy said, laughing. "You're too easy!"

Kris uttered an angry growl. "Why are you always so mean to me?"

"Me? Mean?" Lindy looked up in wide-eyed innocence. "I'm an angel. Ask anyone."

Exasperated, Kris turned back to her mother, who was stuffing socks into a dresser drawer. "Mom, when am I going to get my own room?"

"On the Twelfth of Never," Mrs Powell replied, grinning.

Kris groaned. "That's what you always say."

Her mother shrugged. "You know we don't have a spare inch, Kris." She turned to the bedroom window. Bright sunlight streamed through the filmy curtains. "It's a beautiful day. What are you two doing inside?"

"Mom, we're not little girls," Lindy said, rolling her eyes. "We're twelve. We're too old to go out and play."

"Did I get it all?" Kris asked again, still scraping pink patches of bubble gum off her chin.

"Leave it. It improves your complexion," Lindy told her.

"I wish you girls would be nicer to each other,"

Mrs Powell said with a sigh.

They suddenly heard shrill barking coming from downstairs. "What's Barky excited about now?" Mrs Powell fretted. The little black terrier was always barking about something. "Why not take Barky for a walk?"

"Don't feel like it," Lindy muttered, nose in her book.

"What about those beautiful new bikes you got for your birthday?" Mrs Powell said, hands on hips. "Those bikes you just couldn't live without. You know, the ones that have been sitting in the garage since you got them."

"OK, OK. You don't have to be sarcastic, Mom," Lindy said, closing her book. She stood up, stretched, and tossed the book on to her bed.

"You want to?" Kris asked Lindy.

"Want to what?"

"Go for a bike ride. We could ride to the playground, see if anyone's hanging out at school."

"You just want to see if Robby is there," Lindy said, making a face.

"So?" Kris said, blushing.

"Go on. Get some fresh air," Mrs Powell urged. "I'll see you later. I'm off to the supermarket."

Kris peered into the dresser mirror. She had got most of the gum off. She brushed her short hair back with both hands. "Come on. Let's go

6

out," she said. "Last one out is a rotten egg." She darted to the doorway, beating her sister by half a step.

As they burst out the back door, with Barky yipping shrilly behind them, the afternoon sun was high in a cloudless sky. The air was still and dry. It felt more like summer than spring.

Both girls were wearing shorts and sleeveless T-shirts. Lindy bent to pull open the garage door, then stopped. The house next door caught her eye.

"Look – they've got the walls up," she told Kris, pointing across their garden.

"That new house is going up so quickly. It's amazing," Kris said, following her sister's gaze.

The builders had knocked down the old house during the winter. The new concrete foundation had been put down in March. Lindy and Kris had walked around on it when no workers were there, trying to figure out where the different rooms would go.

And now the walls had been built. The construction suddenly looked like a real house, rising up in the midst of tall stacks of lumber, a big mound of red-brown earth, a pile of concrete blocks, and an assortment of power saws, tools and machinery.

"No one's working today," Lindy said.

They took a few steps towards the new house.

"Who do you think will move in?" Kris wondered. "Maybe some great-looking guy our age. Maybe great-looking twin guys!"

"Yuck!" Lindy made a disgusted face. "Twin guys? How drippy can you get! I can't believe you and I are in the same family."

Kris was used to Lindy's sarcasm. Both girls liked being twins and hated being twins at the same time. Because they shared nearly everything – their looks, their clothing, their room – they were closer than most sisters ever get.

But because they were so much alike, they also managed to drive each other crazy a lot of the time.

"No one's around. Let's check out the new house," Lindy said.

Kris followed her across the garden. A squirrel, halfway up the wide trunk of a maple tree, watched them warily.

They made their way through an opening in the low shrubs that divided the two gardens. Then, walking past the stacks of lumber and the tall mound of earth, they climbed the concrete porch.

A sheet of heavy plastic had been nailed over the opening where the front door would go. Kris pulled one end of the plastic up, and they slipped into the house.

It was dark and cool inside and had a fresh

wood smell. The plaster walls were up but hadn't been painted.

"Careful," Lindy warned. "Nails." She pointed to the large nails scattered over the floor. "If you step on one, you'll get lockjaw and die."

"You wish," Kris said.

"I don't want you to die," Lindy replied. "Just get lockjaw." She sniggered.

"Ha-ha," Kris said sarcastically. "This must be the living room," she said, making her way carefully across the front room to the fireplace against the back wall.

"A cathedral ceiling," Lindy said, staring up at the dark, exposed wooden beams above their heads. "Neat."

"This is bigger than our living room," Kris remarked, peering out the large picture window to the street.

"It smells great," Lindy said, taking a deep breath. "All the sawdust. It smells so piney."

They made their way through the hall and explored the kitchen. "Are those wires on?" Kris asked, pointing to a cluster of black electrical wires suspended from the ceiling beams.

"Why don't you touch one and find out?" Lindy suggested.

"You first," Kris shot back.

"The kitchen isn't very big," Lindy said, bending down to stare into the holes where the kitchen cabinets would go.

She stood up and was about to suggest they check out the upstairs when she heard a sound. "Huh?" Her eyes widened in surprise. "Is someone in here?"

Kris froze in the middle of the kitchen.

They both listened.

Silence.

Then they heard soft, rapid footsteps. Close by. Inside the house.

"Let's go!" Lindy whispered.

Kris was already ducking under the plastic, heading out the doorway opening. She leaped off the back porch and started running towards their garden.

Lindy stopped at the bottom of the porch and turned back to the new house. "Hey – look!" she called.

A squirrel came flying out a side window. It landed on the earth with all four feet moving and scrambled towards the maple tree in the Powells' garden.

Lindy laughed. "Just a dumb squirrel."

Kris stopped near the low shrubs. "You sure?" She hesitated, watching the windows of the new house. "That was a pretty loud squirrel."

When she turned back from the house, she was surprised to find that Lindy had disappeared.

"Hey – where'd you go?"

"Over here," Lindy called. "I see something!"

It took Kris a while to locate her sister. Lindy was half hidden behind a large black skip at the far end of the garden.

Kris shielded her eyes with one hand to see better. Lindy was bent over the side of the skip. She appeared to be rummaging through some rubbish.

"What's in there?" Kris called.

Lindy was tossing things around and didn't seem to hear her.

"What *is* it?" Kris called, taking a few reluctant steps towards the skip.

Lindy didn't reply.

Then, slowly, she pulled something out. She started to hold it up. Its arms and legs dangled down limply. Kris could see a head with brown hair.

A head? Arms and legs?

"Oh, no!" Kris cried aloud, raising her hands to her face in horror.

A child?

Kris uttered a silent gasp, staring in horror as Lindy lifted him out of the skip.

She could see his face, frozen in a wide-eyed stare. His brown hair stood stiffly on top of his head. He seemed to be wearing some sort of grey suit.

His arms and legs dangled lifelessly.

"Lindy!" Kris called, her throat tight with fear. "Is it – is he . . . *alive*?"

Her heart pounding, Kris started to run to her sister. Lindy was cradling the poor thing in her arms.

"Is he alive?" Kris repeated breathlessly.

She stopped short when her sister started to laugh.

"No. Not alive!" Lindy called gleefully.

And then Kris realized that it wasn't a child after all. "A dummy!" she shrieked.

Lindy held it up. "A ventriloquist's dummy,"

12

she said. "Someone threw him out. Do you believe it? He's in perfect shape."

It took Lindy a while to notice that Kris was breathing hard, her face bright red. "Kris, what's your problem? Oh, wow. Did you think he was a real kid?" Lindy laughed scornfully.

"No. Of course not," Kris insisted.

Lindy held the dummy up and examined his back, looking for the string to pull to make his mouth move. "I *am* a real kid!" Lindy made him say. She was speaking in a high-pitched voice through gritted teeth, trying not to move her lips.

"Dumb," Kris said, rolling her eyes.

"I am *not* dumb. You're dumb!" Lindy made the dummy say in a high, squeaky voice. When she pulled the string in his back, the wooden lips moved up and down, clicking as they moved. She moved her hand up his back and found the control to make his painted eyes shift from side to side.

"He's probably filled with bugs," Kris said, making a disgusted face. "Throw him back, Lindy."

"No way," Lindy insisted, rubbing her hand tenderly over the dummy's wooden hair. "I'm keeping him."

"She's keeping me," she made the dummy say.

Kris stared suspiciously at the dummy. His

brown hair was painted on his head. His blue eyes moved only from side to side and couldn't blink. He had bright red painted lips, curved up into an eerie smile. The lower lip had a chip on one side so that it didn't quite match the upper lip.

The dummy wore a grey double-breasted suit over a white shirt collar. The collar wasn't attached to a shirt. Instead, the dummy's wooden chest was painted white. Big brown leather shoes were attached to the ends of his thin, dangling legs.

"My name is Slappy," Lindy made the dummy say, moving his grinning mouth up and down.

"Dumb," Kris repeated, shaking her head. "Why Slappy?"

"Come over here and I'll slap you!" Lindy made him say, trying not to move her lips.

Kris groaned. "Are we going to ride our bikes to the playground or not, Lindy?"

"Afraid poor Robby misses you?" Lindy made Slappy ask.

"Put that ugly thing down," Kris replied impatiently.

"I'm not ugly," Slappy said in Lindy's squeaky voice, sliding his eyes from side to side. "You're ugly!"

"Your lips are moving," Kris told Lindy. "You're a lousy ventriloquist."

"I'll get better," Lindy insisted.

"You mean you're really keeping it?" Kris cried.

"I like Slappy. He's cute," Lindy said, cuddling the dummy against the front of her T-shirt.

"I'm cute," she made him say. "And you're ugly."

"Shut up," Kris snapped to the dummy.

"You shut up!" Slappy replied in Lindy's tight, high-pitched voice.

"What do you want to keep him for?" Kris asked, following her sister towards the street.

"I've always liked puppets," Lindy recalled. "Remember those marionettes I used to have? I played with them for hours at a time. I made up long plays with them."

"I always played with the marionettes, too," Kris remembered.

"You got the strings all tangled up," Lindy said, frowning. "You weren't any good at it."

"But what are you going to *do* with this dummy?" Kris demanded.

"I don't know. Maybe I'll work up an act," Lindy said thoughtfully, shifting Slappy to her other arm. "I'll bet I could earn some money with him. You know. Appear at kids' birthday parties. Put on shows."

"Happy birthday!" she made Slappy declare. "Hand over some money!"

Kris didn't laugh.

The two girls walked along the street in front

15

of their house. Lindy cradled Slappy in her arms, one hand up his back.

"I think he's creepy," Kris said, kicking a large pebble across the street. "You should put him back in the skip."

"No way," Lindy insisted.

"No way," she made Slappy say, shaking his head, his glassy blue eyes moving from side to side. "I"ll put *you* in the skip!"

"Slappy sure is mean," Kris remarked, frowning at Lindy.

Lindy laughed. "Don't look at me," she teased. "Complain to Slappy."

Kris scowled.

"You're jealous," Lindy said. "Because I found him and you didn't."

Kris started to protest, but they both heard voices. Kris looked up to see the two Marshall kids from down the street running towards them. They were cute redheaded kids that Lindy and Kris sometimes babysat for.

"What's that?" Amy Marshall asked, pointing at Slappy.

"Does he talk?" her younger brother, Ben, asked, staying several metres away, an uncertain expression on his freckled face.

"Hi, I'm Slappy!" Lindy made the dummy call out. She cradled Slappy in one arm, making him sit up straight, his arms dangling at his sides.

"Where'd you get him?" Amy asked.

"Do his eyes move?" Ben asked, still hanging back.

"Do *your* eyes move?" Slappy asked Ben.

Both Marshall kids laughed. Ben forgot his reluctance. He stepped up and grabbed Slappy's hand.

"Ouch! Not so hard!" Slappy cried.

Ben dropped the hand with a gasp. Then he and Amy collapsed in gleeful laughter.

"Hahahaha!" Lindy made Slappy laugh, tilting his head back and opening his mouth wide.

The two kids thought that was a riot. They laughed even harder.

Pleased by the response she was getting, Lindy glanced at her sister. Kris was sitting on the kerb, cradling her head in her hands, a dejected look on her face.

She's jealous, Lindy realized. *Kris sees that the kids really like Slappy and that I'm getting all the attention. And she's totally jealous.*

I'm definitely *keeping Slappy!* Lindy told herself, secretly pleased at her little triumph.

She stared into the dummy's bright blue painted eyes. To her surprise, the dummy seemed to be staring back at her, a twinkle of sunlight in his eyes, his grin wide and knowing.

17

3

"Who was that on the phone?" Mr Powell asked, shovelling another forkful of spaghetti into his mouth.

Lindy slipped back into her place at the table. "It was Mrs Marshall. Down the street."

"Does she want you to babysit?" Mrs Powell asked, reaching for the salad bowl. She turned to Kris. "Don't you want any salad?"

Kris wiped spaghetti sauce off her chin with her napkin. "Maybe later."

"No," Lindy answered. "She wants me to perform. At Amy's birthday party. With Slappy."

"Your first job," Mr Powell said, a smile crossing his slender face.

"Amy and Ben liked Slappy so much, they insisted on him," Lindy said. "Mrs Marshall is going to pay me twenty dollars."

"That's great!" their mother exclaimed. She passed the salad bowl across the table to her husband.

It had been a week since Lindy rescued Slappy from the skip. Every day after school, she had spent hours up in her room rehearsing with him, working on his voice, practising not moving her lips, thinking up jokes to perform with him.

Kris kept insisting the whole thing was stupid. "I can't believe you're being such a nerd," she told her sister. She refused to be an audience for Lindy's routines.

But when Lindy brought Slappy into school on Friday, Kris's attitude began to change. A group of kids had gathered around Lindy outside her locker.

As Lindy made Slappy talk for them, Kris watched from down the hall. *She's going to make a total fool of herself*, Kris thought.

But to her surprise, the kids hooted and howled. They thought Slappy was a riot. Even Robby Martin, the guy Kris had had a crush on for two years, thought Lindy was terrific.

Watching Robby laugh along with the other kids made Kris think hard. Becoming a ventriloquist might be fun.

And profitable. Lindy was going to earn twenty dollars at the Marshalls' birthday party. And when word got around, she'd probably perform at a lot of parties and earn even more money.

After dinner that evening, Lindy and Kris

washed and dried the dishes. Then Lindy asked her parents if she could practise her new comedy routine on them. She hurried up to her room to get Slappy.

Mr and Mrs Powell took a seat on the living room sofa. "Maybe Lindy will be a TV star," Mrs Powell said.

"Maybe," Mr Powell agreed, settling back on the sofa, a pleased smile on his face. Barky yapped and climbed between Mr and Mrs Powell, his tiny stub of a tail wagging furiously.

"You know you're not allowed on the sofa," Mrs Powell said, sighing. But she made no move to push Barky off.

Kris sat down away from the others, on the floor by the steps, cradling her chin in her hands.

"You're looking glum this evening," her father remarked.

"Can I get a dummy, too?" Kris asked. She hadn't really planned to say it. The question just popped out of her mouth.

Lindy came back into the room, carrying Slappy around the waist. "Ready?" she asked. She pulled a dining room chair into the centre of the living room and sat down on it.

"Well, can I?" Kris repeated.

"You really want one, too?" Mrs Powell asked, surprised.

"Want *what*?" Lindy asked, confused.

"Kris says she wants a dummy, too," Mrs Powell reported.

"No way," Lindy said heatedly. "Why do you want to be such a copycat?"

"It looks like fun," Kris replied, her cheeks turning bright pink. "If you can do it, I can do it, too," she added shrilly.

"You always copy everything I do," Lindy protested angrily. "Why don't you find something of your own for once? Go upstairs and work on your junk jewellery collection. That's *your* hobby. Let *me* be the ventriloquist."

"Girls"– Mr Powell started, raising a hand for quiet –"please, don't fight over a dummy."

"I really think I'd be better at it," Kris said. "I mean, Lindy isn't very funny."

"Everyone thinks I'm funny," Lindy insisted.

"That's not very nice, Kris," Mrs Powell scolded.

"Well, I just think if Lindy has one, I should be able to have one, too," Kris said to her parents.

"Copycat," Lindy repeated, shaking her head. "You've been putting me down all week. You said it was nerdy. But I know why you changed your mind. You're upset because I'm going to earn some money and you're not."

"I really wish you two wouldn't argue about *everything*," Mr Powell said disgustedly.

"Well, can I have a dummy?" Kris asked him.

"They're expensive," Mr Powell replied, glancing at his wife. "A good one will cost more than a hundred dollars. I really don't think we can afford to buy one now."

"Why don't you both share Slappy?" Mrs Powell suggested.

"Huh?" Lindy's mouth dropped open in protest.

"You two always share everything," Mrs Powell continued. "So why don't you share Slappy?"

"But, Mom—" Lindy whined unhappily.

"Excellent idea," Mr Powell interrupted. He motioned to Kris. "Try it out. After you share him for a while, I'm sure one of you will lose interest in him. Maybe even both of you."

Kris climbed to her feet and walked over to Lindy. She reached out for the dummy. "I don't mind sharing," she said quietly, searching her sister's eyes for approval of the idea. "Can I hold him for just a second?"

Lindy held on to Slappy tightly.

Suddenly the dummy's head tilted back and his mouth opened wide. *"Beat it, Kris!"* he snarled in a harsh, raspy voice. *"Get lost, you stupid moron!"*

Before Kris could back away, Slappy's wooden hand shot up, and he slapped her hard across the face.

"Ow!"

Kris screamed and raised her hand to her cheek, which was bright pink. She stepped back. "Stop it, Lindy! That *hurt*!"

"Me?" Lindy cried. "I didn't do it! Slappy did!"

"Don't be dumb," Kris protested, rubbing her cheek. "You really hurt me."

"But I didn't do it!" Lindy cried. She turned Slappy's face towards her. "Why were you so rude to Kris?"

Mr Powell jumped up from the sofa. "Stop acting dumb and apologize to your sister," he ordered.

Lindy bowed Slappy's head. "I'm sorry," she made the dummy say.

"No. In your own voice," Mr Powell insisted, crossing his arms in front of his chest. "Slappy didn't hurt Kris. You did."

"OK, OK," Lindy muttered, blushing. She

avoided Kris's angry stare. "I'm sorry. Here." She dumped Slappy into Kris's arms.

Kris was so surprised, she nearly dropped the dummy. Slappy was heavier than she'd imagined.

"Now what am I supposed to do with him?" Kris asked Lindy.

Lindy shrugged and crossed the room to the sofa, where she dropped down beside her mother.

"Why'd you make such a fuss?" Mrs Powell whispered, leaning close to Lindy. "That was so babyish."

Lindy blushed. "Slappy is *mine*! Why can't something be mine for once?"

"Sometimes you girls are so nice to each other, and sometimes. . ." Mrs Powell's voice trailed off.

Mr Powell took a seat on the padded arm of the chair across the room.

"How do I make his mouth work?" Kris asked, tilting the dummy upside down to examine its back.

"There's a string in his back, inside the slit in his jacket," Lindy told her grudgingly. "You just pull it."

I don't want Kris to work Slappy, Lindy thought unhappily.

I don't want to share Slappy.

Why can't I have something that just belongs

24

to me? Why do I have to share everything with her?

Why does Kris always want to copy me?

She gritted her teeth and waited for her anger to fade.

Later that night, Kris sat straight up in bed. She'd had a bad dream.

I was being chased, she remembered, her heart still pounding. Chased by what? By whom?

She couldn't remember.

She glanced around the shadowy room, waiting for her heartbeat to return to normal. The room felt hot and stuffy, even though the window was open and the curtains were fluttering.

Lindy lay sound asleep on her side in the twin bed next to Kris's. She was snoring softly, her lips slightly parted, her long hair falling loose about her face.

Kris glanced at the clock radio on the bedside table between the two twin beds. It was nearly three in the morning.

Even though she was now wide awake, the nightmare wouldn't completely fade away. She still felt uncomfortable, a little frightened, as if she were still being chased by someone or something. The back of her neck felt hot and prickly.

She turned and fluffed up her pillow, propping

25

it higher on the headboard. As she lay back on it, something caught her eye.

Someone sitting in the chair in front of the bedroom window. Someone staring at her.

After a sharp intake of breath, she realized it was Slappy.

Yellow moonlight poured over him, making his staring eyes glow. He was sitting up in the chair, tilted to the right at a slight angle, one arm resting on the slender arm of the chair.

His mouth locked in a wide, mocking grin, his eyes seemed to be staring right at Kris.

Kris stared back, studying the dummy's expression in the eerie yellow moonlight. Then, without thinking, without even realizing what she was doing, she climbed silently out of bed.

Her foot got tangled in the bedsheet and she nearly tripped. Kicking the sheet away, she made her way quickly across the room to the window.

Slappy stared up at her as her shadow fell over him. His grin seemed to grow wider as Kris leaned closer.

A gust of wind made the soft curtains flutter against her face. Kris pushed them away and peered down at the dummy's painted head.

She reached a hand out and rubbed his wooden hair, shining in the moonlight. His head felt warm, warmer than she'd imagined.

Kris quickly jerked her hand away.

What was that sound?

Had Slappy sniggered? Had he laughed at her?

No. Of course not.

Kris realized she was breathing hard.

Why am I so freaked out by this stupid dummy? she thought.

In the bed behind her, Lindy made a gurgling sound and rolled on to her back.

Kris stared hard into Slappy's big eyes, gleaming in the light from the window. She waited for him to blink or to roll his eyes from side to side.

She suddenly felt foolish.

He's just a stupid wooden dummy, she told herself.

She reached out and pushed him over.

The stiff body swung to the side. The hard head made a soft *clonk* as it hit the wooden arm of the chair.

Kris stared down at him, feeling strangely satisfied, as if she'd somehow taught him a lesson.

The curtains rustled against her face again. She pushed them away.

Feeling sleepy, she started back to bed.

She had only gone one step when Slappy reached up and grabbed her wrist.

"Oh!" As the hand tightened around her wrist, Kris cried out and spun around.

To her surprise, Lindy was crouched beside her. Lindy had a tight grip on Kris's wrist.

Kris jerked her hand from Lindy's grasp.

Moonlight through the window lit up Lindy's devilish grin. "Gotcha again!" she declared.

"You didn't scare me!" Kris insisted. But her voice came out a trembling whisper.

"You jumped a mile!" Lindy exclaimed gleefully. "You really thought the dummy grabbed you."

"Did not!" Kris replied. She hurried to her bed.

"What were you doing up, anyway?" Lindy demanded. "Were you messing with Slappy?"

"No. I . . . uh . . . had a bad dream," Kris told her. "I just went to look out the window."

Lindy sniggered. "You should've seen the look on your face."

"I'm going back to sleep. Leave me alone," Kris snapped. She pulled the covers up to her chin.

Lindy pushed the dummy back to a sitting position. Then she returned to her bed, still chuckling over the scare she'd given her sister.

Kris rearranged her pillows, then glanced across the room to the window. The dummy's face was half covered in shadow now. But the eyes glowed as if he were alive. And they stared into hers as if they were trying to tell her something.

Why does he have to grin like that? Kris asked herself, trying to rub away the prickling feeling on the back of her neck.

She pulled up the sheet, settled into the bed, and turned on her side, away from the wide staring eyes.

But even with her back turned, she could feel them gazing at her. Even with her eyes closed and the covers pulled up to her head, she could picture the shadowy, distorted grin, the unblinking eyes. Staring at her. Staring. Staring.

She drifted into an uncomfortable sleep, drifted into another dark nightmare. Someone was chasing her. Someone very evil was chasing her.

But who?

On Monday afternoon, Lindy and Kris both

stayed after school to rehearse for the spring concert. It was nearly five when they arrived home, and they were surprised to see their dad's car in the driveway.

"You're home so early!" Kris exclaimed, finding him in the kitchen helping their mother prepare dinner.

"I'm leaving tomorrow for a sales conference in Portland," Mr Powell explained, peeling an onion over the sink with a small paring knife. "So I only worked half a day today."

"What's for dinner?" Lindy asked.

"Meat loaf," Mrs Powell replied, "if your father ever gets the onion peeled."

"There's a trick to not crying when you peel an onion," Mr Powell said, tears rolling down his cheeks. "Wish I knew it."

"How was chorus rehearsal?" Mrs Powell asked, kneading a big ball of red minced beef in her hands.

"Boring," Lindy complained, opening the refrigerator and taking out a can of Coke.

"Yeah. We're doing all these Russian and Yugoslavian songs," Kris said. "They're so sad. They're all about sheep or something. We don't really know what they're about. There's no translation."

Mr Powell rushed to the sink and began splashing cold water on his red, runny eyes. "I can't take this!" he wailed. He tossed the half-peeled onion back to his wife.

"Crybaby," she muttered, shaking her head.

Kris headed up the stairs to drop her backpack in her room. She tossed it on to the desk she shared with Lindy, then turned to go back downstairs.

But something by the window caught her eye.

Spinning around, she gasped.

"Oh, no!" The startled cry escaped her lips.

Kris raised her hands to her cheeks and stared in disbelief.

Slappy was propped up in the chair in front of the window, grinning at her with his usual wide-eyed stare. And seated beside him was another dummy, also grinning at her.

And they were holding hands.

"What's going on here?" Kris cried aloud.

"Do you like him?"

At first, Kris thought that Slappy had asked the question.

She gaped in stunned disbelief.

"Well? What do you think of him?"

It took Kris a long moment to realize that the voice was coming from behind her. She turned to find her father standing in the doorway, still dabbing at his eyes with a wet dishtowel.

"The – the new dummy?" Kris stammered.

"He's for you," Mr Powell said, stepping into the room, the wet towel pressed against both eyes.

"Really?" Kris hurried over to the chair and picked the new dummy up to examine him.

"There's a tiny pawnshop on the corner across from my office," Mr Powell said, lowering the towel. "I was walking past and, believe it or not, this guy was in the window. He was cheap, too. I think the pawnbroker was glad to get rid of him."

"He's . . . cute," Kris said, searching for the right word. "He looks just like Lindy's dummy, except his hair is bright red, not brown."

"Probably made by the same company," Mr Powell said.

"His clothes are better than Slappy's," Kris said, holding the dummy out at arm's length to get a good view. "I hate that stupid grey suit on Lindy's dummy."

The new dummy wore blue denim jeans and a red and green flannel shirt. And instead of the formal-looking, shiny brown shoes, he had white high-top trainers on his feet.

"So you like him?" Mr Powell asked, smiling.

"I *love* him!" Kris cried happily. She crossed the room and gave her dad a hug.

Then she picked up the dummy and ran out of the room, down the stairs, and into the kitchen. "Hey, everybody! Meet Mr Wood!" she declared happily, holding the grinning dummy up in front of her.

Barky yapped excitedly, leaping up to nip at the dummy's trainers. Kris pulled her dummy away.

"Hey!" Lindy cried in surprise. "Where'd you get that?"

"From Daddy," Kris said, her grin wider than the dummy's. "I'm going to start practising with him after dinner, and I'm going to be a better ventriloquist than you."

"Kris!" Mrs Powell scolded. "Everything isn't a competition, you know!"

"I already have a job with Slappy," Lindy said with a superior sneer. "And you're just getting started. You're just a beginner."

"Mr Wood is much better-looking than Slappy," Kris said, mirroring her twin's sneer. "Mr Wood is cool-looking. That grey suit on your dummy is the pits."

"You think that ratty old shirt is cool-looking?" Lindy scoffed, making a disgusted face. "Yuck. That old dummy probably has worms!"

"*You* have worms!" Kris exclaimed.

"Your dummy won't be funny," Lindy said nastily, "because you don't have a sense of humour."

"Oh, yeah?" Kris replied, tossing Mr Wood over her shoulder. "I *must* have a sense of humour. I put up with *you*, don't I?"

"Copycat! Copycat!" Lindy cried angrily.

"Out of the kitchen!" Mrs Powell ordered with an impatient shriek. "Out! Get out! You two are impossible! The dummies have better personalities than either of you!"

"Thanks, Mom," Kris said sarcastically.

"Call me for dinner," Lindy called back. "I'm going upstairs to practise my act with Slappy for the birthday party on Saturday."

It was the next afternoon, and Kris was sitting at the dressing table she shared with Lindy.

Kris rummaged in the jewellery box and pulled out another string of brightly coloured beads. She slipped them over her head and untangled them from the other three strands of beads she was wearing. Then she gazed at herself in the mirror, shaking her head to better see the long dangly earrings.

I love my junk jewellery collection, she thought, digging into the depths of the wooden jewellery box to see what other treasures she could pull out.

Lindy had no interest in the stuff. But Kris could spend hours trying on the beads, fingering the dozens of little charms, running her fingers over the plastic bracelets, jangling the earrings. Her jewellery collection always cheered her up.

She shook her head again, making the long earrings jangle. A knock on the bedroom door made her spin around.

"Hey, Kris, how's it going?" Her friend Cody Matthews stepped into the room. He had straight white-blond hair and pale grey eyes in a slender, serious face. Cody always looked as if he were deep in thought.

"You ride your bike over?" Kris asked, removing several strands of beads at once and tossing them into the jewellery box.

"No. Walked," Cody replied. "Why'd you call? You just want to hang out?"

"No." Kris jumped to her feet. She walked over to the chair by the window and grabbed Mr Wood. "I want to practise my act."

Cody groaned. "I'm the guinea pig?"

"No. The audience. Come on."

She led him out to the bent old maple tree in the middle of her garden. The afternoon sun was just beginning to lower itself in the clear spring-blue sky.

She raised one foot against the tree trunk and propped Mr Wood on her knee. Cody sprawled on his back in the shade. "Tell me if this is funny," she instructed.

"OK. Shoot," Cody replied, narrowing his eyes in concentration.

Kris turned Mr Wood to face her. "How are you today?" she asked him.

"Pretty good. Knock wood," she made the dummy say.

She waited for Cody to laugh, but he didn't. "Was that funny?" she asked.

"Kinda," he replied without enthusiasm. "Keep going."

"OK." Kris lowered her head so that she was face-to-face with her dummy. "Mr Wood," she said, "why were you standing in front of the mirror with your eyes closed?"

"Well," answered the dummy in a high-pitched, squeaky voice, "I wanted to see what I look like when I'm asleep!"

36

Kris tilted the dummy's head back and made him look as if he were laughing. "How about that joke?" she asked Cody.

Cody shrugged. "Better, I guess."

"Aw, you're no help!" Kris screamed angrily. She lowered her arms, and Mr Wood crumpled on to her lap. "You're supposed to tell me if it's funny or not."

"I guess *not*," Cody said thoughtfully.

Kris groaned. "I need some good joke books," she said. "That's all. Some good joke books with some really funny jokes. Then I'd be ready to perform. Because I'm a pretty good ventriloquist, right?"

"I guess," Cody replied, pulling up a handful of grass and letting the moist green blades sift through his fingers.

"Well, I don't move my lips very much, *do* I?" Kris demanded.

"Not too much," Cody allowed. "But you don't really throw your voice."

"No one can throw her voice," Kris told him. "It's just an illusion. You make people *think* you're throwing your voice. You don't *really* throw it."

"Oh," Cody said, pulling up another handful of grass.

Kris tried out several more jokes. "What do you think?" she asked Cody.

"I think I have to go home," Cody said. He

tossed a handful of grass at her.

Kris brushed the green blades off Mr Wood's wooden head. She rubbed her hand gently over the dummy's painted red hair. "You're hurting Mr Wood's feelings," she told Cody.

Cody climbed to his feet. "Why do you want to mess with that thing, anyway?" he asked, pushing his white-blond hair back off his forehead.

"Because it's fun," Kris replied.

"Is that the real reason?" Cody demanded.

"Well . . . I guess I want to show Lindy that I'm better at it than she is."

"You two are *weird*!" Cody declared. "See you in school." He gave her a little wave, then turned and headed for his home down the street.

Kris pulled down the blankets and climbed into bed. Pale moonlight filtered in through the bedroom window.

Yawning, she glanced at the clock radio. Nearly ten. She could hear Lindy brushing her teeth in the bathroom across the hall.

Why does Lindy always hum when she brushes her teeth? Kris wondered. *How can one twin sister do so many annoying things?*

She gave Mr Wood one last glance. He was propped in the chair in front of the window, his hands carefully placed in his lap, his white trainers hanging over the chair edge.

He looks like a real person, Kris thought sleepily.

Tomorrow I'm going to check out some good joke books from the library at school. I can be funnier than Lindy. I know *I can.*

She settled back sleepily on her pillow. *I'll be asleep as soon as we turn off the lights*, she thought.

A few seconds later, Lindy entered the room, wearing her nightshirt and carrying Slappy under one arm. "You asleep?" she asked Kris.

"Almost," Kris replied, yawning loudly. "I've been studying for the maths exam all night. Where've you been?"

"Over at Alice's," Lindy told her, setting Slappy down in the chair beside Mr Wood. "Some kids were over, and I practised my act for them. They laughed so hard, I thought they'd split a gut. When Slappy and I did our rap routine, Alice spat her chocolate milk out her nose. What a riot!"

"That's nice," Kris said without enthusiasm. "Guess you and Slappy are ready for Amy's birthday party on Saturday."

"Yeah," Lindy replied. She placed Slappy's arm around Mr Wood's shoulder. "They look so cute together," she said. Then she noticed the clothing neatly draped over the desk chair. "What's that?" she asked Kris.

Kris raised her head from the pillow to see

what her sister was pointing at. "My outfit for tomorrow," she told her. "We're having a dress-up party in Miss Finch's class. It's a farewell party. For Margot. You know. The student teacher."

Lindy stared at the clothes. "Your Betsey Johnson skirt? Your silk blouse?"

"We're supposed to get really dressed up," Kris said, yawning. "Can we go to sleep now?"

"Yeah. Sure." Lindy made her way to her bed, sat down, and clicked off the bedside table lamp. "Are you getting any better with Mr Wood?" she asked, climbing between the sheets.

Kris was stung by the question. It was such an obvious put-down. "Yeah. I'm getting really good. I did some stuff for Cody. Out in the garden. Cody laughed so hard, he couldn't breathe. Really. He was holding his sides. He said Mr Wood and I should be on TV."

"Really?" Lindy replied after a long moment's hesitation. "That's weird. I never thought Cody had much of a sense of humour. He's always so grim. I don't think I've ever seen him laugh."

"Well, he was laughing at Mr Wood and me," Kris insisted, wishing she were a better liar.

"Awesome," Lindy muttered. "I can't wait to see your act."

Neither can I, Kris thought glumly.

A few seconds later, they were both asleep. Their mother's voice, calling from downstairs, awoke them at seven the next morning. Bright morning-orange sunlight poured in through the window. Kris could hear birds chirping happily in the old maple tree.

"Rise and shine! Rise and shine!" Every morning, Mrs Powell shouted up the same words.

Kris rubbed the sleep from her eyes, then stretched her arms high over her head. She glanced across the room, then uttered a quiet gasp. "Hey – what's going on?" She reached across to Lindy's bed and shook Lindy by the shoulder. "What's going on?"

"Huh?" Lindy, startled, sat straight up.

"What's the joke? Where is he?" Kris demanded.

"Huh?"

Kris pointed to the chair across the room.

Sitting straight up in the chair, Slappy grinned back at them, bathed in morning sunlight.

But Mr Wood was gone.

7

Kris blinked several times and pushed herself up in bed with both hands. Her left hand tingled. She must have been sleeping on it, she realized.

"What? What's wrong?" Lindy asked, her voice fogged with sleep.

"Where's Mr Wood?" Kris demanded impatiently. "Where'd you put him?"

"Huh? Put him?" Lindy struggled to focus her eyes. She saw Slappy sitting stiffly on the chair across the room. By himself.

"It's not funny," Kris snapped. She climbed out of bed, pulled down the hem of her nightshirt, and made her way quickly to the chair in front of the window. "Don't you ever get tired of playing stupid jokes?"

"Jokes? Huh?" Lindy lowered her feet to the floor.

Kris bent down to search the floor under the chair. Then she moved to the foot of the bed and got down on her knees to search under both twin beds.

"Where *is* he, Lindy?" she asked angrily, on her knees at the foot of the bed. "I don't think this is funny. I really don't."

"Well, neither do I," Lindy insisted, standing up and stretching.

Kris climbed to her feet. Her eyes went wide as she spotted the missing dummy.

"Oh!"

Lindy followed her sister's startled gaze.

Mr Wood grinned at them from the doorway. He appeared to be standing, his skinny legs bent at an awkward angle.

He was wearing Kris's dress-up clothes, the Betsey Johnson skirt and the silk blouse.

Her mouth wide open in surprise, Kris made her way quickly to the doorway. She immediately saw that the dummy wasn't really standing on his own. He had been propped up, the doorknob shoved into the opening in his back.

She grabbed the dummy by the waist and pulled him away from the door. "My blouse. It's all wrinkled!" she cried, holding it so Lindy could see. She narrowed her eyes angrily at her sister. "This was so obnoxious of you, Lindy."

"Me?" Lindy shrieked. "I swear, Kris, I didn't do it. I slept like a rock last night. I didn't move. I didn't get up till you woke me. I didn't do it. Really!"

Kris stared hard at her sister, then lowered her eyes to the dummy.

In her blouse and skirt, Mr Wood grinned up at her, as if enjoying her bewilderment.

"Well, Mr Wood," Kris said aloud, "I guess you put on my clothes and walked to the door all by yourself!"

Lindy started to say something. But their mother's voice from downstairs interrupted. "Are you girls going to school today? Where *are* you? You're late!"

"Coming!" Kris called down, casting an angry glance at Lindy. She carefully set Mr Wood down on his back on her bed and pulled her skirt and blouse off him. She looked up to see Lindy making a mad dash across the hall to be first in the bathroom.

Sighing, Kris stared down at Mr Wood. The dummy grinned up at her, a mischievous grin on his face.

"Well? What's going on?" she asked the dummy. "I didn't dress you up and move you. And Lindy swears *she* didn't do it."

But if we didn't do it, she thought, *who did?*

"Tilt his head forward," Lindy instructed. "That's it. If you bounce him up and down a little, it'll make it look like he's laughing."

Kris obediently bounced Mr Wood on her lap, making him laugh.

"Don't move his mouth so much," Lindy told her.

"I think you're both crazy," Lindy's friend Alice said.

"So what else is new?" Cody joked.

All four of them were sitting in a small patch of shade under the bent old maple tree in the Powells' garden. It was a hot Saturday afternoon, the sun high in a pale blue sky, streaks of yellow light filtering down through the shifting leaves above their heads.

Barky sniffed busily around the garden, his little tail wagging non-stop.

Kris sat on a folding chair, which leaned back against the gnarled tree trunk. She had Mr

45

Wood on her lap.

Lindy and Alice stood at the edge of the shade, their hands crossed over their chests, watching Kris's performance with frowns of concentration on their faces.

Alice was a tall, skinny girl with straight black hair down to her shoulders, a snub nose, and a pretty, heart-shaped mouth. She was wearing white shorts and a bright blue midriff top.

Cody was sprawled on his back in the grass, his hands behind his head, a long blade of grass between his teeth.

Kris was trying to show off her ventriloquist skills. But Lindy kept interrupting with "helpful" suggestions. When she wasn't making suggestions, Lindy was nervously glancing at her watch. She didn't want to be late for her job at Amy's birthday party at two o'clock.

"I think you're way weird," Alice told Lindy.

"Hey, no way," Lindy replied. "Slappy is a lot of fun. And I'm going to make a lot of money with him. And maybe I'll be a comedy star or something when I'm older." She glanced at her watch again.

"Well, everyone at school thinks that both of you are weird," Alice said, swatting a fly off her bare arm.

"Who cares?" Lindy replied sharply. "They're all weird, too."

"And so are you," Kris made Mr Wood say.

"I could see your lips move," Lindy told Kris.

Kris rolled her eyes. "Give me a break. You've been giving me a hard time all morning."

"Just trying to help," Lindy said. "You don't have to be so defensive, do you?"

Kris uttered an angry growl.

"Was that your stomach?" she made Mr Wood say.

Cody laughed.

"At least *one* person thinks you're funny," Lindy said dryly. "But if you want to do parties, you really should get some better jokes."

Kris let the dummy slump to her lap. "I can't find any good joke books," she said dejectedly. "Where do you find your jokes?"

A superior sneer formed on Lindy's face. She tossed her long hair behind her shoulder. "I make up my own jokes," she replied snootily.

"You *are* a joke!" Cody said.

"Ha-ha. Remind me to laugh later," Lindy said sarcastically.

"I can't believe you don't have *your* dummy out here," Alice told Lindy. "I mean, don't you want to rehearse for the party?"

"No need," Lindy replied. "I've got my act down. I don't want to over-rehearse."

Kris groaned loudly.

"Some of the other parents are staying at the

birthday party to watch Slappy and me," Lindy continued, ignoring Kris's sarcasm. "If the kids like me, their parents might hire me for *their* parties."

"Maybe you and Kris should do an act together," Alice suggested. "That could be really awesome."

"Yeah. What an act! Then there'd be *four* dummies!" Cody joked.

Alice was the only one to laugh.

Lindy made a face at Cody. "That might actually be fun," she said thoughtfully. And then she added, "When Kris is ready."

Kris drew in her breath and prepared to make an angry reply.

But before she could say anything, Lindy grabbed Mr Wood from her hands. "Let me give you a few pointers," Lindy said, putting one foot on Kris's folding chair and arranging Mr Wood on her lap. "You have to hold him up straighter, like this."

"Hey – give him back," Kris demanded, reaching for her dummy.

As she reached up, Mr Wood suddenly lowered his head until he was staring down at her. "*You're a jerk!*" he rasped in Kris's face, speaking in a low, throaty growl.

"Huh?" Kris pulled back in surprise.

"*You're a stupid jerk!*" Mr Wood repeated nastily in the same harsh growl.

"Lindy – stop it!" Kris cried.

Cody and Alice both stared in open-mouthed surprise.

"Stupid moron! Get lost! Get lost, stupid jerk!" the dummy rasped in Kris's face.

"Whoa!" Cody exclaimed.

"Make him stop!" Kris screamed at her sister.

"I can't!" Lindy cried in a trembling voice. Her face became pale, her eyes wide with fear. "I can't make him stop, Kris! He – he's speaking for himself!"

The dummy glared at Kris, its grin ugly and evil.

"I – I can't make him stop. I'm not doing it," Lindy cried. Tugging with all her might, she pulled Mr Wood out of Kris's face.

Cody and Alice flashed each other bewildered glances.

Frightened, Kris raised herself from the folding chair and backed up against the tree trunk. "He – he's talking on his own?" She stared hard at the grinning dummy.

"I – I think so. I'm . . . all mixed up!" Lindy declared, her cheeks bright pink.

Barky yipped and jumped on Lindy's legs, trying to get her attention. But she kept her gaze on Kris's frightened face.

"This is a joke – right?" Cody asked hopefully.

"What's going on?" Alice demanded, her arms crossed in front of her chest.

Ignoring them, Lindy handed Mr Wood back

to Kris. "Here. Take him. He's yours. Maybe *you* can control him."

"But, Lindy—" Kris started to protest.

Lindy glared at her watch. "Oh, no! The party! I'm late!" Shaking her head, she took off towards the house. "Later!" she called without looking back.

"But, Lindy—" Kris called.

The kitchen door slammed behind Lindy.

Holding Mr Wood by the shoulders, Kris lowered her eyes to his face. He grinned up at her, a devilish grin, his eyes staring intently into hers.

Kris swung easily, leaning back and raising her feet into the air. The chains squeaked with every swing. The old garden swing set, half covered with rust, hadn't been used much in recent years.

The early evening sun was lowering itself behind the house. The aroma of a roasting chicken floated out from the kitchen window. Kris could hear her mother busy in the kitchen preparing dinner.

Barky yapped beneath her. Kris dropped her feet to the ground and stopped the swing to avoid kicking him. "Dumb dog. Don't you know you could get hurt?"

She looked up to see Lindy come running up the driveway, holding Slappy under her arm. From the smile on Lindy's face, Kris knew at once that the birthday party had been a triumph. But she had to ask anyway. "How'd it go?"

"It was awesome!" Lindy exclaimed. "Slappy and I were *great*!"

Kris pulled herself off the swing and forced a smile to her face. "That's nice," she offered.

"The kids thought we were a riot!" Lindy continued. She pulled Slappy up. "Didn't they, Slappy?"

"They liked me. Hated you!" Slappy declared in Lindy's high-pitched voice.

Kris forced a laugh. "I'm glad it went OK," she said, trying hard to be a good sport.

"I did a sing-along with Slappy, and it went over really well. Then Slappy and I did our rap routine. What a hit!" Lindy gushed.

She's spreading it on a little thick, Kris thought bitterly. Kris couldn't help feeling jealous.

"The kids all lined up to talk to Slappy," Lindy continued. "Didn't they, Slappy?"

"Everyone loved me," she made the dummy say. "Where's my share of the loot?"

"So you got paid twenty dollars?" Kris asked, kicking at a clump of weeds.

"Twenty-five," Lindy replied. "Amy's mom said I was so good, she'd pay me extra. Oh. And guess what else? You know Mrs Evans? The woman who always wears the leopardskin trousers? You know – Anna's mom? She asked

52

me to do Anna's party next Sunday. She's going to pay me *thirty* dollars! I'm going to be rich!"

"Wow. Thirty dollars," Kris muttered, shaking her head.

"I get twenty. You get ten," Lindy made Slappy say.

"I have to go tell Mom the good news!" Lindy said. "What have you been doing all afternoon?"

"Well, after you left, I was pretty upset," Kris replied, following Lindy to the house. "You know. About Mr Wood. I – I put him upstairs. Alice and Cody went home. Then Mom and I went to the mall."

His tail wagging furiously, Barky ran right over their feet, nearly tripping both of them. "Barky, look out!" Lindy yelled.

"Oh. I nearly forgot," Kris said, stopping on the back porch. "Something good happened."

Lindy stopped, too. "Something good?"

"Yeah. I ran into Mrs Berman at the mall." Mrs Berman was their music teacher and organizer of the spring concert.

"Thrills," Lindy replied sarcastically.

"And Mrs Berman asked if Mr Wood and I wanted to be master of ceremonies for the spring concert." Kris smiled at her sister.

Lindy swallowed hard. "She asked *you* to host the concert?"

"Yeah. I get to perform with Mr Wood in front

53

of everyone!" Kris gushed happily. She saw a flash of jealousy on Lindy's face, which made her even happier.

Lindy pulled open the screen door. "Well, good luck," she said dryly. "With that weird dummy of yours, you'll *need* it."

Dinner was spent talking about Lindy's performance at Amy Marshall's birthday party. Lindy and Mrs Powell chatted excitedly. Kris ate in silence.

"At first I thought the whole thing was strange, I have to admit," Mrs Powell said, scooping ice cream into bowls for dessert. "I just couldn't believe you'd be interested in ventriloquism, Lindy. But I guess you have a flair for it. I guess you have some talent."

Lindy beamed. Mrs Powell normally wasn't big on compliments.

"I found a book in the school library about ventriloquism," Lindy said. "It had some pretty good tips in it. It even had a comedy routine to perform." She glanced at Kris. "But I like making up my own jokes better."

"You should watch your sister's act," Mrs Powell told Kris, handing her a bowl of ice cream. "I mean, you could probably pick up some pointers for the concert at school."

"Maybe," Kris replied, trying to hide how annoyed she was.

After dinner, Mr Powell called from Portland,

and they all talked with him. Lindy told him about her success with Slappy at the birthday party. Kris told him about being asked to host the concert with Mr Wood. Her father promised he wouldn't schedule any road trips so that he could attend the concert.

After watching a video their mother had rented at the mall, the two sisters went up to their room. It was a little after eleven.

Kris clicked on the light. Lindy followed her in.

They both glanced across the room to the chair where they kept the two dummies – and gasped.

"Oh, no!" Lindy cried, raising one hand to her wide-open mouth.

Earlier that night, the dummies had been placed side by side in a sitting position.

But now Slappy was upside down, falling out of the chair, his head on the floor. His brown shoes had been pulled off his feet and tossed against the wall. His suit jacket had been pulled halfway down his arms, trapping his hands behind his back.

"L-look!" Kris stammered, although her sister was already staring in horror at the scene. "Mr Wood – he's. . ." Kris's voice caught in her throat.

Mr Wood was sprawled on top of Slappy. His hands were wrapped around Slappy's throat, as if he were strangling him.

10

"I – I don't believe this!" Kris managed to whisper. She turned and caught the frightened expression on Lindy's face.

"What's going *on*?" Lindy cried.

Both sisters hurried across the room. Kris grabbed Mr Wood by the back of the neck and pulled him off the other dummy. She felt as if she were separating two fighting boys.

She held Mr Wood up in front of her, examining him carefully, staring at his face as if half expecting him to talk to her.

Then she lowered the dummy and tossed it face down on to her bed. Her face was pale and taut with fear.

Lindy stooped and picked up Slappy's brown shoes from the floor. She held them up and studied them, as if they would offer a clue as to what had happened.

"Kris – did you do this?" Lindy asked softly.

"Huh? Me?" Kris reacted with surprise.

"I mean, I *know* you're jealous of Slappy and me—" Lindy started.

"Whoa. Wait a minute," Kris replied angrily in a shrill, trembling voice. "I didn't do this, Lindy. Don't accuse me."

Lindy glared at her sister, studying her face. Then her expression softened and she sighed. "I don't get it. I just don't get it. Look at Slappy. He's nearly been torn apart."

She set the shoes down on the chair and picked the dummy up gently, as if picking up a baby. Holding him in one hand, she struggled to pull his suit jacket up with the other.

Kris heard her sister mutter something. It sounded like "Your dummy is evil."

"What did you say?" Kris demanded.

"Nothing," Lindy replied, still struggling with the jacket. "I'm . . . uh . . . I'm kind of scared about this," Lindy confessed, blushing, avoiding Kris's eyes.

"Me, too," Kris admitted. "Something weird is going on. I think we should tell Mom."

Lindy buttoned the jacket. Then she sat down on the bed with Slappy on her lap and started to replace the dummy's shoes. "Yeah. I guess we should," she replied. "It – it's just so creepy."

Their mother was in bed, reading a Stephen King novel. Her bedroom was dark except for a tiny reading lamp on her headboard that threw

57

down a narrow triangle of yellow light.

Mrs Powell uttered a short cry as her two daughters appeared out of the shadows. "Oh! You startled me. This is such a scary book, and I think I was just about to fall asleep."

"Can we talk to you?" Kris asked eagerly in a low whisper.

"Something weird is going on," Lindy added.

Mrs Powell yawned and closed her book. "What's wrong?"

"It's about Mr Wood," Kris said. "He's been doing a lot of strange things."

"Huh?" Mrs Powell's eyes opened wide. She looked pale and tired under the harsh light from the reading lamp.

"He was strangling Slappy," Lindy reported. "And this afternoon, he said some really gross things. And—"

"Stop!" Mrs Powell ordered, raising one hand. "Just stop."

"But, Mom—" Kris started.

"Give me a break, girls," their mother said wearily. "I'm tired of your silly competitions."

"You don't understand," Lindy interrupted.

"Yes, I *do* understand," Mrs Powell said sharply. "You two are even competing with those ventriloquist dummies."

"Mom, please!"

"I want it to stop right now," Mrs Powell

insisted, tossing the book on to her bedside table. "I mean it. I don't want to hear another word from either of you about those dummies. If you two have problems, settle it between yourselves."

"Mom, listen—"

"And if you can't settle it, I'll take the dummies away. Both of them. I'm serious." Mrs Powell reached above her head and clicked off the reading light, throwing the room into darkness. "Good night," she said.

The girls had no choice but to leave the room. They slunk down the hall in silence.

Kris hesitated at the doorway to their bedroom. She expected to find Mr Wood strangling Slappy again. She breathed a sigh of relief when she saw the two dummies on the bed, where they had been left.

"Mom wasn't too helpful," Lindy said dryly, rolling her eyes. She picked up Slappy and started to arrange him in the chair in front of the window.

"I think she was asleep and we woke her up," Kris replied.

She picked up Mr Wood and started towards the chair with him – then stopped. "You know what? I think I'm going to put him in the closet tonight," she said thoughtfully.

"Good idea," Lindy said, climbing into bed.

Kris glanced down at the dummy, half

...act. To complain. To start

...od grinned up at her, his painted
...nd lifeless.

...felt a chill of fear.

*...m becoming afraid of a stupid ventriloquist's
dummy,* she thought.

*I'm shutting him up in the closet tonight
because I'm afraid.*

She carried Mr Wood to the closet. Then, with
a groan, she raised him high above her head and
slid him on to the top shelf. Carefully closing the
closet door, listening for the click, she made her
way to her bed.

She slept fitfully, tossing on top of the covers,
her sleep filled with disturbing dreams. She awoke
to find her nightshirt completely twisted, cutting
off the circulation to her right arm. She struggled
to straighten it, then fell back to sleep.

She awoke early, drenched in sweat. The sky
was still dawn-grey outside the window.

The room felt hot and stuffy. She sat up slowly,
feeling weary, as if she hadn't slept at all.

Blinking away the sleep, her eyes focused on
the chair in front of the window.

There sat Slappy, exactly where Lindy had
placed him.

And beside him sat Mr Wood, his arm around
Slappy's shoulder, grinning triumphantly at Kris
as if he had just pulled off a wonderful joke.

"Now, Mr Wood, do you go to school?"

"Of course I do. Do you think I'm a dummy?"

"And what's your favourite class?"

"Woodshop, of course!"

"What project are you building in shop class, Mr Wood?"

"I'm building a *girl* dummy! What else? Ha-ha! Think I want to spend the rest of my life on *your* lap?!"

Kris sat in front of the dressing table mirror with Mr Wood on her lap, studying herself as she practised her routine for the school concert.

Mr Wood had been well-behaved for two days. No frightening, mysterious incidents. Kris was beginning to feel better. Maybe everything would go OK from now on.

She leaned close to the mirror, watching her lips as she made the dummy talk.

61

The b's and the m's were impossible to pronounce without moving her lips. She'd just have to avoid those sounds as best she could.

I'm getting better at switching from Mr Wood's voice back to mine, she thought happily. *But I've got to switch faster. The faster he and I talk, the funnier it is.*

"Let's try it again, Mr Wood," she said, pulling her chair closer to the mirror.

"Work, work, work," she made the dummy grumble.

Before she could begin the routine, Lindy came rushing breathlessly into the room. Kris watched her sister in the mirror as she came up behind her, her long hair flying loosely over her shoulders, an excited smile on her face.

"Guess what?" Lindy asked.

Kris started to reply, but Lindy didn't give her a chance.

"Mrs Petrie was at Amy Marshall's birthday party," Lindy gushed excitedly. "She works for Channel Three. You know. The TV station. And she thinks I'm good enough to go on *Talent Search*, the show they have every week."

"Huh? Really?" was all Kris could manage in reply.

Lindy leaped excitedly in the air and cheered. "Slappy and I are going to be on TV!" she cried. "Isn't that *fabulous*?"

62

Staring at her sister's jubilant reflection in the mirror, Kris felt a stab of jealousy.

"I've got to tell Mom!" Lindy declared. "Hey, Mom! Mom!" She ran from the room. Kris heard her shouting all the way down the stairs.

"Aaaaaargh!" Kris couldn't hold it in. She uttered an angry cry.

"Why does everything good happen to Lindy?" Kris screamed aloud. "I'm hosting a stupid concert for maybe a hundred parents – and she's going to be on TV! I'm just as good as she is. Maybe better!"

In a rage, she raised Mr Wood high over her head and slammed him to the floor.

The dummy's head made a loud *clonk* as it hit the hardwood floor. The wide mouth flew open as if about to scream.

"Oh." Kris struggled to regain her composure.

Mr Wood, crumpled at her feet, stared up at her accusingly.

Kris lifted him up and cradled the dummy against her. "There, there, Mr Wood," she whispered soothingly. "Did I hurt you? Did I? I'm so sorry. I didn't mean to."

The dummy continued to stare up at her. His painted grin hadn't changed, but his eyes seemed cold and unforgiving.

It was a still night. No breeze. The curtains in front of the open bedroom window didn't flutter

63

or move. Pale silver moonlight filtered in, creating long purple shadows that appeared to creep across the girls' bedroom.

Lindy had been sleeping fitfully, a light sleep filled with busy, colourful dreams. She was startled awake by a sound. A gentle *thud*.

"Huh?" She raised her head from the damp pillow and turned.

Someone was moving in the darkness.

The sounds she'd heard were footsteps.

"Hey!" she whispered, wide awake now. "Who is it?"

The figure turned in the doorway, a shadow against even blacker shadows. "It's only me," came a whispered reply.

"Kris?"

"Yeah. Something woke me up. My throat is sore," Kris whispered from the doorway. "I'm going down to the kitchen for a glass of water."

She disappeared into the shadows. Her head still raised off the pillow, Lindy listened to her footsteps padding down the stairs.

When the sounds faded, Lindy shut her eyes and lowered her head to the pillow.

A few seconds later, she heard Kris's scream of horror.

Her heart pounding, Lindy struggled out of bed. The sheet tangled around her legs, and she nearly fell.

Kris's blood-curdling scream echoed in her ears.

She practically leaped down the dark stairway, her bare feet thudding hard on the thin carpet of the steps.

It was dark downstairs, except for a thin sliver of yellow light from the kitchen.

"Kris – Kris – are you OK?" Lindy called, her voice sounding small and frightened in the dark hallway.

"Kris?"

Lindy stopped at the kitchen doorway.

What was that eerie light?

It took her a while to focus. Then she realized she was staring at the dim yellow light from inside the refrigerator.

The refrigerator door was wide open.

And . . . the refrigerator was empty.

"What – what's going on here?"

She took a step into the kitchen. Then another.

Something cold and wet surrounded her foot.

Lindy gasped and, looking down, saw that she had stepped into a wide puddle.

An overturned milk carton beside her foot revealed that the puddle was spilled milk.

She raised her eyes to Kris, who was standing in darkness across the room, her back against the wall, her hands raised to her face in horror.

"Kris, what on earth—"

The scene was coming into focus now. It was all so weird, so . . . *wrong*. It was taking Lindy a long time to see the whole picture.

But now, following Kris's horrified stare, Lindy saw the mess on the floor. And realized why the refrigerator was empty.

Everything inside it had been pulled out and dumped on the kitchen floor. An orange juice bottle lay on its side in a puddle of orange juice. Eggs were scattered everywhere. Fruits and vegetables were strewn over the floor.

"Oh!" Lindy moaned in utter disbelief.

Everything seemed to sparkle and gleam.

What was all that shiny stuff among the food?

Kris's jewellery!

There were earrings and bracelets and strands of beads tossed everywhere, mixed with the spilled, strewn food like some kind of bizarre salad.

"Oh, no!" Lindy shrieked as her eyes came to rest on the figure on the floor.

Sitting upright in the middle of the mess was Mr Wood, grinning gleefully at her. He had several strands of beads around his neck, long dangling earrings hanging from his ears, and a platter of leftover chicken on his lap.

"Kris, are you *OK*?" Lindy cried, turning her eyes away from the grinning, jewellery-covered dummy.

Kris didn't seem to hear her.

"Are you OK?" Lindy repeated the question.

"Wh-what's going on?" Kris stammered, her back pressed against the wall, her expression taut with terror. "Who – who *did* this? Did Mr Wood—?"

Lindy started to reply. But their mother's howl of surprise from the doorway cut off her words. "Mom—" Lindy cried, spinning around.

Mrs Powell clicked on the ceiling light. The kitchen seemed to flare up. All three of them blinked, struggling to adjust to the sudden brightness.

"What on earth!" Mrs Powell cried. She started to call her husband, then remembered he wasn't home. "I – I don't believe this!"

Barky came bounding into the room, his tail

68

wagging. He lowered his head and started to lick up some spilled milk.

"Out you go," Mrs Powell said sternly. She picked up the dog, carried him out, and closed the kitchen door. Then she strode into the centre of the room, shaking her head, her bare feet narrowly missing the puddle of milk.

"I came down for a drink, and I – I found this mess," Kris said in a trembling voice. "The food. My jewellery. Everything. . ."

"Mr Wood did it," Lindy accused. "Look at him!"

"*Stop it! Stop it!*" Mrs Powell screamed. "I've had enough."

Mrs Powell surveyed the mess, frowning and tugging at a strand of blonde hair. Her eyes stopped on Mr Wood, and she uttered a groan of disgust.

"I knew it," she said in a low voice, raising her eyes accusingly to the two girls. "I knew this had something to do with those ventriloquist dummies."

"Mr Wood did it, Mom," Kris said heatedly, stepping away from the wall, her hands tensed into fists. "I know it sounds dumb, but—"

"Stop it," Mrs Powell ordered, narrowing her eyes. "This is just sick. Sick!" She stared hard at the jewel-bedecked dummy, who grinned up at her over the big platter of chicken.

"I'm going to take the dummies away from

you both," Mrs Powell said, turning back to Lindy and Kris. "This whole thing has just got out of control."

"No!" Kris cried.

"That's not fair!" Lindy declared.

"I'm sorry. They have to be put away," Mrs Powell said firmly. She let her eyes move over the cluttered floor and let out another weary sigh. "Look at my kitchen."

"But I didn't do anything!" Lindy screamed.

"I need Mr Wood for the spring concert!" Kris protested. "Everyone is counting on me, Mom."

Mrs Powell glanced from one to the other. Her eyes stayed on Kris. "That's *your* dummy on the floor, right?"

"Yeah," Kris told her. "But I didn't do this. I swear!"

"You both swear you didn't do it, right?" Mrs Powell said, suddenly looking very tired under the harsh ceiling light.

"Yes," Lindy answered quickly.

"Then you both lose your dummies. I'm sorry," Mrs Powell said. "One of you is lying. I – I really can't believe this."

A heavy silence blanketed the room as all three Powells stared down in dismay at the mess on the floor.

Kris was the first to speak. "Mom, what if Lindy and I clean everything up?"

Lindy caught on quickly. Her face brightened.

"Yeah. What if we put everything back? Right now. Make the kitchen just like normal. Make it spotless. Can we keep our dummies?"

Mrs Powell shook her head. "No. I don't think so. Look at this mess. All the vegetables are spoiled. And the milk."

"We'll replace it all," Kris said quickly. "With our allowance. And we'll clean it up perfectly. Please. If we do that, give us one more chance?"

Mrs Powell twisted her face in concentration, debating with herself. She stared at her daughters' eager faces. "OK," she replied finally. "I want the kitchen spotless when I come down in the morning. All the food, all the jewellery. Everything back where it goes."

"OK," both girls said in unison.

"And I don't want to see either of those dummies down here in my kitchen again," Mrs Powell demanded. "If you can do that, I'll give you one more chance."

"Great!" both girls cried at once.

"And I don't want to hear any more arguments about those dummies," Mrs Powell continued. "No more fights. No more competing. No more blaming everything on the dummies. I don't want to hear *anything* about them. Ever."

"You won't," Kris promised, glancing at her sister.

"Thanks, Mom," Lindy said. "You go to bed.

We'll clean up." She gave her mother a gentle shove towards the doorway.

"Not another word," Mrs Powell reminded them.

"Right, Mom," the twins agreed.

Their mother disappeared towards her room. They began to clean up. Kris pulled a large rubbish bag from the drawer and held it open while Lindy tossed in empty cartons and spoiled food.

Kris carefully collected her jewellery and carried it upstairs.

Neither girl spoke. They worked in silence, picking up, scrubbing, and mopping until the kitchen was clean. Lindy closed the refrigerator door. She yawned loudly.

Kris inspected the floor on her hands and knees, making sure it was spotless. Then she picked up Mr Wood. He grinned back at her as if it was all a big joke.

This dummy has been nothing but trouble, Kris thought.

Nothing but trouble.

She followed Lindy out of the kitchen, clicking off the light as she left. The two girls climbed the stairs silently. Neither of them had spoken a word.

Pale moonlight filtered into their room through the open window. The air felt hot and steamy.

Kris glanced at the clock. It was a little past

three in the morning.

Slappy sat slumped in the chair in front of the window, moonlight shining on his grinning face. Lindy, yawning, climbed into bed, pushed down the blanket, and pulled up the sheet. She turned her face away from her sister.

Kris lowered Mr Wood from her shoulder. *You're nothing but trouble*, she thought angrily, holding him in front of her and staring at his grinning face.

Nothing but trouble.

Mr Wood's wide, leering grin seemed to mock her.

A chill of fear mixed with her anger.

I'm beginning to hate this dummy, she thought.

Fear him and hate him.

Angrily, she pulled open the closet door and tossed the dummy into the closet. It fell in a crumpled heap on the floor.

Kris slammed the closet door shut.

Her heart thudding, she climbed into bed and pulled up the covers. She suddenly felt very tired. Her entire body ached from weariness.

She buried her face in the pillow and shut her eyes.

She had just about fallen asleep when she heard the tiny voice.

"Let me out! Let me out of here!" it cried. A muffled voice, coming from inside the closet.

"Let me out! Let me out!" the high-pitched voice called angrily.

Kris sat up with a jolt. Her entire body convulsed in a shudder of fear.

Her eyes darted to the other bed. Lindy hadn't moved.

"Did – did you hear it?" Kris stammered.

"Hear what?" Lindy asked sleepily.

"The voice," Kris whispered. "In the closet."

"Huh?" Lindy asked sleepily. "What are you talking about? It's three in the morning. Can't we get some sleep?"

"But, Lindy—" Kris lowered her feet to the floor. Her heart was thudding in her chest. "Wake up. Listen to me! Mr Wood was calling to me. He was *talking*!"

Lindy raised her head and listened.

Silence.

"I don't hear anything, Kris. Really. Maybe you were dreaming."

"No!" Kris shrieked, feeling herself lose control. "It wasn't a dream! I'm so scared, Lindy. I'm just so *scared*!"

Suddenly, Kris was trembling all over, and hot tears were pouring down her cheeks.

Lindy stood up and moved to the edge of her sister's bed.

"Something h-horrible is going on here, Lindy," Kris stammered through her tears.

"And I know who's doing it," Lindy whispered, leaning over her twin, putting a comforting hand on her quivering shoulder.

"Huh?"

"Yes. I know who's been doing it all," Lindy whispered. "I know who it is."

"Who?" Kris asked breathlessly.

"Who?" Kris repeated, letting the tears run down her cheeks. "Who?"

"*I* have," Lindy said. Her smile spread into a grin almost as wide as Slappy's. She closed her eyes and laughed.

"Huh?" Kris didn't understand. "What did you say?"

"I said I have been doing it," Lindy repeated. "Me. Lindy. It was all a joke, Kris. I gotcha again." She nodded as if confirming her words.

Kris gaped at her twin in disbelief. "It was all a joke?"

Lindy kept nodding.

"You moved Mr Wood during the night? You dressed him in my clothes and made him say those gross things to me? You put him in the kitchen? You made that horrible mess?"

Lindy chuckled. "Yeah. I really scared you, didn't I?"

Kris balled her hands into angry fists.

"But – but—" she sputtered. "*Why?*"

"For fun," Lindy replied, dropping back on to her bed, still grinning.

"Fun?"

"I wanted to see if I could scare you," Lindy explained. "It was just a joke. You know. I can't *believe* you fell for that voice in the closet just now! I must be a really good ventriloquist!"

"But, Lindy—"

"You really believed Mr Wood was alive or something!" Lindy said, laughing, enjoying her victory. "You're such a nit!"

"Nit?"

"Half a nitwit!" Lindy burst into wild laughter.

"It isn't funny," Kris said softly.

"I know," Lindy replied. "It's a riot! You should've seen the look on your face when you saw Mr Wood downstairs in your precious beads and earrings!"

"How – how did you ever *think* of such a mean joke?" Kris demanded.

"It just came to me," Lindy answered with some pride. "When you got your dummy."

"You didn't want me to get a dummy," Kris said thoughtfully.

"You're right," Lindy quickly agreed. "I wanted something that would be mine for a change. I'm so tired of you being a copycat. So—"

"So you thought of this mean joke," Kris accused.

Lindy nodded.

Kris strode angrily to the window and pressed her forehead against the glass. "I – I can't believe I was so stupid," she muttered.

"Neither can I," Lindy agreed, grinning again.

"You really made me start thinking that Mr Wood was alive or something," Kris said, staring out the window to the garden below. "You really made me afraid of him."

"Aren't I brilliant!" Lindy proclaimed.

Kris turned to face her sister. "I'm never speaking to you again," she said angrily.

Lindy shrugged. "It was just a joke."

"No," Kris insisted. "It was too mean to be just a joke. I'm never speaking to you again. Never."

"Fine," Lindy replied curtly. "I thought you had a sense of humour. Fine." She slid into bed, her back to Kris, and pulled the covers up over her head.

I've got to find a way to pay her back for this, Kris thought. *But how?*

After school a few days later, Kris walked home with Cody. It was a hot, humid afternoon. The trees were still and seemed to throw little shade on the pavement. The air above the road shimmered in the heat.

"Wish we had a swimming pool," Kris muttered, pulling her backpack off her shoulder.

"I wish you had one, too," Cody said, wiping his forehead with the sleeve of his red T-shirt.

"I'd like to dive into an enormous pool of iced tea," Kris said, "like in the TV commercials. It always looks so cold and refreshing."

Cody made a face. "Swim in iced tea? With ice cubes and lemon?"

"Forget it," Kris muttered.

They crossed the street. A couple of kids they knew rode by on their bikes. Two men in white uniforms were up on ladders, leaning against the corner house, painting the guttering.

"Bet they're hot," Cody remarked.

"Let's change the subject," Kris suggested.

"How are you doing with Mr Wood?" Cody asked.

"Not bad," Kris said. "I think I've got some pretty good jokes. I should be ready for the concert tomorrow night."

They stopped at the corner and let a large blue van rumble past.

"Are you talking to your sister?" Cody asked as they crossed the street. The bright sunlight made his white-blond hair glow.

"A little," Kris said, making a face. "I'm talking to her. But I haven't forgiven her."

"That was such a dumb stunt she pulled," Cody said sympathetically. He wiped the sweat off his forehead with the sleeve of his T-shirt.

"It just made me feel like such a dork," Kris admitted. "I mean, I was so stupid. She really had me believing that Mr Wood was doing all that stuff." Kris shook her head. Thinking about it made her feel embarrassed all over again.

Her house came into view. She unzipped the back compartment of her backpack and searched for the keys.

"Did you tell your mom about Lindy's practical joke?" Cody asked.

Kris shook her head. "Mom is totally disgusted. We're not allowed to mention the dummies to her. Dad got home from Portland last night, and

80

Mom told him what was going on. So we're not allowed to mention the dummies to him, either!" She found the keys and started up the drive. "Thanks for walking home with me."

"Yeah. Sure." Cody gave her a little wave and continued on towards his house up the street.

Kris pushed the key into the front door lock. She could hear Barky jumping and yipping excitedly on the other side of the door. "I'm coming, Barky," she called in. "Hold your horses."

She pushed open the door. Barky began leaping on her, whimpering as if she'd been away for months. "OK, OK!" she cried, laughing.

It took several minutes to calm the dog down. Then Kris got a snack from the kitchen and headed up to her room to practise with Mr Wood.

She hoisted the dummy up from the chair, where it had spent the day beside Lindy's dummy. A can of Coke in one hand, the dummy over her shoulder, she headed to the dressing table and sat down in front of the mirror.

This was the best time of day to rehearse, Kris thought. No one was home. Her parents were at work. Lindy was at some after-school activity.

She arranged Mr Wood on her lap. "Time to go to work," she made him say, reaching into his back to move his lips. She made his eyes slide back and forth.

A button on his plaid shirt had come unbuttoned. Kris leaned him down against the dressing table and started to fasten it.

Something caught her eye. Something yellow inside the pocket.

"Weird," Kris said aloud. "I never noticed anything in there."

Slipping two fingers into the slender pocket, she pulled out a yellowed sheet of paper, folded up.

Probably just the receipt for him, Kris thought.

She unfolded the sheet of paper and held it up to read it.

It wasn't a receipt. The paper contained a single sentence handwritten very cleanly in bold black ink. It was in a language Kris didn't recognize.

"Did someone send you a love note, Mr Wood?" she asked the dummy.

It stared up at her lifelessly.

Kris lowered her eyes to the paper and read the strange sentence out loud:

"Karru marri odonna loma molonu karrano."

What language is that? Kris wondered.

She glanced down at the dummy and uttered a low cry of surprise.

Mr Wood appeared to blink.

But that wasn't possible – *was* it?

Kris took a deep breath, then let it out slowly.

The dummy stared up at her, his painted eyes as dull and wide open as ever.

Let's not get paranoid, Kris scolded herself.

"Time to work, Mr Wood," she told him. She folded up the piece of yellow paper and slipped it back into his shirt pocket. Then she raised him to a sitting position, searching for the eye and mouth controls with her hand.

"How are things around *your* house, Mr Wood?"

"Not good, Kris. I've got termites. I need termites like I need another hole in my head! Ha-ha!"

"Lindy! Kris! Could you come downstairs, please?" Mr Powell called from the foot of the stairs.

It was after dinner, and the twins were up in their room. Lindy was sprawled on her stomach on the bed, reading a book for school. Kris was in front of the dressing table mirror, rehearsing quietly with Mr Wood for tomorrow night's concert.

"What do you want, Dad?" Lindy shouted down, rolling her eyes.

"We're kind of busy," Kris shouted, shifting the dummy on her lap.

"The Millers are here, and they're dying to see your ventriloquist acts," their father shouted up.

Lindy and Kris both groaned. The Millers were the elderly couple who lived next door. They were very nice people, but very boring.

The twins heard Mr Powell's footsteps on the stairs. A few seconds later, he poked his head into their room. "Come on, girls. Just put on a short show for the Millers. They came over for coffee, and we told them about your dummies."

"But I have to rehearse for tomorrow night," Kris insisted.

"Rehearse on them," her father suggested. "Come on. Just do five minutes. They'll get a real kick out of it."

Sighing loudly, the girls agreed. Carrying their dummies over their shoulders, they followed their father down to the living room.

Mr and Mrs Miller were side by side on the sofa, coffee mugs in front of them on the low coffee table. They smiled and called out cheerful greetings as the girls appeared.

Kris was always struck by how much the Millers looked alike. They both had slender pink faces topped with spongy white hair. They both wore silver-framed bifocals, which slipped down on nearly identical pointy noses. They both had the same smile. Mr Miller had a small grey moustache. Lindy always joked that he grew it so the Millers could tell each other apart.

Is that *what happens to you when you've been*

married a long time? Kris found herself thinking. *You start to look exactly alike?*

The Millers were even dressed alike, in loose-fitting tan Bermuda shorts and white cotton sports shirts.

"Lindy and Kris took up ventriloquism a few weeks ago," Mrs Powell was explaining, twisting herself forward to see the girls from the armchair. She motioned them to the centre of the room. "And they both seem to have some talent for it."

"Have you girls ever heard of Bergen and McCarthy?" Mrs Miller asked, smiling.

"Who?" Lindy and Kris asked in unison.

"Before your time," Mr Miller said, chuckling. "They were a ventriloquist act."

"Can you do something for us?" Mrs Miller asked, picking up her coffee mug and setting it in her lap.

Mr Powell pulled a dining room chair into the centre of the room. "Here. Lindy, why don't you go first?" He turned to the Millers. "They're very good. You'll see," he said.

Lindy sat down and arranged Slappy on her lap. The Millers applauded. Mrs Miller nearly spilled her coffee, but she caught the mug just in time.

"Don't applaud – just throw money!" Lindy made Slappy say. Everyone laughed as if they'd never heard that before.

Kris watched from the stairway as Lindy did

85

a short routine. Lindy was really good, she had to admit. Very smooth. The Millers were laughing so hard, their faces were bright red. An identical shade of red. Mrs Miller kept squeezing her husband's knee when she laughed.

Lindy finished to big applause. The Millers gushed about how wonderful she was. Lindy told them about the TV show she might be on, and they promised they wouldn't miss it. "We'll tape it," Mr Miller said.

Kris took her place on the chair and sat Mr Wood in her lap. "This is Mr Wood," she told the Millers. "We're going to be the hosts of the spring concert at school tomorrow night. So I'll give you a preview of what we're going to say."

"That's a nice-looking dummy," Mrs Miller said quietly.

"You're a nice-looking dummy, too!" Mr Wood declared in a harsh, raspy growl of a voice.

Kris's mother gasped. The Millers' smiles faded.

Mr Wood leaned forward on Kris's lap and stared at Mr Miller. *"Is that a moustache, or are you eating a rat?"* he asked nastily.

Mr Miller glanced uncomfortably at his wife, then forced a laugh. They both laughed.

"Don't laugh so hard. You might drop your false teeth!" Mr Wood shouted. *"And how do you get your teeth that disgusting shade of*

yellow? Does your bad breath do that?"

"Kris!" Mrs Powell shouted. "That's enough!"

The Millers' faces were bright red now, their expressions bewildered.

"That's not funny. Apologize to the Millers," Mr Powell insisted, crossing the room and standing over Kris.

"I – I didn't say any of it!" Kris stammered. "Really, I—"

"Kris – apologize!" her father demanded angrily.

Mr Wood turned to the Millers. *"I'm sorry,"* he rasped. *"I'm sorry you're so ugly! I'm sorry you're so old and stupid, too!"*

The Millers stared at each other unhappily. "I don't get her humour," Mrs Miller said.

"It's just crude insults," Mr Miller replied quietly.

"Kris – what is *wrong* with you?" Mrs Powell demanded. She had crossed the room to stand beside her husband. "Apologize to the Millers right now! I don't *believe* you!"

"I – I—" Gripping Mr Wood tightly around the waist, Kris rose to her feet. "I – I—" She tried to utter an apology, but no words would come out.

"Sorry!" she finally managed to scream. Then, with an embarrassed cry, she turned and fled up the stairs, tears streaming down her face.

"You *have* to believe me!" Kris cried in a trembling voice. "I really didn't say any of those things. Mr Wood was talking by himself!"

Lindy rolled her eyes. "Tell me another one," she muttered sarcastically.

Lindy had followed Kris upstairs. Down in the living room, her parents were still apologizing to the Millers. Now Kris sat on the edge of her bed, wiping tears off her cheeks. Lindy stood with her arms crossed in front of the dressing table.

"I don't make insulting jokes like that," Kris said, glancing at Mr Wood, who lay crumpled in the centre of the floor where Kris had tossed him. "You know that isn't my sense of humour."

"So why'd you do it?" Lindy demanded. "Why'd you want to make everyone mad?"

"But I *didn't*!" Kris shrieked, tugging at the sides of her hair. "Mr Wood said those things!

I didn't!"

"How can you be such a copycat?" Lindy asked disgustedly. "I already *did* that joke, Kris. Can't you think of something original?"

"It's not a joke," Kris insisted. "Why don't you believe me?"

"No way," Lindy replied, shaking her head, her arms still crossed in front of her chest. "No way I'm going to fall for the same gag."

"Lindy, please!" Kris pleaded. "I'm frightened. I'm really frightened."

"Yeah. Sure," Lindy said sarcastically. "I'm shaking all over, too. Wow. You really fooled me, Kris. Guess you showed me you can play funny tricks, too."

"Shut up!" Kris snapped. More tears formed in the corners of her eyes.

"Very good crying," Lindy said. "But it doesn't fool me, either. And it won't fool Mom and Dad." She turned and picked up Slappy. "Maybe Slappy and I should practise some jokes. After your performance tonight, Mom and Dad might not let you do the concert tomorrow night."

She slung Slappy over her shoulder and, stepping over the crumpled form of Mr Wood, hurried from the room.

It was hot and noisy backstage in the auditorium. Kris's throat was dry, and she kept walking over to the water fountain and slurping mouthfuls of the warm water.

The voices of the audience on the other side of the curtain seemed to echo off all four walls and the ceiling. The louder the noise became as the auditorium filled, the more nervous Kris felt.

How am I ever going to do my act in front of all those people? she asked herself, pulling the edge of the curtain back a few centimetres and peering out. Her parents were off to the side, in the third row.

Seeing them brought memories of the night before flooding back to Kris. Her parents had grounded her for two weeks as punishment for insulting the Millers. They almost hadn't let her come to the concert.

Kris stared at the kids and adults filing into the large auditorium, recognizing a lot of faces. She realized her hands were ice-cold. Her throat was dry again.

Don't think of it as an audience, she told herself. *Think of it as a bunch of kids and parents, most of whom you know.*

Somehow that made it worse.

She let go of the curtain, hurried to get one last drink from the fountain, then retrieved Mr Wood from the table she had left him on.

The room suddenly grew quiet on the other side of the curtain. The concert was about to begin.

"Break a leg!" Lindy called across to her as

she hurried to join the other chorus members.

"Thanks," Kris replied weakly. She pulled up Mr Wood and straightened his shirt. "Your hands are clammy!" she made him say.

"No insults tonight," Kris told him sternly.

To her shock, the dummy blinked.

"Hey!" she cried. She hadn't touched his eye controls.

She had a stab of fear that went beyond stage fright. *Maybe I shouldn't go on with this*, she thought, staring intently at Mr Wood, watching for him to blink again.

Maybe I should say I'm ill and not perform with him.

"Are you nervous?" a voice whispered.

"Huh?" At first, she thought it was Mr Wood. But then she quickly realized that it was Mrs Berman, the music teacher.

"Yeah. A little," Kris admitted, feeling her face grow hot.

"You'll be terrific," Mrs Berman gushed, squeezing Kris's shoulder with a sweaty hand. She was a heavyset woman with several chins, a red lipsticked mouth, and flowing black hair. She was wearing a long, loose-fitting dress of red and blue flower patterns. "Here goes," she said, giving Kris's shoulder one more squeeze.

Then she stepped onstage, blinking against the harsh white light of the spotlight, to introduce Kris and Mr Wood.

91

Am I really doing this? Kris asked herself. Can *I do this?*

Her heart was pounding so hard, she couldn't hear Mrs Berman's introduction. Then, suddenly, the audience was applauding, and Kris found herself walking across the stage to the microphone, carrying Mr Wood in both hands.

Mrs Berman, her flowery dress flowing around her, was heading offstage. She smiled at Kris and gave her an encouraging wink as they passed each other.

Squinting against the bright spotlight, Kris walked to the middle of the stage. Her mouth felt as dry as cotton. She wondered if she could make a sound.

A folding chair had been set up for her. She sat down, arranging Mr Wood on her lap, then realized that the microphone was much too high.

This drew titters of soft laughter from the audience.

Embarrassed, Kris stood up and, holding Mr Wood under one arm, struggled to lower the microphone.

"Are you having trouble?" Mrs Berman called from the side of the stage. She hurried over to help Kris.

But before the music teacher got halfway across the stage, Mr Wood leaned into the microphone. *"What time does the blimp go up?"*

he rasped nastily, staring at Mrs Berman's dress.

"What?" She stopped in surprise.

"Your face reminds me of a wart I had removed!" Mr Wood growled at the startled woman.

Her mouth dropped open in horror. "Kris!"

"If we count your chins, will it tell us your age?"

There was laughter floating up from the audience. But it was mixed with gasps of horror.

"Kris – that's enough!" Mrs Berman cried, the microphone picking up her angry protest.

"You're more than enough! You're enough for two!" Mr Wood declared nastily. *"If you got any bigger, you'd need your own postcode!"*

"Kris – really! I'm going to ask you to apologize," Mrs Berman said, her face bright red.

"Mrs Berman, I – I'm not doing it!" Kris stammered. "I'm not saying these things!"

"Please apologize. To me and to the audience," Mrs Berman demanded.

Mr Wood leaned into the microphone. *"Apologize for THIS!"* he screamed.

The dummy's head tilted back. His jaw dropped. His mouth opened wide.

And a thick green liquid came spewing out.

"Yuck!" someone screamed.

It looked like pea soup. It spurted up out of Mr Wood's open mouth like water rushing from a fire hose.

Voices screamed and cried out their surprise as the thick green liquid showered over the people in the front rows.

"Stop it!"

"Help!"

"Somebody – turn it off!"

"It stinks!"

Kris froze in horror, staring as more and more of the disgusting substance poured from her dummy's gaping mouth.

A putrid stench – the smell of sour milk, of rotten eggs, of burning rubber, of decayed meat – rose up from the liquid. It puddled over the stage and showered over the front seats.

Blinded by the spotlight, Kris couldn't see the audience in front of her. But she could hear the choking and the gagging, the frantic cries for help.

"Clear the auditorium! Clear the auditorium!" Mrs Berman was shouting.

Kris heard the rumble and scrape of people shoving their way up the aisles and out the doors.

"It stinks!"

"I'm ill!"

"Somebody – help!"

Kris tried to clamp her hand over the dummy's

mouth. But the force of the putrid green liquid frothing and spewing out was too strong. It pushed her hand away.

Suddenly, she realized she was being shoved from behind. Off the stage. Away from the shouting people fleeing the auditorium. Out of the glaring spotlight.

She was backstage before she realized that it was Mrs Berman who was pushing her.

"I – I don't know how you did that. Or why!" Mrs Berman shouted angrily, frantically wiping splotches of the disgusting green liquid off the front of her dress with both hands. "But I'm going to see that you're suspended from school, Kris! And if I have my way," she sputtered, "you'll be suspended for *life*!"

"That's right. Close the door," Mr Powell said sternly, glaring with narrowed eyes at Kris.

He stood a few centimetres behind her, arms crossed in front of him, making sure she followed his instructions. She had carefully folded Mr Wood in half and shoved him to the back of her closet shelf. Now she closed the closet, making sure it was completely shut, as he ordered.

Lindy watched silently from her bed, her expression troubled.

"Does the closet door lock?" Mr Powell asked.

"No. Not really," Kris told him, lowering her head.

"Well, that will have to do," he said. "On Monday, I'm taking him back to the pawnshop. Do not take him out until then."

"But, Dad—"

He raised a hand to silence her.

"We have to talk about this," Kris pleaded.

"You have to listen to me. What happened tonight – it wasn't a practical joke. I—"

Her father turned away from her, a scowl on his face. "Kris, I'm sorry. We'll talk tomorrow. Your mother and I – we're both too angry and too upset to talk now."

"But, Dad—"

Ignoring her, he stormed out of the room. She listened to his footsteps, hard and hurried, down the stairs. Then Kris slowly turned to Lindy. "Now do you believe me?"

"I – I don't know what to believe," Lindy replied. "It was just so . . . unbelievably gross."

"Lindy, I – I—"

"Dad's right. Let's talk tomorrow," Lindy said. "I'm sure everything will be clearer and calmer tomorrow."

But Kris couldn't sleep. She shifted from side to side, uncomfortable, wide awake. She pulled the pillow over her face, held it there for a while, welcoming the soft darkness, then tossed it to the floor.

I'm never going to sleep again, she thought.

Every time she closed her eyes, she saw the hideous scene in the auditorium once again. She heard the astonished cries of the audience, the kids and their parents. And she heard the cries of shock turn to groans of disgust as the putrid gunk poured out over everyone.

Sickening. So totally sickening.

And everyone blamed her.

My life is ruined, Kris thought. *I can never go back there again. I can never go to school. I can never show my face* anywhere.

Ruined. My whole life. Ruined by that stupid dummy.

In the next bed, Lindy snored softly, in a slow, steady rhythm.

Kris turned her eyes to the bedroom window. The curtains hung down over the window, filtering the pale moonlight from outside. Slappy sat in his usual place in the chair in front of the window, bent in two, his head between his knees.

Stupid dummies, Kris thought bitterly. *So stupid.*

And now my life is ruined

She glanced at the clock. One twenty. Outside the window, she heard a low, rumbling sound. A soft whistle of brakes. Probably a large truck going by.

Kris yawned. She closed her eyes and saw the gross green gunk spewing out of Mr Wood's mouth.

Will I see that every time I close my eyes? she wondered.

What on earth was *it? How could everyone blame* me *for something so . . . so. . .*

The rumbling of the truck faded into the distance.

But then Kris heard another sound. A rustling sound.

A soft footstep.

Someone was moving.

She sucked in her breath and held it, listening hard.

Silence now. Silence so heavy, she could hear the loud thudding of her heart.

Then another soft footstep.

A shadow moved.

The closet door swung open.

Or was it just shadows shifting?

No. Someone was moving. Moving from the open closet. Someone was creeping towards the bedroom door. Creeping so softly, so silently.

Her heart pounding, Kris pulled herself up, trying not to make a sound. Realizing that she'd been holding her breath, she let it out slowly, silently. She took another breath, then sat up.

The shadow moved slowly to the door.

Kris lowered her feet to the floor, staring hard into the darkness, her eyes staying with the silent, moving figure.

What's happening? she wondered.

The shadow moved again. She heard a scraping sound, the sound of a sleeve brushing the door frame.

Kris pushed herself to her feet. Her legs felt shaky as she crept to the door, following the moving shadow.

Out into the hallway. Even darker out here because there were no windows.

Towards the stairway.

The shadow moved more quickly now.

Kris followed, her bare feet moving lightly over the thin carpet.

What's happening? What's happening?

She caught up to the shadowy figure on the landing. "Hey!" she called, her voice a tight whisper.

She grabbed the shoulder and turned the figure around.

And stared into the grinning face of Mr Wood.

Mr Wood blinked, then hissed at her, an ugly sound, a menacing sound. In the darkness of the stairwell, his painted grin became a threatening leer.

In her fright, Kris squeezed the dummy's shoulder, wrapping her fingers around the harsh fabric of his shirt.

"This – this is impossible!" she whispered.

He blinked again. He giggled. His mouth opened, making his grin grow wider.

He tried to tug out of Kris's grasp, but she hung on without even realizing she was holding him.

"But – you're a *dummy*!" she squealed.

He giggled again. "So are you," he replied. His voice was a deep growl, like the angry snarl of a large dog.

"You can't walk!" Kris cried, her voice trembling.

The dummy giggled its ugly giggle again.

"You can't be alive!" Kris exclaimed.

"Let go of me – *now!*" the dummy growled.

Kris held on, tightening her grip. "I'm dreaming," Kris told herself aloud. "I have to be dreaming."

"I'm not a dream. I'm a nightmare!" the dummy exclaimed, and tossed back his wooden head, laughing.

Still gripping the shoulder of the shirt, Kris stared through the darkness at the grinning face. The air seemed to grow heavy and hot. She felt as if she couldn't breathe, as if she were suffocating.

What was that sound?

It took her a while to recognize the strained gasps of her own breathing.

"Let go of me," the dummy repeated. "Or I'll throw you down the stairs." He tried once again to tug out of her grasp.

"No!" Kris insisted, holding tight. "I – I'm putting you back in the closet."

The dummy laughed, then pushed his painted face close to Kris's face. "You can't keep me there."

"I'm locking you in. I'm locking you in a box. In *something!*" Kris declared, panic clouding her thoughts.

The darkness seemed to descend over her, choking her, weighing her down.

"Let go of me." The dummy pulled hard.

Kris reached out her other hand and grabbed him around the waist.

"Let go of me," he snarled in his raspy, deep rumble of a voice. "I'm in charge now. You will listen to me. This is *my* house now."

He pulled hard.

Kris encircled his waist.

They both fell on to the stairs, rolling down a few steps.

"Let go!" the dummy ordered. He rolled on top of her, his wild eyes glaring into hers.

She pushed him off, tried to pin his arms behind his back.

He was surprisingly strong. He pulled back one arm, then shoved a fist hard into the pit of her stomach.

"Ohhh." Kris groaned, feeling the breath knocked out of her.

The dummy took advantage of her momentary weakness and pulled free. Grasping the banister with one hand, he tried to pull himself past her and down the stairs.

But Kris shot out a foot and tripped him.

Still struggling to breathe, she pounced on to his back. Then she pulled him away from the banister and pushed him down hard on to a step.

"Oh!" Kris gasped loudly as the overhead hall light flashed on. She closed her eyes against the sudden harsh intrusion. The dummy struggled to pull out from under her, but she pushed down on his back with all her weight.

"Kris – what on earth—?!" Lindy's startled voice called down from the top step.

"It's Mr Wood!" Kris managed to cry up to her. "He's . . . *alive!*" She pushed down hard, sprawled over the dummy, keeping him pinned beneath her.

"Kris – what are you doing?" Lindy demanded. "Are you OK?"

"No!" Kris exclaimed. "I'm not OK! Please – Lindy! Go get Mom and Dad! Mr Wood – he's alive!"

"It's just a dummy!" Lindy called down, taking a few reluctant steps towards her sister. "Get up, Kris! Have you lost your mind?"

"*Listen to me!*" Kris shrieked at the top of her lungs. "Get Mom and Dad! Before he escapes!"

But Lindy didn't move. She stared down at her sister, her long hair falling in tangles about her face, her features twisted in horror. "Get up, Kris," she urged. "Please – get up. Let's go back to bed."

"I'm *telling* you, he's *alive!*" Kris cried desperately. "You've got to believe me, Lindy. You've *got* to!"

The dummy lay lifelessly beneath her, his face buried in the carpet, his arms and legs sprawled out to the sides.

"You had a nightmare," Lindy insisted, climbing down step by step, holding her long nightshirt up above her ankles until she was standing right above Kris. "Come back to bed, Kris. It was just a nightmare. The horrible thing that happened at the concert – it gave you a nightmare, that's all."

Gasping for breath, Kris lifted herself up and twisted her head to face her sister. Grabbing the banister with one hand, she raised herself a little.

The instant she lightened up on him, the dummy grabbed the edge of the stair with both hands and pulled himself out from under her. Half falling, half crawling, he scrambled down the rest of the stairs.

"No! No! I don't *believe* it!" Lindy shrieked, seeing the dummy move.

"Go get Mom and Dad!" Kris said. "Hurry!"

Her mouth wide open in shocked disbelief, Lindy turned and headed back up the stairs, screaming for her parents.

Kris dived off the step, thrusting her arms in front of her.

She tackled Mr Wood from behind, wrapping her arms around his waist.

His head hit the carpet hard as they both crumpled to the floor.

He uttered a low, throaty cry of pain. His eyes closed. He didn't move.

Dazed, her chest heaving, her entire body trembling, Kris slowly climbed to her feet. She quickly pressed a foot on the dummy's back to hold him in place.

"Mom and Dad – where *are* you?" she cried aloud. "Hurry."

The dummy raised its head. He let out an angry growl and started to thrash his arms and legs wildly.

Kris pressed her foot hard against his back.

"Let go!" he growled viciously.

Kris heard voices upstairs.

"Mom? Dad? Down here!" she called up to them.

Both of her parents appeared at the upstairs landing, their faces filled with worry.

"Look!" Kris cried, frantically pointing down to the dummy beneath her foot.

"Look at *what*?" Mr Powell cried, adjusting his pyjama top.

Kris pointed down to the dummy under her foot. "He – he's trying to get away," she stammered.

But Mr Wood lay lifeless on his stomach.

"Is this supposed to be a joke?" Mrs Powell demanded angrily, hands at the waist of her cotton nightgown.

"I don't get it," Mr Powell said, shaking his head.

"Mr Wood – he ran down the stairs," Kris said frantically. "He's been doing everything. He—"

"This isn't funny," Mrs Powell said wearily, running a hand back through her blonde hair. "It isn't funny at all, Kris. Waking everyone up in the middle of the night."

"I really think you've lost your mind. I'm very worried about you," Mr Powell added. "I mean, after what happened at school tonight—"

"Listen to me!" Kris shrieked. She bent down and pulled Mr Wood up from the floor. Holding him by the shoulders, she shook him hard. "He moves! He runs! He talks! He – he's *alive*!"

She stopped shaking the dummy and let go. He slumped lifelessly to the floor, falling in an unmoving heap at her feet.

"I think maybe you need to see a doctor," Mr Powell said, his face tightening with concern.

"No. I *saw* him, too!" Lindy said, coming to Kris's aid. "Kris is right. The dummy *did* move." But then she added, "I mean, I *think* it moved!"

You're a big help, Lindy, Kris thought, suddenly feeling weak, drained.

"Is this just another stupid prank?" Mrs Powell asked angrily. "After what happened at school tonight, I'd think that would be enough."

"But, Mom—" Kris started, staring down at the lifeless heap at her feet.

"Back to bed," Mrs Powell ordered. "There's no school tomorrow. We'll have plenty of time to discuss punishments for you two."

"*Me?*" Lindy cried, outraged. "What did *I* do?"

"Mom, we're telling the truth!" Kris insisted.

"I still don't get the joke," Mr Powell said, shaking his head. He turned to his wife. "Were we supposed to believe her or something?"

"Get to bed. Both of you. Now!" their mother snapped. She and their father disappeared from the upstairs landing, heading angrily back down the hall to their room.

Lindy remained, one hand on the top of the banister, staring down regretfully at Kris.

"You believe me, don't you?" Kris called up to her.

"Yeah. I guess," Lindy replied doubtfully, lowering her eyes to the dummy at Kris's feet.

Kris looked down, too. She saw Mr Wood blink. He started to straighten up.

"Whoa!" She uttered an alarmed cry and grabbed him by the neck. "Lindy – hurry!" she called. "He's moving again!"

"Wh-what should we do?" Lindy stammered, making her way hesitantly down the stairs.

"I don't know," Kris replied as the dummy thrashed his arms and legs against the carpet, trying desperately to free himself from her two-handed grip on his neck. "We've got to—"

"There's *nothing* you can do," Mr Wood snarled. "You will be my slaves now. I'm alive once again! Alive!"

"But – how?" Kris demanded, staring at him in disbelief. "I mean, you're a dummy. How—?"

109

The dummy sniggered. "*You* brought me back to life," he told her in his raspy voice. "You read the ancient words."

The ancient words? What was he talking about?

And then Kris remembered. She had read the strange-sounding words from the sheet of paper in the dummy's shirt pocket.

"I am back, thanks to you," the dummy growled. "And now you and your sister will serve me."

As she stared in horror at the grinning dummy, an idea popped into Kris's mind.

The paper. She had tucked it back into his pocket.

If I read the words again, Kris thought, *it will put him back to sleep.*

She reached out and grabbed him. He tried to jerk away, but she was too quick.

The folded sheet of yellow paper was in her hand.

"Give me that!" he cried. He swiped at it, but Kris swung it out of his reach.

She unfolded it quickly. And before the dummy could grab the paper out of her hands, she read the strange words aloud:

"*Karru marri odonna loma molonu karrano.*"

Both sisters stared at the dummy, waiting for him to collapse.

But he gripped the banister and tossed his head back in an amused, scornful laugh. "Those are the words of the ancient sorcerer to bring me to life!" he proclaimed. "Those aren't the words to kill me!"

Kill him?

Yes, Kris thought frantically. She tossed down the yellow paper disgustedly.

We have no choice.

"We have to kill him, Lindy."

"Huh?" Her sister's face filled with surprise.

Kris grabbed the dummy by the shoulders and held on tightly. "I'll hold him. You pull his head off."

Lindy was beside her now. She had to duck away from Mr Wood's thrashing feet.

"I'll hold him still," Kris repeated. "Grab his

111

head. Pull it off."

"You – you're sure?" Lindy hesitated, her features tight with fear.

"*Just do it!*" Kris screamed.

She let her hands slide down around Mr Wood's waist.

Lindy grabbed his head in both hands.

"*Let go of me!*" the dummy rasped.

"Pull!" Kris cried to her terrified sister.

Holding the dummy tightly around the waist, she leaned back, pulling him away from her sister.

Lindy's hands were wrapped tightly around the dummy's head. With a loud groan, she pulled hard.

The head didn't come off.

Mr Wood uttered a high-pitched giggle. "Stop. You're tickling me!" he rasped.

"Pull harder!" Kris ordered her sister.

Lindy's face was bright red. She tightened her grip on the head and pulled again, tugging with all her strength.

The dummy giggled his shrill, unpleasant giggle.

"It – it won't come off," Lindy said, sighing in defeat.

"Twist it off!" Kris suggested frantically.

The dummy thrashed out with his feet, kicking Kris in the stomach. But she held on. "Twist the head off!" she cried.

Lindy tried to turn the head.

The dummy giggled.

"It won't twist!" Lindy cried in frustration. She let go of the head and took a step back.

Mr Wood raised his head, stared up at Lindy, and grinned. "You can't kill me. I have powers."

"What do we do?" Lindy cried, raising her eyes to Kris.

"This is my house now," the dummy rasped, grinning at Lindy as it struggled to wriggle out of Kris's arms. "You will do as I say now. Put me down."

"What do we *do*?" Lindy repeated.

"Take him upstairs. We'll *cut* his head off," Kris replied.

Mr Wood swung his head around, his eyes stretched open in an evil glare.

"Ow!" Kris cried out in surprise as the dummy snapped his jaws over her arm, biting her. She pulled her arm away and, without thinking, slapped the dummy's wooden head with the palm of her hand.

The dummy giggled in response. "Violence! Violence!" he said in a mock scolding tone.

"Get those sharp scissors. In your drawer," Kris instructed her sister. "I'll carry him up to our room."

Her arm throbbed where he had bitten her. But she held on to him tightly and carried him up to their bedroom.

Lindy had already pulled the long metal scissors from the drawer. Her hand trembled as she opened and closed the blades.

"Below the neck," Kris said, holding Mr Wood tightly by the shoulders.

He hissed furiously at her. She dodged as he tried to kick her with both feet.

Holding the scissors with two hands, Lindy tried cutting the head off at the neck. The scissors didn't cut, so she tried a sawing motion.

Mr Wood giggled. "I told you. You can't kill me."

"It isn't going to work," Lindy cried, tears of frustration running down her cheeks. "Now what?"

"We'll put him in the closet. Then we can think," Kris replied.

"You have no need to think. You are my slaves," the dummy rasped. "You will do whatever I ask. I will be in charge from now on."

"No way," Kris muttered, shaking her head.

"What if we *won't* help you?" Lindy demanded.

The dummy turned to her, casting her a hard, angry stare. "Then I'll start hurting the ones you love," he said casually. "Your parents. Your friends. Or maybe that disgusting dog that's always yapping at me." He tossed back his head and a dry, evil laugh escaped his wooden lips.

"Lock him in the closet," Lindy suggested. "Till we figure out how to get rid of him."

"You *can't* get rid of me," Mr Wood insisted. "Don't make me angry. I have powers. I'm warning you. I'm starting to get tired of your stupid attempts to harm me."

"The closet doesn't lock – remember?" Kris cried, struggling to hold on to the wriggling dummy.

"Oh. Wait. How about this?" Lindy hurried to the closet. She pulled out an old suitcase from the back.

"Perfect," Kris said.

"I'm warning you—" Mr Wood threatened. "You are becoming very tiresome."

With a hard tug, he pulled himself free of Kris.

She dived to tackle him, but he darted out from under her. She fell face down on to her bed.

The dummy ran to the centre of the room, then turned his eyes to the doorway, as if trying to decide where to go. "You must do as I tell you," he said darkly, raising a wooden hand towards Lindy. "I will not run from you two. You are to be my slaves."

"No!" Kris cried, pushing herself up.

She and her sister both dived at the dummy. Lindy grabbed his arms. Kris ducked to grab his ankles.

Working together, they stuffed him into the open suitcase.

"You will regret this," he threatened, kicking his legs, struggling to hit them. "You will pay dearly for this. Now someone will die!"

He continued screaming after Kris latched the suitcase and shoved it into the closet. She quickly closed the closet door, then leaned her back against it, sighing wearily.

"Now what?" she asked Lindy.

"We'll bury him," Kris said.

"Huh?" Lindy stifled a yawn.

They had been whispering together for what seemed like hours. As they tried to come up with a plan, they could hear the dummy's muffled cries from inside the closet.

"We'll bury him. Under that huge mound of earth," Kris explained, her eyes going to the window. "You know. Next door, at the side of the new house."

"Yeah. OK. I don't know," Lindy replied. "I'm so tired, I can't think straight." She glanced at the bedside table clock. It was nearly three thirty in the morning. "I still think we should wake up Mom and Dad," Lindy said, fear reflected in her eyes.

"We can't," Kris told her. "We've been over that a hundred times. They won't believe us. If we wake them up, we'll be in even bigger trouble."

"How could we be in *bigger* trouble?" Lindy demanded, gesturing with her head to the closet where Mr Wood's angry cries could still be heard.

"Get dressed," Kris said with renewed energy. "We'll bury him under all that earth. Then we'll never have to think about him again."

Lindy shuddered and turned her eyes to her dummy, folded up in the chair. "I can't bear to look at Slappy any more. I'm so sorry I got us interested in dummies."

"*Ssshhh*. Just get dressed," Kris said impatiently.

A few minutes later, the two girls crept down the stairs in the darkness. Kris carried the suitcase in both arms, trying to muffle the sound of Mr Wood's angry protests.

They stopped at the bottom of the stairs and listened for any sign that they had awakened their parents.

Silence.

Lindy pulled open the front door and they slipped outside.

The air was surprisingly cool and wet. A heavy dew had begun to fall, making the front lawn glisten under the light of a half-moon. Blades of wet grass clung to their trainers as they made their way to the garage.

As Kris held on to the suitcase, Lindy slowly, quietly, pulled open the garage door. When it was halfway up, she ducked and slipped inside.

A few seconds later she emerged, carrying a large snow shovel. "This should do it," she said, whispering even though no one was around.

Kris glanced down the street as they headed across the garden to the plot next door. The heavy morning dew misted the glow of the street lamps, making the pale light appear to bend and flicker like candles. Everything seemed to shimmer under the dark purple sky.

Kris set the suitcase down beside the tall mound of earth. "We'll dig right down here," she said, pointing towards the bottom of the mound. "We'll shove him in and cover him."

"I'm warning you," Mr Wood threatened, listening inside the suitcase. "Your plan won't work. I have powers!"

"You dig first," Kris told her sister, ignoring the dummy's threat. "Then I'll take a turn."

Lindy dug into the pile and heaved up a shovelful of earth. Kris shivered. The heavy dew felt cold and damp. A cloud floated over the moon, darkening the sky from purple to black.

"Let me out!" Mr Wood called. "Let me out now, and your punishment won't be too severe."

"Dig faster," Kris whispered impatiently.

"I'm going as fast as I can," Lindy replied. She had dug a pretty good-sized square-shaped hole at the base of the mound. "How much deeper, do you think?"

"Deeper," Kris said. "Here. Watch the suitcase. I'll take a turn." She changed places with Lindy and started to dig.

Something scampered heavily near the low shrubs that separated the gardens. Kris looked up, saw a moving shadow, and gasped.

"Raccoon, I think," Lindy said with a shudder. "Are we going to bury Mr Wood in the suitcase, or are we going to take him out?"

"Think Mom will notice the suitcase is gone?" Kris asked, tossing a shovelful of wet earth to the side.

Lindy shook her head. "We never use it."

"We'll bury him in the suitcase," Kris said. "It'll be easier."

"You'll be sorry," the dummy rasped. The suitcase shook and nearly toppled on to its side.

"I'm so sleepy," Lindy moaned, tossing her socks on to the floor, then sliding her feet under the covers.

"I'm wide awake," Kris replied, sitting on the edge of her bed. "I guess it's because I'm so happy. So happy we got rid of that awful creature."

"It's all so weird," Lindy said, adjusting her pillow behind her head. "I don't blame Mom and Dad for not believing it. I'm not sure I believe it, either."

"You put the shovel back where you found it?" Kris asked.

Lindy nodded. "Yeah," she said sleepily.

"And you closed the garage door?"

"*Ssshhh*. I'm asleep," Lindy said. "At least there's no school tomorrow. We can sleep late."

"I hope I can fall asleep," Kris said doubtfully. "I'm just so *pumped*. It's all like some kind of hideously gross nightmare. I just think . . . Lindy? Lindy – are you still awake?"

No. Her sister had fallen asleep.

Kris stared up at the ceiling. She pulled the blankets up to her chin. She still felt chilled. She couldn't shake the cold dampness of the early morning air.

After a short while, with thoughts of everything that had happened that night whirring crazily in her head, Kris fell asleep, too.

The rumble of machines woke her up at eight thirty the next morning. Stretching, trying to rub the sleep from her eyes, Kris stumbled to the window, leaned over the chair holding Slappy, and peered out.

It was a grey, cloudy day. Two enormous yellow steamrollers were rolling over the plot next door behind the newly constructed house, flattening the land.

I wonder if they're going to flatten that big mound of earth, Kris thought, staring down at them. That would really be *excellent*.

Kris smiled. She hadn't slept very long, but she felt refreshed.

Lindy was still sound asleep. Kris tiptoed past her, pulled her dressing gown on, and headed downstairs.

"Morning, Mom," she called brightly, tying the belt to her dressing gown as she entered the kitchen.

Mrs Powell turned from the sink to face her. Kris was surprised to see an angry expression on her face.

She followed her mother's stare to the breakfast counter.

"Oh!" Kris gasped when she saw Mr Wood. He was seated at the counter, his hands in his lap. His hair was matted with red-brown earth, and he had dirt smears on his cheeks and forehead.

Kris raised her hands to her face in horror.

"I thought you were told never to bring that thing down here!" Mrs Powell scolded. "What do I have to do, Kris?" She turned angrily back to the sink.

The dummy winked at Kris and flashed her a wide, evil grin.

As Kris stared in horror at the grinning dummy, Mr Powell suddenly appeared in the kitchen doorway. "Ready?" he asked his wife.

Mrs Powell hung the dishtowel on the rack and turned around, brushing a lock of hair off her forehead. "Ready. I'll get my bag." She brushed past him into the front hallway.

"Where are you going?" Kris cried, her voice revealing her alarm. She kept her eyes on the dummy at the counter.

"Just doing a little shopping at the garden store," her father told her, stepping into the room, peering out the kitchen window. "Looks like rain."

"Don't go!" Kris pleaded.

"Huh?" He turned towards her.

"Don't go – please!" Kris cried.

Her father's eyes landed on the dummy. He walked over to him. "Hey – what's the big idea?" her father asked angrily.

"I thought you wanted to take him back to the pawnshop," Kris replied, thinking quickly.

"Not till Monday," her father replied. "Today is Saturday, remember?"

The dummy blinked. Mr Powell didn't notice.

"Do you have to go shopping now?" Kris asked in a tiny voice.

Before her father could answer, Mrs Powell reappeared in the doorway. "Here. Catch," she called, and tossed the car keys to him. "Let's go before it pours."

Mr Powell started to the door. "Why don't you want us to go?" he asked.

"The dummy—" Kris started. But she knew it was hopeless. They'd never listen. They'd never believe her. "Never mind," she muttered.

A few seconds later, she heard their car back down the driveway. They were gone.

And she was alone in the kitchen with the grinning dummy.

Mr Wood turned towards her slowly, swivelling the tall counter stool. His big eyes locked angrily on Kris's.

"I warned you," he rasped.

Barky came trotting into the kitchen, his toenails clicking loudly on the linoleum. He sniffed the floor as he ran, searching for breakfast scraps someone might have dropped.

124

"Barky, where've you been?" Kris asked, glad to have company.

The dog ignored her and sniffed under the stool Mr Wood sat on.

"He was upstairs, waking me up," Lindy said, rubbing her eyes as she walked into the kitchen. She was wearing white tennis shorts and a sleeveless magenta T-shirt. "Stupid dog."

Barky licked at a spot on the linoleum.

Lindy cried out as she spotted Mr Wood. "Oh, no!"

"I'm back," the dummy rasped. "And I'm very unhappy with you two slaves."

Lindy turned to Kris, her mouth open in surprise and terror.

Kris kept her eyes trained on the dummy. *What does he plan to do?* she wondered. *How can I stop him?*

Burying him under all that earth hadn't kept him from returning. Somehow he had freed himself from the suitcase and pulled himself out.

Wasn't there any way to defeat him? Any way at all?

Grinning his evil grin, Mr Wood dropped down to the floor, his trainers thudding hard on the floor. "I'm very unhappy with you two slaves," he repeated in his growly voice.

"What are you going to do?" Lindy cried in a shrill, frightened voice.

"I have to punish you," the dummy replied. "I have to prove to you that I am serious."

"Wait!" Kris cried.

But the dummy moved quickly. He reached down and grabbed Barky by the neck with both hands.

As the dummy tightened his grip, the frightened terrier began to howl in pain.

"I warned you," Mr Wood snarled over the howls of the little black terrier. "You will do as I say – or one by one, those you love will suffer!"

"No!" Kris cried.

Barky let out a high-pitched *whelp*, a bleat of pain that made Kris shudder.

"Let go of Barky!" Kris screamed.

The dummy giggled.

Barky uttered a hoarse gasp.

Kris couldn't stand it any longer. She and Lindy leaped at the dummy from two sides. Lindy tackled his legs. Kris grabbed Barky and tugged.

Lindy dragged the dummy to the floor. But his wooden hands held a tight grip on the dog's throat.

Barky's howls became a muffled whimper as he struggled to breathe.

"Let go! Let *go*!" Kris shrieked.

"I *warned* you!" the dummy snarled as

Lindy held tight to his kicking legs. "The dog must die now!"

"No!" Kris let go of the gasping dog. She slid her hands down to the dummy's wrists. Then, with a fierce tug, she pulled the wooden hands apart.

Barky dropped to the floor, wheezing. He scampered to the corner, his paws sliding frantically over the smooth floor.

"You'll pay now!" Mr Wood growled. Jerking free from Kris, he swung his wooden hand up, landing a hard blow on Kris's forehead.

She cried out in pain and raised her hands to her head.

She heard Barky yipping loudly behind her.

"Let go of me!" Mr Wood demanded, turning back to Lindy, who still held on to his legs.

"No way!" Lindy cried. "Kris – grab his arms again."

Her head still throbbing, Kris lunged forward to grab the dummy's arms.

But he lowered his head as she approached and clamped his wooden jaws around her wrist.

"Owww!" Kris howled in pain and pulled back.

Lindy lifted the dummy up by the legs, then slammed his body hard against the floor. He uttered a furious growl and tried to kick free of her.

Kris lunged again, and this time grabbed one arm, then the other. He lowered his head to bite once more, but she dodged away and pulled his arms tight behind his back.

"I'm warning you!" he bellowed. "I'm warning you!"

Barky yipped excitedly, hopping up on Kris.

"What do we *do* with him?" Lindy cried, shouting over the dummy's angry threats.

"Outside!" Kris yelled, pressing the arms more tightly behind Mr Wood's back.

She suddenly remembered the two steamrollers she had seen moving over the garden next door, flattening the ground. "Come on," she urged her sister. "We'll crush him!"

"I'm warning you! I have powers!" the dummy screamed.

Ignoring him, Kris pulled open the kitchen door and they carried their wriggling captive outside.

The sky was charcoal-grey. A light rain had begun to fall. The grass was already wet.

Over the low shrubs that separated the gardens, the girls could see the two enormous yellow steamrollers, one in the back, one at the side of the next-door plot. They looked like huge lumbering animals, their giant black rollers flattening everything in their path.

"This way! Hurry!" Kris shouted to her sister, holding the dummy tightly as she ran. "Toss him

129

under that one!"

"Let me go! Let me go, slaves!" the dummy screamed. "This is your last chance!" He swung his head hard, trying to bite Kris's arm.

Thunder rumbled, low in the distance.

The girls ran at full speed, slipping on the wet grass as they hurried towards the fast-moving steamroller.

They were just a few metres away from the enormous machine when they saw Barky. His tail wagging furiously, he scampered ahead of them.

"Oh, no! How'd he get out?" Lindy cried.

Gazing back at them, his tongue hanging out of his mouth, prancing happily in the wet grass, the dog was running right into the path of the rumbling steamroller.

"No, Barky!" Kris shrieked in horror. "No! Barky – no!"

Letting go of Mr Wood, both girls dived towards the dog. Hands outstretched, they slid on their stomachs on the wet grass.

Unaware of any problem, enjoying the game of tag, Barky scampered away.

Lindy and Kris rolled out of the path of the steamroller.

"Hey – get away from there!" the angry operator shouted through the high window of the steamroller. "Are you girls crazy?"

They leaped to their feet and turned back to Mr Wood.

The rain began to come down a little harder. A jagged streak of white lightning flashed high in the sky.

"I'm free!" the dummy cried, hands raised victoriously above his head. "Now you will pay!"

"Get him!" Kris shouted to her sister.

The rain pelted their hair and shoulders. The

two girls lowered their heads, leaned into the rain, and began to chase after the dummy.

Mr Wood turned and started to run.

He never saw the other steamroller.

The gigantic black wheel rolled right over him, pushing him on to his back, then crushing him with a loud *crunch*.

A loud *hiss* rose up from under the machine, like air escaping from a large balloon.

The steamroller appeared to rock back and forth.

A strange green gas spurted up from beneath the wheel, into the air, spreading out in an eerie, mushroom-shaped cloud.

Barky stopped scampering and stood frozen in place, his eyes following the green gas as it floated up against the nearly black sky.

Lindy and Kris stared in open-mouthed wonder.

Pushed by the wind and the rain, the green gas floated over them.

"Yuck! It stinks!" Lindy declared.

It smelled like rotten eggs.

Barky uttered a low whimper.

The steamroller backed up. The driver jumped out and came running towards them. He was a short, stocky man with big muscular arms bulging out from the sleeves of his T-shirt. His face was bright red under a short blond flat-top, his eyes wide with horror.

"A kid?" he cried. "I – I ran over a kid?"

"No. He was a dummy," Kris told him. "He wasn't alive."

He stopped. His face faded from red to flour-white. He uttered a loud, grateful sigh. "Oh, man," he moaned. "Oh, man. I thought it was a kid."

He took a deep breath and let it out slowly. Then he bent to examine the area beneath his wheel. As the girls came near, they saw the remains of the dummy, crushed flat inside its jeans and flannel shirt.

"Hey, I'm real sorry," the man said, wiping his forehead with his T-shirt sleeve as he straightened up to face them. "I couldn't stop in time."

"That's OK," Kris said, a wide smile forming on her face.

"Yeah. Really. It's OK," Lindy quickly agreed.

Barky moved close to sniff the crushed dummy.

The man shook his head. "I'm so relieved. It looked like it was running. I really thought it was a kid. I was so scared."

"No. Just a dummy," Kris told him.

"Whew!" The man exhaled slowly. "Close one." His expression changed. "What are you girls doing out in the rain, anyway?"

Lindy shrugged. Kris shook her head. "Just walking the dog."

The man picked up the crushed dummy. The

head crumbled to powder as he lifted it. "You want this thing?"

"You can throw it in the rubbish bin," Kris told him.

"Better get out of the rain," he told them. "And don't scare me like that again."

The girls apologized, then headed back to the house. Kris cast a happy grin at her sister. Lindy grinned back.

I may grin for ever, Kris thought. *I'm so happy. So relieved.*

They wiped their wet trainers on the mat, then held the kitchen door open for Barky. "Wow. What a morning!" Lindy declared.

They followed the dog into the kitchen. Outside, a flash of bright lightning was followed by a roar of thunder.

"I'm drenched," Kris said. "I'm going up to get changed."

"Me, too." Lindy followed her up the stairs.

They entered their bedroom to find the window wide open, the curtains slapping wildly, rain pouring in. "Oh, no!" Kris hurried across the room to shut the window.

As she leaned over the chair to grab the window frame, Slappy reached up and grabbed her arm. "Hey, slave – is that other guy gone?" the dummy asked in a throaty growl. "I thought he'd never leave!"

BEHIND THE SCREAMS

NIGHT of the LIVING DUMMY

CONTENTS

Bonus material
written and compiled
by Joshua Gee

About the Author

R.L. Stine's books are read all over the world. So far, his books have sold more than 300 million copies, making him one of the most popular children's authors in history. Besides Goosebumps, R.L. Stine has written the teen series Fear Street, the funny series Rotten School, as well as the Mostly Ghostly series, The Nightmare Room series, and the two-book thriller *Dangerous Girls*. R.L. Stine lives in New York with his wife, Jane, and Minnie, his King Charles spaniel. You can learn more about him at www. RLStine.com.

Q & A with R.L. Stine

What inspired you to write *Night of the Living Dummy*?

R.L. Stine (RLS): *I've always thought dummies are scary. There's something about those dead wooden eyes staring at you and then suddenly coming to life. Creepy!*

Do you own a ventriloquist's dummy? If so, has it ever insulted, chased, or attacked you?

RLS: *I do own a ventriloquist's dummy. It looks just like me! So far, it hasn't ever chased me or attacked me. But you know, people have told me that dogs always sense ghosts and evil things before humans do. Well, my dog, Minnie, who is normally a very quiet, calm dog, is absolutely terrified of the dummy. She barks at it and shivers with fear whenever she sees him! So now I can't help wondering if she knows something about the dummy that I don't know. . .*

Slappy is a villain that the fans love to fear. What makes him so popular?

RLS: *Face it – all of us would like to be a little mean and a little rude sometimes. Slappy is mean and rude ALL the time. I think that's why the fans love him.*

You're presently writing the first all-new Goosebumps books in a very long time. Will new villains appear in Goosebumps HorrorLand?

RLS: *You* bet *there will be new villains and some old favourites in HorrorLand. Some are so scary I don't even want to THINK about them! (Watch out for Dr Maniac and Mister Slither!)*

How many Goosebumps HorrorLand books will there be? Can you reveal one secret about future books in the series?

RLS: *There will be twelve new books in the Goosebumps HorrorLand series. Here's a secret that you'll be the first to hear: don't let anyone tell you there's no such thing as quicksand. In HorrorLand, Quicksand Beach is a popular attraction at the Black Lagoon Water Park. But kids who innocently step out on to the sand quickly learn there IS such a thing as quicksand! In Book One, the sinking kids are given good advice: when you start to drop underground, the best way to survive is to HOLD YOUR BREATH for as long as you can!*

Fright Gallery: Slappy the Dummy

FIRST APPEARANCE *Night of the Living Dummy*

OTHER APPEARANCES *Night of the Living Dummy II and III; Goosebumps 2000: Bride of the Living Dummy; Goosebumps 2000: Slappy's Nightmare*

ORIGINS In the late 1800s, an ancient sorcerer built two dummies from the wood of a stolen coffin. The wood was cursed. *Very* cursed! Many years later, one of the wicked dummies, Mr Wood, was finally defeated. But it only made the other dummy twice as wicked . . . and a *thousand* times ruder! That other dummy was Slappy.

SPECIAL POWERS Some people believe that Slappy has the power to control people's minds and turn *people* into puppets.

WEAKNESSES *"Karru marri odonna loma molonu karrano."* Those six words have an eerie and often surprising effect on dummies.

LIVING OR DEAD? Both!

FAVOURITE PHRASE "Thanks for waking me up, SLAVE!"

HOBBIES & INTERESTS Daydreaming about what he'll do when he becomes Supreme Ruler of the Human Race.

LAST SEEN Goosebumps HorrorLand 1: *Revenge of the Living Dummy*

SPLAT STATS

STRENGTH										
INTELLIGENCE										
SPEED										
ATTACK SKILLS										
HUMOUR										
EVIL										

A Dummy's Guide to Ventriloquism

Ventriloquism is the art of "throwing" your voice so that it sounds like it's coming from somewhere else. You don't need to be a smarty-pants to learn how. Dummies do it all the time.

1.) Shut your mouth.

Look in a mirror and part your lips slightly. Relax your jaw so that your top teeth just barely touch your bottom teeth.

2.) Know your A-B-Cs!

Here comes the hard part: speaking without moving your lips. That might sound impossible, but some ventriloquists can actually make it look like they're drinking a glass of water while their dummies talk at the same time. Beginners usually start by pronouncing 19 letters over and over again:

A, C, D, E, G, H, I, J, K, L, N, O, Q, R, S, T, U, X, Z

Keep looking in the mirror. Can you see your lips move?

3.) Practice makes perfect.

Most full sentences are extremely tough to say at first. (In fact, one good example is "Practice makes perfect.") If you want to become a true Puppet

Master, keep practising individual letters. When you're ready, try seven more letters. . . .

B, F, M, P, V, W, Y

They're the toughest letters of all.

4.) Cheat!

Instead of saying the toughest letters like you normally would, try making sounds that are similar.

Letter	Say this sound	Example
B	"duh"	**"dunny raddit"**
F	"th" or "eth"	**"athraid"**
M	"nuh"	**"nonster"**
P	"tuh"	**"Goose-dunts"**
V	"the"	**"rethenge"**
W	"oh"	**"ohaffle"**
Y	"oh-eye" or "yuh"	**"oh-eye are you scared?"**

5.) Find a puppet . . . before it finds YOU!

Actually, old-fashioned ventriloquist's dummies are pretty rare these days, and the nice ones cost as much as £600. However, you can practise ventriloquism with almost any type of puppet. You can even draw some eyes on an old sock. Night of the Living . . . *Sock Puppet*? It won't be as evil as Slappy, but it will be just as creepy!

Slappy's Greatest Wisecracks

Sticks and stones will break your bones, but Slappy's insults hurt even more. Don't believe us? Keep reading! And just be glad that Slappy wasn't talking to you. . .

"Is that your head – or are you hatching an ostrich egg on your neck?"

Slappy: *"Knock knock."*
Human: *"Who's there?"*
Slappy: *"Jane."*
Human: *"Jane who?"*
Slappy: *"Jane jer clothes. You stink!"*

"Is your hair red? Or are you starting to rust?"

"Hey – you're pretty. Pretty ugly!"

"I like your perfume. What is it – flea and tick spray?"

"Pinch me. I'm having a nightmare. Or is that really your face?"

"How about a game of Kick the Dummy Down the Stairs? We'll take turns being the dummy. You can go first!"

"I've seen PIMPLES that were prettier than you!"

Goosebumps®

DEEP TROUBLE

There I was, sixty metres under the sea.

I was on the hunt of my life. The hunt for the Great White Stingray.

That's what they called him at Coast Guard headquarters. But me, I called him Joe.

The giant stingray had already stung ten swimmers. People were afraid to step into the water. Panic spread all up and down the coast.

That's why they sent for me.

William Deep, Jr, of Baltimore, Maryland.

Yes, William Deep, Jr, world-famous twelve-year-old undersea explorer. Solver of scary ocean problems.

I captured the Great White Shark that terrorized Myrtle Beach. I proved he wasn't so great!

I fought the giant octopus that ate the entire California Championship Surfing Team.

I unplugged the electric eel that sent shock waves all over Miami.

But now I faced the fight of my life. Joe, the Great White Stingray.

Somewhere down deep under the sea, he lurked.

I had everything I needed: scuba suit, flippers, mask, oxygen tank and poison-dart gun.

Wait – did something move? Just behind that giant clam?

I raised my dart gun and waited for an attack.

Then, suddenly, my mask clouded. I couldn't breathe.

I strained for breath. No air came.

My oxygen tank! Someone must have tampered with it!

There was no time to lose. Sixty metres down – and no air! I had to surface – fast!

I kicked my legs, desperately trying to pull myself to the surface.

Holding my breath. My lungs about to burst. I was losing strength, getting dizzy.

Would I make it? Or would I die right here, deep under the ocean, Joe the Stingray's dinner?

Panic swept over me like an ocean tide. I searched through the fogged mask for my diving partner. Where was she when I needed her?

Finally, I spotted her swimming up at the surface, near the boat.

Help me! Save me! No air! I tried to tell her, waving my arms like a maniac.

Finally, she noticed me. She swam towards me and dragged my dazed and limp body to the surface.

I ripped off my mask and sucked in mouthfuls of air.

"What's your problem, Aqua Man?" she cried. "Did a jellyfish sting you?"

My diving partner is very brave. She laughs in the face of danger.

I struggled to catch my breath. "No air. Someone – cut off – tank—"

Then everything went black.

My diving partner shoved my head back under the water. I opened my eyes and came up sputtering.

"Get real, Billy," she said. "Can't you snorkel without acting like a total jerk?"

I sighed. She was no fun.

My "diving partner" was really just my bratty sister, Sheena. I was only pretending to be William Deep, Jr, undersea explorer.

But would it kill Sheena to go along with it just once?

My name actually *is* William Deep, Jr, but everybody calls me Billy. I'm twelve – I think I mentioned that already.

Sheena is ten. She looks like me. We both have straight black hair, but mine is short and hers goes down to her shoulders. We're both skinny, with knobby knees and elbows, and long, narrow feet. We both have dark blue eyes and thick, dark eyebrows.

Other than that, we're not alike at all.

Sheena has no imagination. She was never afraid of monsters in her closet when she was little. She didn't believe in Santa Claus or the tooth fairy, either. She loves to say, "There's no such thing."

I dived underwater and pinched Sheena's leg. *Attack of the Giant Lobster Man!*

"Stop it!" she screamed. She kicked me in the shoulder. I came up for air.

"Hey, you two," my uncle said. "Be careful down there."

My uncle stood on the deck of his sea lab boat, the *Cassandra*. He peered down at Sheena and me snorkelling nearby.

My uncle's name is George Deep, but everybody calls him Dr D. Even my dad, who is his brother, calls him Dr D. Maybe that's because he looks just the way a scientist should.

Dr D is short, thin, wears glasses and a very serious, thoughtful expression. He has curly brown hair and a bald spot at the back of his head. Anyone who saw him would say, "I bet you're a scientist."

Sheena and I were visiting Dr D on the *Cassandra*. Every year our parents let us spend our summer holiday with Dr D. It sure beats hanging out at home. This summer, we were anchored just off a tiny island called Ilandra, in the Caribbean Sea.

Dr D is a marine biologist. He specializes in tropical marine life. He studies the habits of tropical fish and looks for new kinds of ocean plants and fish that haven't been discovered yet.

The *Cassandra* is a big and sturdy boat. It is about fifteen metres long. Dr D uses most of the space for labs and research rooms. Up on deck is a cockpit, where he steers the boat. He keeps a dinghy tied to the starboard, or right side of the deck, and a huge glass tank on the port, or left side.

Sometimes Dr D catches very big fish and keeps them temporarily in the glass tank – usually just long enough to tag the fish for research, or care for them if they are ill or injured.

The rest of the deck is open space, good for playing catch or sunbathing.

Dr D's research takes him all over the world. He isn't married and doesn't have any kids. He says he's too busy staring at fish.

But he likes kids. That's why he invites me and Sheena to visit him every summer.

"Stick close together, kids," Dr D said. "And don't swim off too far. Especially you, Billy."

He narrowed his eyes at me. That's his "I mean it" look. He never narrows his eyes at Sheena.

"There've been reports of some shark sightings in the area," he said.

"Sharks! Wow!" I cried.

Dr D frowned at me. "Billy," he said. "This is serious. Don't leave the boat. And don't go near the reef."

I knew he was going to say that.

Clamshell Reef is a long red coral reef just a few hundred metres away from where we were anchored. I'd been dying to explore it ever since we got there.

"Don't worry about me, Dr D," I called up to him. "I won't get into trouble."

Sheena muttered under her breath, "Yeah, right."

I reached out to give her another lobster pinch, but she dived underwater.

"Good," said Dr D. "Now don't forget – if you see a shark fin, try not to splash around a lot. Movement will attract it. Just slowly, steadily return to the boat."

"We won't forget," said Sheena, who had come up behind me, splashing like crazy.

I couldn't help feeling just a little bit excited. I'd always wanted to see a real, live shark.

I'd seen sharks at the aquarium, of course. But they were trapped in a glass tank, where they just swam around restlessly, perfectly harmless.

Not very exciting.

I wanted to spot a shark's fin on the horizon, floating over the water, closer, closer, heading right for us. . .

In other words, I wanted adventure.

The *Cassandra* was anchored out in the ocean, a few hundred metres away from Clamshell Reef. The reef surrounded the island. Between the reef and the island stretched a beautiful lagoon.

Nothing was going to stop me from exploring that lagoon – no matter what Dr D said.

"Come on, Billy," Sheena called, adjusting her mask. "Let's check out that school of fish."

She pointed to a patch of tiny ripples in the water near the bow of the boat. She slid the mouthpiece into her mouth and lowered her head into the water. I followed her to the ripples.

Soon Sheena and I were surrounded by hundreds of tiny neon-blue fish.

Underwater, I always felt as if I were in a faraway world. *Breathing through the snorkel, I could live down here with the fish and the dolphins,* I thought. *After a while, maybe I would grow flippers and a fin.*

The tiny blue fish began to swim away, and I swam with them. They were so great-looking! I didn't want them to leave me behind.

Suddenly, the fish all darted from view. I tried to follow, but they were too fast.

They had vanished!

Had something scared them away?

I glanced around. Clumps of seaweed floated near the surface. Then I saw a flash of red.

I floated closer, peering through the mask. A few metres ahead of me I saw bumpy red formations. Red coral.

Oh, no, I thought. *Clamshell Reef. Dr D told me not to swim this far.*

I began to turn around. I knew I should swim back to the boat.

But I was tempted to stay and explore a little. After all, I was already there.

The reef looked like a red sandcastle, filled with underwater caves and tunnels. Small fish darted in and out of them. The fish were bright yellow and blue.

Maybe I could swim over and explore one of those tunnels, I thought. *How dangerous could it be?*

Suddenly, I felt something brush against my leg. It tickled and sent a tingle up my leg.

A fish?

I glanced around, but I didn't see anything.

Then I felt it again.

A tingling against my leg.

And then it clutched me.

Again I turned to see what it was. Again I saw nothing.

My heart began to race. I knew it was probably nothing dangerous. But I wished I could see it.

I turned and started back for the boat, kicking hard.

But something grabbed my right leg – and held on!

I froze in fear. Then I frantically kicked my leg as hard as I could.

Let go! Let go of me!

I couldn't see it – and I couldn't pull free!

The water churned and tossed as I kicked with all my strength.

Overcome with terror, I lifted my head out of the water and choked out a weak cry: "Help!"

But it was no use.

Whatever it was, it kept pulling me down. Down.

Down to the bottom of the sea.

"Help!" I cried out again. "Sheena! Dr D!"

I was dragged below the surface again. I felt the slimy tentacle tighten around my ankle.

As I sank underwater, I turned – and saw it.

It loomed huge and dark.

A sea monster!

Through the churning waters, it glared at me with one giant brown eye. The terrifying creature floated underwater like an enormous dark green balloon. Its mouth opened in a silent cry, revealing two rows of jagged, sharp teeth.

An enormous octopus! But it had at least *twelve* tentacles!

Twelve long, slimy tentacles. One was wrapped around my ankle. Another one slid towards me.

NO!

My arms thrashed in the water.

I gulped in mouthfuls of air.

I struggled to the surface – but the huge creature dragged me down again.

I couldn't believe it. As I sank, scenes from my life actually flashed before my eyes.

I saw my parents, waving to me as I boarded the yellow school bus for my first day of school.

Mom and Dad! I'll never see them again!

What a way to go, I thought. *Killed by a sea monster!*

No one will believe it.

Everything started to turn red. I felt dizzy, weak.

But something was pulling me, pulling me up.

Up to the surface. Away from the tentacled monster.

I opened my eyes, choking and sputtering.

I stared up at Dr D!

"Billy! Are you all right?" Dr D studied me with concern.

I coughed and nodded. I kicked my right leg. The slimy tentacle was gone.

The dark creature had vanished.

"I heard you screaming and saw you thrashing about," said Dr D. "I swam over from the boat as fast as I could. What happened?"

Dr D had a yellow life jacket over his shoulders. He slipped a rubber lifesaver right over my head. I floated easily now, the life ring under my arms.

I had lost my flippers in the struggle. My mask and snorkel dangled around my neck.

Sheena swam over and floated beside me, treading water.

"It grabbed my leg!" I cried breathlessly. "It tried to pull me under!"

"What grabbed your leg, Billy?" asked Dr D. "I don't see anything around here—"

"It was a sea monster," I told him. "A huge one! I felt its slimy tentacle grabbing my leg... *Ouch!*"

Something pinched my toe.

"It's back!" I shrieked in horror.

Sheena popped out of the water and shook her wet hair, laughing.

"That was me, you dork!" she cried.

"Billy, Billy," Dr D murmured. "You and your wild imagination." He shook his head. "You nearly scared me to death. Please – don't ever do that again. Your leg probably got tangled in a piece of seaweed, that's all."

"But – but— !" I sputtered.

He dipped his hand in the water and pulled up a handful of slimy green strings. "There's seaweed everywhere.

"But I saw it!" I shouted. "I saw its tentacles, its big pointy teeth!"

"There's no such thing as sea monsters," said Sheena. Miss Know-It-All.

"Let's discuss it on the boat," my uncle said, dropping the clump of seaweed back in the water.

"Come on. Swim back with me. And stay away from the reef. Swim around it."

He turned around and started swimming towards the *Cassandra*. I saw that the sea monster had pulled me into the lagoon. The reef lay between us and the boat. But there was a break in the reef we could swim through.

I followed them, thinking angry thoughts.

Why didn't they believe me?

I had seen the creature grab my leg. It wasn't a stupid clump of seaweed. It wasn't my imagination.

I was determined to prove them wrong. I'd find that creature and show it to them myself – someday. But not today.

Now I was ready to get back to the safety of the boat.

I swam up to Sheena and called, "Race you to the boat."

"Last one there is a chocolate-covered jellyfish!" she cried.

Sheena can't refuse a race. She started speeding towards the boat, but I caught her by the arm.

"Wait," I said. "No fair. You're wearing flippers. Take them off."

"Too bad!" she cried, and pulled away. "See you at the boat!" I watched her splash away, building up a good lead.

She's not going to win, I decided.

I stared at the reef up ahead.

It would be faster just to swim over the reef. A short cut.

I turned and started to swim straight towards the red coral.

"Billy! Get back here!" Dr D shouted.

I pretended I didn't hear him.

The reef loomed ahead. I was almost there.

I saw Sheena splashing ahead of me. I kicked extra hard. I knew she'd never have the guts to swim over the reef. She'd swim around the end of it. I would cut through and beat her.

But my arms suddenly began to ache. I wasn't used to swimming so far.

Maybe I can stop at the reef and rest my arms for a second, I thought.

I reached the reef. I turned around. Sheena was swimming to the left, around the reef. I figured I had a few seconds to rest.

I stepped on to the red coral reef –

– and screamed in horror!

My foot burned as if it were on fire. The throbbing pain shot up my leg.

I screamed and dived into the water.

When I surfaced, I heard Sheena yelling, "Dr D! Come quick!"

My foot burned, even in the cold ocean water.

Dr D came up beside me. "Billy, what's the problem now?" he demanded.

"I saw him do something really stupid," Sheena said, smirking.

If my foot hadn't been burning up, I definitely would have punched out her lights.

"My foot!" I moaned. "I stepped on the reef – and – and—"

Dr D held on to the lifesaver ring around my waist. "Ow. That's painful," he said, reaching up to pat my shoulder. "But you'll be all right. The burning will stop in a little while."

He pointed to the reef. "All that bright red coral is fire coral."

"Huh? Fire coral?" I stared back at it.

"Even I knew that!" Sheena said.

"It's covered with a mild poison," my uncle continued. "When it touches your skin, it burns like fire."

Now *he tells me*, I thought.

"Don't you know *anything*?" Sheena asked sarcastically.

She was asking for it. She really was.

"You're lucky you only burned your foot," Dr D said. "Coral can be very sharp. You could have cut your foot and got poison into your bloodstream. Then you'd *really* be in trouble."

"Wow! What kind of trouble?" Sheena asked. She seemed awfully eager to hear about all the terrible things that could have happened to me.

Dr D's expression turned serious. "The poison could paralyse you," he said.

"Oh, great," I said.

"So keep away from the red coral from now on," Dr D warned. "And stay away from the lagoon, too."

"But that's where the sea monster lives!" I protested. "We have to go back there. I have to show it to you!"

Sheena bobbed in the blue-green water. "No such thing, no such thing," she chanted. Her favourite phrase. "No such thing – right, Dr D?"

"Well, you never know," Dr D replied thoughtfully. "We don't know all of the creatures

161

that live in the oceans, Sheena. It's better to say that scientists have never seen one."

"So there, She-Ra," I said.

Sheena spat a stream of water at me. She hates it when I call her She-Ra.

"Listen, kids – I'm serious about staying away from this area," said Dr D. "There may not be a sea monster in that lagoon, but there could be sharks, poisonous fish, electric eels. Any number of dangerous creatures. Don't swim over there."

He paused and frowned at me, as if to make sure I'd been paying attention.

"How's your foot feeling, Billy?" he asked.

"It's a little better now," I told him.

"Good. Enough adventure for one morning. Let's get back to the boat. It's almost lunch time."

We all started swimming back to the *Cassandra*.

As I kicked, I felt something tickle my leg again.

Seaweed?

No.

It brushed against my thigh like – *fingers*.

"Cut it out, Sheena," I shouted angrily. I spun around to splash water in her face.

But she wasn't there. She wasn't anywhere near me.

She was up ahead, swimming beside Dr D.

Sheena couldn't possibly have tickled me.

But something definitely *did*.

I stared down at the water, suddenly gripped with terror.

What was down there?

Why was it teasing me like that?

Was it preparing to grab me again and pull me down for ever?

Alexander DuBrow, Dr D's assistant, helped us aboard the boat.

"Hey, I heard shouting," Alexander said. "Is everything OK?"

"Everything is fine, Alexander," said Dr D. "Billy stepped on some fire coral, but he's all right."

As I climbed up the ladder, Alexander grabbed my hands and pulled me aboard.

"Wow, Billy," he said. "Fire coral. I accidentally bumped into the fire coral my first day here. I saw stars. I really did, man. You sure you're OK?"

I nodded and showed him my foot. "It feels better now. But that wasn't the worst thing that happened. I was almost eaten by a sea monster!"

"No such thing, no such thing," Sheena chanted.

"I really saw it," I insisted. "They don't believe

me. But it was there. In the lagoon. It was big and green and—"

Alexander smiled. "If you say so, Billy," he said. He winked at Sheena.

I wanted to punch out his lights, too.

Big deal science student. What did *he* know?

Alexander was in his early twenties. But, unlike Dr D, he didn't look like a scientist.

He looked more like a football player. He was very tall, about six feet four inches, and muscular. He had thick, wavy blond hair and blue eyes that crinkled in the corners. He had broad shoulders and big powerful-looking hands. He spent a lot of time in the sun and had a smooth, dark tan.

"I hope you're all hungry," Alexander said. "I made chicken salad sandwiches for lunch."

"Oh. Great," Sheena said, rolling her eyes.

Alexander did most of the cooking. He thought he was good at it. But he wasn't.

I went below decks to my cabin to change out of my wet swimming trunks. My cabin was really just a tiny sleeping cubby with a cupboard for my things. Sheena had one just like it. Dr D and Alexander had bigger cabins that they could actually walk around in.

We ate in the galley, which was what Dr D called the boat's kitchen. It had a built-in table and built-in seats, and a small area for cooking.

When I entered the galley, Sheena was already sitting at the table. There was a big sandwich on a plate in front of her and one waiting for me.

Neither of us was too eager to try Alexander's chicken salad. The night before, we had eaten Brussels sprouts casserole. For breakfast this morning, he served us whole wheat pancakes that sank to the bottom of my stomach like the *Titanic* going down!

"You first," I whispered to my sister.

"Uh-uh," Sheena said, shaking her head. "You try it. You're older."

My stomach growled. I sighed. There was nothing to do but taste it.

I sank my teeth into the sandwich and started chewing.

Not bad, I thought at first. A little chicken, a little mayonnaise. It actually tasted like a regular chicken salad sandwich.

Then, suddenly, my tongue started to burn. My whole mouth was on fire!

I let out a cry and grabbed for the glass of iced tea in front of me. I downed the entire glass.

"Fire coral!" I screamed. "You put fire coral in the chicken salad!"

Alexander laughed. "Just a little chilli pepper. For taste. You like it?"

"I think I'd rather have cereal for lunch," Sheena said, setting down her sandwich. "If you don't mind."

"You can't have cereal for every meal," Alexander replied, frowning. "No wonder you're so skinny, Sheena. You never eat anything but cereal. Where's your spirit of adventure?"

"I think I'll have cereal, too," I said sheepishly. "Just for a change of pace."

Dr D came into the galley. "What's for lunch?" he asked.

"Chicken salad sandwiches," said Alexander. "I made them spicy."

"*Very* spicy," I warned him.

Dr D glanced at me and raised an eyebrow. "Oh, really?" he said. "You know, I'm not very hungry. I think I'll just have cereal for lunch."

"Maybe Billy and I could make dinner tonight," Sheena offered. She poured cereal into a bowl and added milk. "It's not fair for Alexander to cook *all* the time."

"That's a nice idea, Sheena," said Dr D. "What do you two know how to make?"

"I know how to make brownies from a mix," I offered.

"And I know how to make fudge," said Sheena.

"Hmm," said Dr D. "Maybe *I'll* cook tonight. How does grilled fish sound?"

"Great!" I said.

*　　*　　*

167

After lunch, Dr D went into his office to go over some notes. Alexander led Sheena and me into the main lab to show us around.

The work lab was really cool. It had three big glass tanks along the wall filled with weird, amazing fish.

The smallest tank held two bright yellow sea horses and an underwater trumpet. The underwater trumpet was a long red and white fish shaped like a tube. There were also a lot of guppies swimming around in this tank.

Another tank held some flame angelfish, which were orange-red like fire, and a harlequin tuskfish with orange and aqua tiger stripes for camouflage.

The biggest tank held a long black and yellow snakelike thing with a mouth full of teeth.

"Ugh!" Sheena made a disgusted face as she stared at the long fish. "That one is really gross!"

"That's a black ribbon eel," said Alexander. "He bites, but he's not deadly. We call him Biff."

I snarled through the glass at Biff, but he ignored me.

I wondered what it would be like to come face-to-face with Biff in the ocean. His teeth looked nasty, but he wasn't nearly as big as the sea monster. I figured William Deep, Jr, world-famous undersea explorer, could handle it.

I turned away from the fish tanks and stood by the control panel, staring at all the knobs and dials.

"What does this do?" I asked. I pushed a button. A loud horn blared. We all jumped, startled.

"It honks the horn," Alexander said, laughing.

"Dr D told Billy not to touch things without asking first," said Sheena. "He's told him a million times. He never listens."

"Shut up, She-Ra!" I said sharply.

"*You* shut up."

"Hey – no problem," said Alexander, raising both hands, motioning for us to chill out. "No harm done."

I turned back to the panel. Most of the dials were lit up, with little red indicators moving across their faces. I noticed one dial that was dark, its red indicator still.

"What's this for?" I asked, pointing to the dark dial. "It looks like you forgot to turn it on."

"Oh, that controls the Nansen bottle," Alexander said. "It's broken."

"What's a Nansen bottle?" asked Sheena.

"It collects samples of seawater from way down deep," said Alexander.

"Why don't you fix it?" I asked.

"We can't afford to," said Alexander.

"Why not?" asked Sheena. "Doesn't the university give you money?"

We both knew that Dr D's research was paid for by a university in Ohio.

"They gave us money for our research," Alexander explained. "But it's almost gone. We're waiting to see if they'll give us more. In the meantime, we don't have the money to fix things."

"What if the *Cassandra* breaks down or something?" I asked.

"Then I guess we'll have to put her in dry dock for a while," said Alexander. "Or else find a new way to get more money."

"Wow," said Sheena. "That would mean no more summer visits."

I hated to think of the *Cassandra* just sitting on a dock. Even worse was the thought of Dr D being stuck on land with no fish to study.

Our uncle was miserable whenever he had to go ashore. He didn't feel comfortable unless he was on a boat. I know, because one Christmas he came to our house to visit.

Usually Dr D is fun to be with. But that Christmas visit was a nightmare.

Dr D spent the whole time pacing through the house. He barked orders at us like a sea captain.

"Billy, sit up straight!" he yelled at me. "Sheena, swab the decks!"

He just wasn't himself.

Finally, on Christmas Eve, my dad couldn't take it any more. He told Dr D to shape up or ship out.

Dr D ended up spending a good part of Christmas Day in the bathtub playing with my old toy boats. As long as he stayed in the water, he was back to normal.

I never wanted to see Dr D stranded on land again.

"Don't worry, kids," Alexander said. "Dr D has always found a way to get by."

I hoped Alexander was right.

I studied another strange dial, marked SONAR PROBES.

"Hey, Alexander," I said. "Will you show me how the sonar probes work?"

"Sure," said Alexander. "Just let me finish a few chores."

He walked over to the first fish tank. He scooped out a few guppies with a small net.

"Who wants to feed Biff today?"

"Not me," said Sheena. "Yuck!"

"No way!" I said as I stepped to a porthole and peered out.

I thought I heard a motor outside. So far we had seen very few other boats. Not many people passed by Ilandra.

A white boat chugged up to the side of the *Cassandra*. It was smaller but newer than our boat. A logo on the side said MARINA ZOO.

A man and a woman stood on the deck of the zoo boat. They were both neatly dressed in khaki trousers and button-down shirts. The man had a short, neat haircut, and the woman's brown hair was pulled back in a ponytail. She carried a black briefcase.

The man waved to someone on the deck of the *Cassandra*. I figured he had to be waving at Dr D.

Now Sheena and Alexander stood beside me at the porthole, watching.

"Who's that?" Sheena asked.

Alexander cleared his throat. "I'd better go see what this is about," he said.

He handed Sheena the net with the guppies in it. "Here," he said. "Feed Biff. I'll be back later."

He left the lab in a hurry.

Sheena looked at the squirming guppies in the net and made a face.

"I'm not going to stay here and watch Biff eat these poor guppies." She stuck the net in my hand and ran out of the cabin.

I didn't want to watch Biff eat the poor fish, either. But I didn't know what else to do with them.

I quickly dumped the guppies into Biff's tank. The eel's head shot forward. His teeth clamped down on a fish. The guppy disappeared. Biff grabbed for another one.

He was a fast eater.

I dropped the net on a table and walked out of the lab.

I made my way down the narrow passageway, planning to go up on deck for some air.

I wondered if Dr D would let me do some more snorkelling this afternoon.

If he said yes, maybe I would swim towards the lagoon, see if I could find any sign of the sea monster.

Was I scared?

Yes.

But I was also determined to prove to my sister and uncle that I wasn't crazy. That I wasn't making it up.

I was passing Dr D's office when I heard voices. I figured Dr D and Alexander must be in there with the two people from the zoo.

I paused for just a second. I didn't mean to eavesdrop, I swear. But the man from the zoo had a loud voice, and I couldn't help but hear him.

And what he said was the most amazing thing I had ever heard in my whole entire life.

"I don't care how you do it, Dr Deep," the man bellowed. "But I want you to find that mermaid!"

A mermaid!

Was he serious?

I couldn't believe it. Did he really want my uncle to find a real, live mermaid?

I knew Sheena would start chanting, "No such thing, no such thing." But here was a grown man, a man who worked for a zoo, talking about a mermaid. It *had* to be real!

My heart started to pound with excitement. *I might be one of the first people on earth ever to see a mermaid!* I thought.

And then I had an even better thought: *What if I was the one to find her?*

I'd be famous! I'd be on TV and everything!

William Deep, Jr, the famous sea explorer!

Well, after I heard that, I couldn't just walk away. I had to hear more.

Holding my breath, I pressed my ear to the door and listened.

"Mr Showalter, Ms Wickman, please understand," I heard Dr D saying. "I'm a scientist, not a circus trainer. My work is serious. I can't waste my time looking for fairy tale creatures."

"We're quite serious, Dr Deep," said Ms Wickman. "There is a mermaid in these waters. And if anyone can find her, you can."

I heard Alexander ask, "What makes you think there's really a mermaid out there?"

"A fisherman from a nearby island spotted her," replied the man from the zoo. "He said he got pretty close to her – and he's sure she's real. He saw her near the reef – *this* reef, just off Ilandra."

The reef! Maybe she lives in the lagoon!

I leaned closer to the door. I didn't want to miss a word of this.

"Some of these fishermen are very superstitious, Mr Showalter," my uncle scoffed. "For years there have been stories . . . but no real reason to believe them."

"We didn't believe the man ourselves," said the woman. "Not at first. But we asked some other fishermen in the area, and they claim to have seen the mermaid, too. And I think they're telling the truth. Their descriptions of her match, down to the smallest detail."

I could hear my uncle's desk chair creak. I imagined him leaning forward as he asked, "And how, exactly, did they describe her?"

"They said she looked like a young girl," Mr Showalter told him. "Except for the" – he cleared his throat – "the fishtail. She's small, delicate, with long blonde hair."

"They described her tail as shiny and bright green," said the woman. "I know it sounds incredible, Dr Deep. But when we spoke to the fishermen, we were convinced that they really saw a mermaid!"

There was a pause.

Was something missing? I pressed my ear to the door. I heard my uncle ask. "And why, exactly, do you want to capture this mermaid?"

"Obviously, a real, live mermaid would be a spectacular attraction at a zoo like ours," said the woman. "People from all over the world would flock to see her. The Marina Zoo would make millions of dollars."

"We are prepared to pay you very well for your trouble, Dr Deep," said Mr Showalter. "I understand you are running out of money. What if the university refuses to give you more? It would be terrible if you had to stop your important work just because of that."

"The Marina Zoo can promise you one million dollars," said the woman. "*If* you find the mermaid. I'm sure your lab could run for a long time on that much money."

A million dollars! I thought. *How could Dr D turn down that kind of money?*

My heart pounded with excitement. I pushed against the door, straining to hear.

What would my uncle's answer be?

Leaning hard against the door, I heard Dr D let out a long, low whistle. "That's quite a lot of money, Ms Wickman," I heard him say.

There was a long pause. Then he continued. "But even if mermaids existed, I wouldn't feel right about capturing one for a zoo to put on display."

"I promise you we would take excellent care of her," replied Mr Showalter. "Our dolphins and whales are very well cared for. The mermaid, of course, would get extra-special treatment."

"And remember, Dr Deep," said Ms Wickman. "If you don't find her, someone else will. And there's no guarantee that they will treat the mermaid as well as we will."

"I suppose you're right," I heard my uncle reply. "It would certainly be a big boost to my research if I found her."

"Then you'll do it?" asked Mr Showalter eagerly.

Say yes, Dr D! I thought. *Say yes!*

I pressed my whole body against the door.

"Yes," my uncle answered. "If there really is a mermaid, I'll find her."

Excellent! I thought.

"Very good," said Ms Wickman.

"Excellent decision," Mr Showalter added enthusiastically. "I knew we had come to the right man for the job."

"We'll be back in a couple of days to see how the search is going. I hope you'll have some good news by then," Ms Wickman said.

"That's not much time," I heard Alexander remark.

"We know," Ms Wickman replied. "But, obviously, the sooner you find her, the better."

"And please," Mr Showalter said, "*please* keep this a secret. No one must know about the mermaid. I'm sure you can imagine what would happen if—"

CRASSSSSSSH!

I lost my balance. I fell against the door.

To my shock, it swung open – and I tumbled into the room.

I landed in a heap in the centre of the cabin floor.

Dr D, Mr Showalter, Ms Wickman and Alexander all gaped at me with their mouths open. I guess they hadn't expected me to drop in.

"Uh . . . hi, everyone," I murmured. I felt my face burning and knew that I was blushing. "Nice day for a mermaid hunt."

Mr Showalter jumped to his feet angrily. He glared at my uncle. "This was supposed to be a secret!"

Alexander strode across the room and helped me to my feet. "Don't worry about Billy," he said. He put a protective arm around me. "You can trust him."

"I'm very embarrassed," Dr D told his visitors. "This is my nephew Billy Deep. He and his sister are visiting me for a few weeks."

"Can they keep our secret?" asked Ms Wickman.

Dr D turned his gaze on Alexander. Alexander nodded.

"Yes, I'm sure they can," said Dr D. "Billy won't say anything to anyone. Right, Billy?"

He narrowed his eyes at me. I really do hate it when he does that. But this time I couldn't blame him.

I shook my head. "No. I won't tell anyone. I swear."

"Just to be on the safe side, Billy," said Dr D, "don't mention the mermaid to Sheena. She's too young to have to keep a big secret like this."

"I promise," I replied solemnly. I raised my right hand as if swearing an oath. "I won't breathe a word to Sheena."

This was *so cool*!

I knew the biggest secret in the world – and Sheena wouldn't have a clue!

The man and woman from the zoo exchanged glances. I could see they were still worried.

Alexander said, "You really can trust Billy. He's very serious for someone his age."

You bet *I'm serious*, I thought.

I'm William Deep, Jr, world-famous mermaid catcher.

Mr Showalter and Ms Wickman seemed to relax a little.

"Good," said Ms Wickman. She shook hands with Dr D, Alexander and me.

Mr Showalter gathered up some papers and put them into the briefcase.

"We'll see you in a few days, then," said Ms Wickman. "Good luck."

I won't need luck, I thought, watching them roar away on their boat a few minutes later.

I won't need luck because I have skill. And daring.

My head spun with all kinds of exciting thoughts.

Would I let Sheena be on TV with me after I single-handedly captured the mermaid?

Probably not.

That night I sneaked off the boat and slipped into the dark water. I swam noiselessly towards the lagoon.

I glanced back at the *Cassandra*. It floated quietly. All the portholes were dark.

Good, I thought. *No one is awake to notice that I'm gone. No one knows I'm out here. No one knows I'm swimming in the sea at night, all alone.*

Swimming steadily, easily, under the silvery moonlight, I made my way around the reef and into the dark lagoon.

I slowed my stroke just past the reef.

My eyes darted eagerly around the lagoon. The waves lapped gently under me. The water sparkled as if a million tiny diamonds floated on the surface.

Where was the mermaid?

I knew she was there. I knew I would find her here.

From deep below me, I heard a low rumble.

I listened hard. The sound, faint at first, grew louder.

The waves tossed as the sound became a steady roar.

It rumbled like an earthquake. An earthquake on the ocean floor.

The waves tumbled and tossed. I struggled to stay on top of them.

What was happening?

Suddenly, from the middle of the lagoon, a huge wave swelled. It rose higher, like a gigantic geyser.

Higher. Over my head. As tall as a building!

A tidal wave?

No.

The wave broke.

The dark creature pushed up underneath it.

Water slid off its grotesque body. Its single eye stared out darkly at me. Its tentacles writhed and stretched.

I screamed.

The monster blinked its muddy brown eye at me.

I tried to turn and swim away.

But it was too fast.

The tentacles whipped out – and grabbed me, tightening, tightening around my waist.

Then a slimy, cold tentacle wrapped around my neck and started to squeeze.

"I – I can't breathe!" I managed to choke out.

I tugged at the tentacle twining around my throat.

"Help me – somebody!"

I opened my eyes – and stared up at the ceiling.

I was lying in bed.

In my cabin.

The sheet was wrapped tightly around me.

I took a deep breath and waited for my heart to stop thudding. A dream.

Only a dream.

I rubbed my eyes, lifted myself, and peered out the porthole. The sun was just rising over the horizon. The sky was morning red. The water a hazy purple.

Squinting past the reef, I saw the lagoon. Perfectly still. Not a sea monster in sight.

I wiped the sweat from my forehead with my pyjama sleeve.

No need to be afraid, I told myself. *It was just a dream. A bad dream.*

I shook my head, trying to forget about the sea monster.

I couldn't let it scare me. I couldn't let it stop me from finding that mermaid.

Was anyone up? Had I yelled out loud in my sleep?

I listened carefully. I could hear only the creaking of the boat, the splash of waves against its side.

The pink morning sunlight cheered me. The dark water looked inviting.

I slipped into my swimming trunks and crept out of my cabin as quietly as I could. I didn't want anyone to hear me.

In the galley I saw a half-empty pot of coffee sitting on the warmer. That meant Dr D was already up.

I tiptoed down the passageway and listened. I could hear him pottering around in the main lab.

I grabbed my snorkel, flippers and mask and went up on deck. Nobody up there.

The coast was clear.

Silently, I climbed down the ladder, slipped into the water, and snorkelled towards the lagoon.

I know it was crazy to sneak away like that. But you can't imagine how excited I was. Even in my wildest daydreams as William Deep, Jr, undersea explorer, I never thought I would see a real, live mermaid!

As I snorkelled towards the lagoon, I tried to imagine what she would look like.

Mr Showalter had said she looked like a young girl with long blonde hair and a green fishtail.

Weird, I thought.

Half-human, half-fish.

I tried to imagine my own legs replaced by a fishtail.

I'd be the greatest swimmer on earth if I had a fishtail, I thought. *I could win the Olympics without even practising.*

I wonder if she's pretty? I thought. *And I wonder if she can talk! I hope she can. She can tell me all kinds of secrets of the oceans.*

I wonder how she breathes underwater?

I wonder if she thinks like a human or like a fish?

So many questions.

This is going to be the greatest adventure of my life, I thought. *After I'm famous, I'll write a book about my undersea adventures. I'll call it* Courage of the Deep, *by William Deep, Jr. Maybe someone will even turn it into a movie.*

I raised my head and saw that I was nearing the reef. I concentrated on keeping away from it. I didn't want to touch that fire coral again.

I couldn't wait to explore the lagoon. I was so

excited, I forgot all about the terrifying dream I had had the night before.

I kicked my legs carefully, watching out for red coral.

I was nearly past the reef when I felt something brush my leg.

"Oh!" I cried out, and swallowed a mouthful of salty water.

Sputtering and choking, I felt something wrap around my ankle.

As it grabbed me, it scratched my ankle.

This time I knew for sure it wasn't seaweed.

Seaweed doesn't have claws!

Ignoring the panic that nearly froze me, I kicked and thrashed with all my strength.

"Stop it! Stop kicking me!" a voice screamed.

The mermaid?

"Hey—!" I cried out angrily as Sheena's head appeared beside me.

She pulled up her snorkelling mask. "I didn't scratch you *that* hard!" she snapped. "You don't have to go crazy!"

"What are *you* doing here?" I cried.

"What are *you* doing here?" she demanded nastily. "You know Dr D told us not to swim here."

"Then you shouldn't be here – *should* you?" I shouted.

"I knew you were up to something, so I followed you," Sheena replied, adjusting her mask.

"I'm not up to anything," I lied. "I'm just snorkelling."

"Sure, Billy. You're just snorkelling at six thirty in the morning exactly where you're not supposed to – *and* where you burned your foot on that fire coral yesterday. You're either up to something or you're totally crazy!" She squinted at me, waiting for a response.

What a choice! I was either up to something or crazy. Which should I admit to?

If I admitted I was up to something, I'd have to tell her about the mermaid – and I couldn't do that.

"OK," I said with a casual shrug. "I guess I'm crazy."

"Well, big news," she muttered sarcastically. "Come on back to the boat, Billy," said Sheena. "Dr D will be looking for us."

"You go back. I'll be there in a little while."

"Billy," said Sheena. "Dr D is going to be very mad. He's probably ready to hop in the dinghy and search for us right now."

I was about to give up and go with her. Then, out of the corner of my eye, I saw a big splash on the other side of the reef.

The mermaid! I thought. *That's got to be her! If I don't go look for her now, I might miss her!*

I turned away from Sheena and started swimming very fast, straight for the reef.

I could hear Sheena screaming, "Billy! Come back! *Billy!*"

190

I thought I heard an extra note of panic in her voice, but I ignored it. *Just Sheena trying to scare me again*, I thought.

"*Billy!*" she screamed again. "*Billy!*"

I kept on swimming.

No way was I going to stop now.

But as it turned out, I should have listened to her.

Swimming fast, I raised my head, searching for a good place to swim safely over the fire coral.

I saw another splash. Across the lagoon. Near the shore.

That's *got* to be the mermaid! I thought excitedly.

I stared hard, trying to catch a glimpse of her.

I thought I saw some kind of fin.

I made my way past the reef into the deep, still waters of the lagoon. I strained to see the mermaid, but my mask had fogged.

Rats! I thought. *What a time for my mask to start leaking!*

I came up for air and pulled off the mask. I hoped I wouldn't lose sight of the mermaid because of this.

I wiped the water from my eyes and, leaving the mask wrapped around my wrist, stared towards the lagoon.

That's when I saw it. A few hundred metres away.

Not the green fishtail of a mermaid.

The fin I saw was a grey-white triangle sticking straight up in the water.

The fin of a hammerhead shark.

As I stared in horror, the fin turned in the water and then ripped towards me, moving steady and straight as a torpedo.

Where was Sheena?

Was she still behind me?

I glanced back. I could see her in the distance, splashing back to the boat.

I was forced to forget about Sheena as the grey fin swiftly moved closer.

I thrashed my arms in the water, trying to swim away.

When the shark swam right past me, I stopped thrashing.

Would it go away? Would it leave me alone?

My heart in my throat, I started swimming in the other direction, towards the reef. Away from the shark.

I kept my eyes on that fin.

It began to turn. The shark's fin streamed towards me in a wide arc.

"Ohhh." I let out a terrified groan as I realized it was circling me.

Now I didn't know which way to go. The shark

swam between me and the boat. If I could turn around and climb on to the reef, maybe I would be safe.

The huge fin slid closer.

I plunged towards the reef. I knew I had to keep distance between me and the shark.

Suddenly, the fin shot up in front of me – between me and the reef.

The shark kept circling, closing in, swimming faster and faster, making the circle smaller as he swam.

I was trapped. But I couldn't stay still. I couldn't just float there, waiting for the shark to eat me.

I had to fight. I kicked my legs in a panic as I swam towards the reef.

I was nearer to the reef now. But the shark's circles grew smaller, smaller.

I breathed in quick, shallow gasps. I couldn't think clearly. I was too terrified. The same two words echoed in my brain: *The shark. The shark.*

Over and over again. *The shark. The shark.*

The shark swam around me in a tight circle. His tail swished, sending up waves of water over me.

The shark. The shark.

I stared at the monster in wide-eyed horror. He swam so close, I could see him clearly. He was big – at least three metres long. His head was wide and hideous, long like the head of a hammer, with an eye on each end.

I heard my voice quivering. "No . . . no. . ."

Something cold brushed my leg.

The shark. The shark.

My stomach lurched. I threw my head back and let out a howl of sheer terror.

"Aaaaaiiii!"

Pain jolted down my spine.

The shark had bumped me with its snout. My body rose out of the water, then hit the surface with a *smack*.

I froze.

The shark was hungry.

It wanted to fight.

It circled me again, then zoomed straight for me.

Its jaws opened. I saw rows and rows of sharp teeth.

I screamed out a hoarse "NO!" I thrashed, panicked. I kicked with all my strength.

The razor teeth brushed by, just missing my leg.

The reef. I had to get to the reef. It was my only chance.

I dived for the coral. The shark plunged towards me. I dodged it once more.

I grabbed the red coral. Pain shot through my hand. The fire coral.

I didn't care.

The top of the reef sat just above the surface of the water. I tried to pull myself up. My whole body stung.

I had almost made it. Soon I'd be safe.

With a mighty kick, I hoisted myself on to the reef – and was yanked back into the water.

My stomach slammed against the side of the reef. I felt a sharp stab of pain in my leg.

I tried to pull my leg away. I couldn't.

It was caught in the jaws of the shark.

My mind screamed with terror.

The shark. The shark.

It's got me!

13

My entire body burned with pain. I slipped heavily into the water.

The shark knew he had me. I had no strength left to fight.

Then something splashed nearby.

The shark released my leg and jerked towards the splash.

I had no time to catch my breath. The shark circled back. It charged at me.

The gaping jaws moved in for the kill.

I shut my eyes and let out a shrill scream of terror.

A second passed. Then another.

Nothing happened.

I heard a loud thump.

I opened my eyes.

Something had come between me and the shark, a few metres in front of me.

I stared. The water churned white. A long, shiny

green fishtail rose out of the water and splashed back down.

Another fish was fighting the shark!

The shark rolled over, then attacked. The green fishtail smacked the shark hard. The shark went under.

I couldn't see what was happening. The water rocked higher, tossing up frothy white waves.

All around me the water bubbled and churned, white with foam. Over the crash of the water, I heard shrill animal squeals.

Sharks don't squeal, do they? I thought. *What is making that sound?*

The shark surfaced, its toothy jaws gaping. It snapped them at something, once, twice. Snapping at air.

The long green fishtail rose out of the water and smacked the shark hard. A direct hit on its broad hammerhead.

The shark shut its jaws and sank below the surface.

Then I heard a loud *bump*! The water stopped churning.

A second later, the huge grey fin surfaced a few metres away, speeding off in the other direction.

The shark was swimming away!

I stared at the green fishtail as it arced over the dark swelling water.

As the waters calmed, I heard a low musical sound. It was beautiful and slightly sad. Whistling and humming at the same time.

It sounded something like a whale. But this creature was much smaller than a whale.

The green tail swung around. Then the creature lifted its head.

A head with long blonde hair.

The mermaid!

Bobbing in the water, I forgot my burning pain as I gaped at her.

To my amazement, the mermaid looked just as the zoo people had said she would.

Her head and shoulders were smaller than mine, but her flashing green tail stretched out, long and powerful. Her wide sea-green eyes sparkled. Her skin gave off a pale pink glow.

I stared at her, unable to speak.

She's real! I thought. *And she's so beautiful!*

At last I found my voice. "You – you saved me," I stammered. "You saved my life. Thank you!"

She shyly lowered her eyes and cooed at me through shell-pink lips. What was she trying to say?

"What can I do in return?" I asked her. "I'll do anything I can."

She smiled and uttered that haunting low hum. She was trying to talk to me. I wished I could understand her.

She reached for my hand and examined it, frowning over the red burns from the fire coral. Her hand felt cool. She passed it over the palm of my hand, and the pain from the burns began to fade away.

"Wow!" I exclaimed. I must have sounded pretty stupid, but I didn't know what else to say. Her touch was like magic. When she held my hand, I could float without treading water. Just as she did.

Was this another dream?

I closed my eyes and opened them again.

I was still floating in the sea, staring at a blonde-haired mermaid.

No. Not a dream.

She smiled again and shook her head, making those low singing sounds.

I could hardly believe that only a few minutes before, I'd been frantically fighting off a hungry shark.

I raised my head and searched the waters. The shark had vanished. The water had calmed, shimmering like gold now under the morning sunlight. And there I was, floating in the sea off a deserted island with a real mermaid.

Sheena will never believe this, I thought. *Not in a million years.*

Suddenly, the mermaid flipped her tail and disappeared under the water.

Startled, I searched around for her. She had left without a trace – not a ripple, not a bubble.

Where did she go? I wondered. *Is she gone, just like that? Will I never see her again?*

I rubbed my eyes and looked for her again. No sign of her. A few fish darted past me.

She had disappeared so instantly, I began to think I had dreamed her up after all.

Just then, I felt a tiny pinch on my foot.

"Ouch!" I yelled, quickly pulling away. I began to panic. The shark was back!

Then, behind me, I heard a small splash and a whistlelike giggle. I turned around.

The mermaid smiled mischievously at me. She snapped her fingers in a pinching motion.

"It was you!" I cried, laughing with relief. "You're worse than my little sister!"

She whistled again and slapped her tail against the surface of the water.

Suddenly, a dark shadow fell across her face. I raised my eyes to see what it was.

Too late.

A heavy net dropped over us. Startled, I thrashed my arms and legs. But that only tangled them more in the rope.

The net tightened over both of us. We were thrown together.

We struggled helplessly as the net jerked us up.

The mermaid's eyes widened and she squealed in terror.

"*EEEEEE!*" she cried.

We were being pulled up out of the water.

"*EEEEEEE!*" The mermaid's frightened wail rose like a siren, drowning out my feeble cries for help.

"Billy – I don't believe it!"

I gazed up through the holes in the net and recognized Dr D and Sheena. They struggled to pull us aboard the dinghy.

Sheena stared down at me and the mermaid in amazement. Dr D's eyes were wide, and his mouth hung open.

"You've found her, Billy!" he said. "You've actually found the mermaid!"

"Just get me out of this net!" I cried. Somehow, I didn't feel so great about capturing the mermaid any more.

"The zoo people were right," Dr D muttered to himself. "It's unbelievable. It's astounding. It's historic. . ."

We landed in a heap on the floor of the dinghy. The mermaid squirmed beside me in the net, making sharp, angry clicking noises.

Dr D watched her closely. He touched her tail.

The mermaid flapped it hard against the bottom of the boat.

"Is there any way this could be a hoax?" he wondered aloud.

"Billy – is this one of your dumb tricks?" Sheena demanded suspiciously.

"It's not a trick," I said. "Now will you get me out of this net? The ropes are digging into my skin."

They ignored me.

Sheena gently reached one finger through the net and touched the scales on the mermaid's tail. "I can't believe it," she murmured. "She's really real!"

"Of course she's real!" I cried. "We're both real, and we're both very uncomfortable!"

"Well, it's hard to believe anything *you* say," Sheena snapped. "After all, you've been talking about sea monsters ever since we got here."

"I *did* see a sea monster!" I cried.

"Quiet, kids," said Dr D. "Let's get our discovery back to the sea lab."

He started the dinghy's motor and we roared back to the big boat.

Alexander stood on deck, waiting for us. "It's really true!" he cried excitedly. "It's really a mermaid!"

Sheena tied the dinghy to the side of the *Cassandra* while Dr D and Alexander hoisted me and the mermaid aboard.

Dr D opened the net and helped me out. The mermaid flopped her tail and got herself even more tangled in the net.

Alexander shook my hand. "I'm proud of you, Billy. How did you do it? This is amazing." He gave me a vigorous pat on the back. "Do you realize this is the greatest ocean find of the century? Maybe of all time?"

"Thanks," I said. "But I didn't do anything. I didn't find her – *she* found *me*."

The mermaid flopped violently on deck. Her squeals became higher-pitched, more frantic.

Alexander's face fell. "We've got to do something for her," he said urgently.

"Dr D, you've got to let her go," I said. "She needs to be in the water."

"I'll fill the big tank with seawater, Dr D," said Alexander. He hurried off to fill the tank.

"We can't let her go just yet, Billy," said Dr D. "Not without examining her first." His eyes were shining with excitement. But he saw how upset I was. "We won't hurt her, Billy. She'll be all right."

His eyes dropped to my leg, and he frowned. He kneeled down to look at it.

"You're bleeding, Billy," he said. "Are you OK?"

"I'm fine," I said. "But the mermaid isn't."

He ignored me.

"How did this happen?" asked Dr D.

"A shark grabbed my leg," I told him. "Just as he was about to clamp down, the mermaid came. She saved my life. You should have seen her fighting that shark."

Dr D turned to the mermaid as if seeing her for the first time.

"Wow," said Sheena. "She fought off a shark? All by herself?"

The mermaid's long green tail pounded angrily on the deck of the boat.

"EEEEE! EEEEEE!" she cried shrilly. She almost sounded as if she were screaming.

"Forget about my leg," I shouted. "You've got to let the mermaid go!"

Dr D stood up, shaking his head. "Billy, I'm a scientist. This mermaid is an extremely important discovery. If I let her go, I'd be letting down the entire scientific community. I'd be letting down the entire world!"

"You just want the million dollars," I muttered.

I knew it was cruel, but I couldn't stop myself. I hated seeing the mermaid so unhappy.

Dr D looked hurt.

"That's not fair, Billy," he said. "I think you know me better than that."

I avoided his gaze. Lowering my head, I pretended to examine the cut on my leg. It wasn't very deep. Alexander had given me some gauze. I pressed it against the cut.

"I only want the money to continue my research," Dr D went on. "I would never use this mermaid to get rich."

That was true. I knew Dr D didn't care about the money for himself. All he wanted was to keep studying fish.

"Just think about it, Billy. You've found a mermaid! A creature we all thought didn't exist! We can't just let her go. We've got to find out a little bit about her," he said excitedly.

I said nothing.

"We won't hurt her, Billy. I promise."

Alexander returned. "The tank is ready, Dr D."

"Thanks." Dr D followed him to the other side of the boat.

I glanced at Sheena to see whose side she was on. Did she want to keep the mermaid? Or let her go?

But Sheena just stood there, watching. Her face was tense. I could tell she wasn't sure which of us was right.

But when I looked at the mermaid, I knew *I* was right.

She had finally stopped squirming and flipping her tail. Now she lay still on the deck, the net draped over her. She was breathing hard and staring out at the ocean with watery, sad eyes.

I wished I'd never tried to find her in the first place. Now all I wanted was to find some way to help her get back to her home.

Dr D and Alexander came back. They lifted the mermaid inside the net. Alexander lifted her tail, and Dr D held her head.

"Don't squirm, little mermaid," Dr D said in a soothing voice. "Keep still."

The mermaid seemed to understand. She didn't flop around. But her eyes rolled wildly, and she uttered low moans.

Dr D and Alexander carried her to the giant glass tank. It stood on the deck now, full of fresh seawater. They gently dropped her into the tank, pulling the net away as she slid into the water. Then they put a screen top over the tank and clamped it shut.

The mermaid churned the water with her tail. Then, gradually, her tail stopped moving. She grew still.

Her body slumped lifelessly to the bottom of the tank.

She didn't move or breathe.

"Noooo!" An angry cry escaped my lips. "She's dead! She's dead! We *killed* her!"

Sheena had moved to the other side of the tank. "Billy, look—!" she called to me.

I hurried around to her.

"The mermaid isn't dead," Sheena reported, pointing. "Look. She – she's crying or something."

My sister was right. The mermaid had slumped to the bottom of the tank and had buried her face in her hands. "Now what do we do?" I asked.

No one answered.

"We have to find a method of feeding her," my uncle said, rubbing his chin, his eyes on the tank.

"Do you think she eats like a person or a fish?" I asked.

"If only she could tell us," said Alexander. "She can't talk, can she, Billy?"

"I don't think so," I said. "She just makes sounds. Whistles and clicks and hums."

"I'll go down to the lab and get some equipment ready," said Alexander. "Maybe we can find out something about her with the sonar monitor."

"Good idea," said Dr D thoughtfully.

Alexander hurried below.

"I think I'd better go to Santa Anita for some supplies," said Dr D. Santa Anita was the nearest inhabited island. "I'll buy lots of different kinds of foods. We can try them out on her until we find something she likes. Would you two like anything while I'm there?"

"How about some peanut butter?" Sheena asked quickly. "There's no way Alexander can ruin a peanut butter sandwich!"

Dr D nodded as he climbed into the dinghy. "Peanut butter it is. Anything else? Billy?"

I shook my head.

"All right," Dr D said. "I'll be back in a few hours."

He started the motor, and the dinghy sped off towards Santa Anita.

"It's so hot," Sheena complained. "I'm going down to my cabin for a while."

"OK," I said, my eyes on the mermaid.

It *was* hot up on deck. There was no breeze, and the white-hot noon sun beat down on my face.

But I couldn't go below deck. I couldn't leave the mermaid.

She floated behind the glass, her long tail

drooping. When she saw me, she pressed her hands and face to the glass and cooed sadly.

I waved to her through the glass.

She cooed and hummed in her low voice, trying to communicate with me. I listened, trying to understand.

"Are you hungry?" I asked her.

She stared at me blankly.

"Are you hungry?" I repeated, rubbing my stomach. "Go like this" – I nodded my head up and down – "for yes. Do this for no." I shook my head back and forth.

I stopped and waited to see what she'd do.

She nodded her head yes.

"Yes?" I said. "You *are* hungry?"

She shook her head no.

"No? You're not hungry?"

She nodded her head yes. Then she shook her head no again.

She's just copying me, I thought. *She doesn't really understand.*

I took a step back and studied her in the tank.

She's young, I thought. *She's a lot like me. That means she* must *be hungry. And she probably likes to eat what I like. Right?*

Maybe. It was worth a try.

I hurried down to the galley. I pulled open a cupboard and took out a packet of chocolate chip cookies.

OK, so it's not exactly seafood, I thought. *But who wouldn't like chocolate chip cookies?*

I grabbed a few cookies and stuffed the packet back in the cupboard. Alexander came through on his way up to the deck. He was carrying some equipment in his arms.

"Getting a snack?" he asked me.

"For the mermaid," I told him. "Do you think she'll like them?"

He shrugged his broad shoulders and said, "Who knows?"

He followed me out on deck, carrying the equipment.

"What's all that stuff?" I asked him.

"I thought we could run a few tests on the mermaid to see what we can find out about her," said Alexander. "But go ahead and feed her first."

"OK," I said. "Here goes."

I held a cookie up to the glass. The mermaid stared at it. I could see that she didn't know what it was.

"Mmmmm," I said, patting my stomach. "Yummy."

The mermaid patted her tummy, imitating me. She stared out at me blankly with those sea-green eyes.

Alexander reached up and unlatched the screen top. I handed him the cookie, and he dropped it into the tank.

214

The mermaid watched it falling towards her through the water. She made no attempt to grab it.

By the time it reached her, it was soggy. It fell apart in the tank.

"Yuck," I said. "Even I wouldn't eat it now."

The mermaid pushed the soggy cookie pieces away.

"Maybe Dr D will have something she likes when he gets back," said Alexander.

"I hope so," I said.

Alexander began to set up his equipment. He put a thermometer inside the tank, and some long white plastic tubes.

"Oh, man," Alexander mumbled, shaking his head. "I forgot my notebook."

He hurried back down to the lab.

I watched the mermaid float sadly in her tank, with all the tubes coming out of it. She reminded me of the fish down in the lab.

No, I thought. *She's not a fish. She shouldn't be treated this way.*

I remembered how she had fought the shark.

She could have been killed, I thought. *Easily. But she fought the shark, anyway, just to help me.*

The mermaid cooed. Then I saw her wipe away the tears that had begun to run down her face.

She's crying again, I thought, feeling guilty and miserable. *She's pleading with me.*

I put my face against the glass, as close to hers as I could get it.

I've got to help her, I thought.

I put a finger to my lips. "*Ssshhh*," I whispered. "Stay quiet. I have to work quickly!"

I knew I was about to do something that would make Dr D very angry.

My uncle would probably never forgive me.

But I didn't care.

I was going to do what I thought was right.

I was going to set the mermaid free.

My hand trembled as I reached up to unlatch the screen at the top of the tank. The tank was taller than I was. I wasn't quite sure how I'd get the mermaid out of there. But I had to find a way.

As I struggled to pull the screen off, the mermaid began to squeal, *"Eeee! EEEEEE!"*

"Sshh! Don't make any noise!" I warned her.

Then I felt a hand grab me by the arm. I gasped, startled.

A deep voice asked, "What are you doing?"

I turned around to see Alexander standing behind me.

I stepped away from the tank, and he let go of my arm.

"Billy, what were you doing?" he asked again.

"I was going to let her go!" I cried. "Alexander, you can't keep her in there! Look how unhappy she is!"

We both stared at the mermaid, who had slumped to the bottom of the tank again. I think

217

she knew that I had tried to help her – and that I had been stopped.

I caught the sadness on Alexander's face. I could tell he felt sorry for her. But he had a job to do.

He turned to me and put an arm around my shoulders. "Billy, you've got to understand how important this mermaid is to your uncle," he said. "He's worked his whole life for a discovery like this. It would break his heart if you let her go."

He slowly led me away from the tank. I turned back to look at the mermaid again.

"But what about *her* heart?" I asked. "I think it's breaking her heart to be stuck in that fish tank."

Alexander sighed. "It's not ideal, I know that. But it's only temporary. Soon she'll have plenty of room to swim and play in."

Sure, I thought bitterly. *As an exhibit at the zoo, with millions of people gawking at her every day.*

Alexander removed his arm from my shoulders and rubbed his chin.

"Your uncle is a very caring man, Billy," he said. "He'll do his best to make sure the mermaid has everything she needs. But it's his duty to study her. The things he can learn from her could help people understand the oceans better – and take better care of them. That's important, right?"

"I guess so," I said.

I knew Alexander had a good point. I loved Dr D, and I didn't want to spoil his big discovery.

But still, the mermaid shouldn't have to suffer for science, I thought.

"Come on, Billy," Alexander said, leading me below deck. "I promised you I'd show you how the sonar probes work, didn't I? Let's go down to the lab, and I'll give you a demonstration."

As we started to climb below, I took one last glance back at the mermaid. She was still slumped forlornly at the bottom of the tank. Her head was lowered, her blonde hair floating limply above it like seaweed.

The sonar probes weren't as interesting as I thought they'd be. All they did was beep whenever the *Cassandra* was in danger of running ashore.

I guess Alexander could tell my mind was not on the sonar probes. "Want some lunch?" he asked me.

Uh-oh. Lunch. I was hungry. But not for spicy chicken salad.

I hesitated. "Well, I had a big breakfast. . . "

"I'll whip up something special," Alexander offered. "We can have a picnic up on deck with the mermaid. Come on."

What could I do? I followed him to the galley.

He opened the small refrigerator and pulled out a bowl.

"This has been marinating all morning," he said.

I looked into the bowl. It was full of thin strips of something white and rubbery-looking. They floated in an oily dark grey liquid.

Whatever it was, I knew I couldn't eat it.

"It's marinated squid," said Alexander. "I added some squid ink for extra flavour. That's what makes it grey."

"Yum," I said, rolling my eyes. "I haven't had squid ink in days!"

"Don't be so sarcastic. You might be surprised," Alexander replied. He handed me the bowl. "Take this up on deck. I'll bring some bread and iced tea."

I carried the bowl of squid up and set it down near the mermaid's tank.

"How are you doing, Mermaid?" I asked her.

She flipped her tail a little. Then she opened and closed her mouth, as if she were chewing.

"Hey," I said. "You *are* hungry, aren't you?"

She kept making that chewing motion. I glanced down at the bowl of squid.

Who knows? I thought. *This might be just what she'd like.*

I stood on a rail and unlatched the top of the tank. Then I dropped in a piece of the rubbery squid.

The mermaid leaped towards it and caught it in her mouth.

She chewed, then smiled.

She liked it!

I gave her some more. She ate it.

I rubbed my stomach. "Do you like it?" I asked her. I nodded yes.

She smiled again. Then she nodded yes.

She understood me!

"What are you doing, Billy?" Alexander asked. He had come up on deck carrying two plates and a loaf of bread.

"Alexander, look!" I cried. "We communicated!"

I dropped another piece of squid into the tank. She ate it. Then she nodded yes.

"That means she likes it!" I said.

"Wow," murmured Alexander. He put down the plates and picked up his notebook. He scribbled some notes.

"Isn't that way cool?" I demanded. "I'm a scientist, too – aren't I, Alexander?"

He nodded but kept writing.

"I mean, I'm the first person on earth to communicate with a mermaid – right?" I insisted.

"If she stays with us long enough, you might be able to talk to her in sign language," he said. "Just think of the things we could learn!"

He spoke aloud as he wrote, "Likes to eat

squid." Then he put down his pencil and said, "Hey, wait! That's our lunch!"

Uh-oh, I thought. I hope his feelings aren't hurt.

He looked at me. He looked at the bowl. He looked at the mermaid.

Then he started laughing.

"At least *somebody* around here likes my cooking!" he exclaimed.

About an hour later, Dr D returned with the groceries and supplies. Luckily, he had bought plenty of seafood in Santa Anita. We fed some of it to the mermaid for supper. While she ate, Dr D checked the readings on the meters Alexander had set up in the tank.

"Interesting," Dr D commented. "She sends out sonar signals through the water. Just as whales do."

"What does that mean?" asked Sheena.

"It means there are probably other mermaids like her," said Dr D. "She must be trying to contact them with underwater sounds."

Poor mermaid, I thought. *She's calling to her friends. She wants to be rescued.*

I went to my cabin after supper and stared out of the little porthole.

An orange sun sank slowly into the purple horizon. A wide carpet of gold light shimmered in the rolling ocean waters. A cool breeze blew in through the porthole.

I watched the sun drop into the ocean. The sky immediately darkened, as if someone had turned off a lamp.

The mermaid is up there all alone, I thought. *She must be so frightened. A prisoner. Trapped in a fish tank in the dark.*

The door to my cabin suddenly burst open. Sheena bounded in, panting, her eyes wide.

"Sheena!" I scolded angrily. "How many times do I have to tell you to knock first?"

She ignored me. "But, Billy!" she gasped. "She's escaped! The mermaid escaped!"

I leaped off my bed, my heart pounding.

"She's not there!" Sheena cried. "She's not in her tank!"

I darted out of the cabin, up the hatch, and out on deck.

Part of me hoped she really had escaped to freedom. But part of me wished she could stay for ever – and make my uncle the most famous scientist in the world and me the most famous nephew of a scientist!

Please let her be OK, I thought.

Up on deck, my eyes adjusted to the evening darkness. Tiny lights glowed all around the edge of the boat.

I squinted across the deck at the giant fish tank.

I ran so fast, I nearly toppled overboard. Sheena was right behind me.

"Hey!" I cried out when I saw the mermaid floating listlessly in the water, her green tail shimmering faintly in the fading light.

It took me a few seconds to realize that Sheena was laughing. "Gotcha!" she shouted gleefully. "Gotcha again, Billy!"

I groaned long and loud. Another one of Sheena's stupid tricks.

"Good one, Sheena," I said bitterly. "Very clever."

"You're just mad because I fooled you again. You're so easy to trick."

The mermaid raised her eyes to me, and a faint smile formed on her pale lips. "*Looorrrooo, looorrrooo,*" she cooed at me.

"She really is pretty," Sheena said.

The mermaid is hoping I'll let her go now, I thought. *Maybe I should. . .*

Sheena could help me, I decided. It would be easier with two of us.

But would my sister cooperate? "Sheena—" I began.

I heard footsteps behind us. "Hey, kids." It was Dr D. "It's almost bedtime," he called. "Ready to go below?"

"We never go to bed this early at home," Sheena whined.

"Maybe not. But I bet you don't get up so early at home, either. Do you?"

Sheena shook her head. We all stood at the tank and watched the mermaid in silence. She gave her tail a little flick and settled back down at the bottom of the tank.

"Don't worry about her," Dr D said. "I'll check on her during the night to make sure she's all right."

The mermaid pressed her tiny hands against the glass wall of the tank. Her eyes pleaded with us, pleaded with us to set her free.

"She'll feel better once she gets to Marina Zoo," Dr D said. "They're building a special lagoon just for her, with a reef and everything. It'll be exactly like the lagoon off Ilandra. She'll be free to swim and play. She'll feel at home."

I hope so, I thought. But I didn't feel so sure.

The *Cassandra* rocked gently on the waves that night, but I couldn't fall asleep.

I lay on my bunk, staring at the ceiling. A pale beam of moonlight fell through the porthole and across my face. I couldn't stop thinking about the mermaid.

I tried to imagine what it would feel like to be trapped in a glass tank for a whole day. It probably wouldn't be that different from being trapped in this tiny cabin, I thought, glancing around. My cabin was about as big as a closet.

It would be terrible, I thought, fiddling with the collar of my pyjama top. I pushed open the porthole to let in more air.

The fish tank might not even be the worst of it, I figured. I know Dr D cares about the mermaid. I know he'd never hurt her.

But what will happen to her when the zoo people take her away? Who will look out for her?

Sure, they're building a fancy fake lagoon. But it won't be the same as the real lagoon. And there will be people around, staring at her all the time. They'll probably expect her to perform tricks or something; maybe jump through hoops like a trained seal.

They'll probably put her in TV commercials, too. And TV shows and movies.

She'll be a prisoner. A lonely prisoner for the rest of her life.

This is all my fault. How could I let this happen?

I have to do something, I decided. I can't let them take her.

Just then I thought I heard something – a low hum. I lay very still and listened. At first I thought it was the mermaid. But I quickly realized it was a motor.

I heard it chugging softly, from a distance. But slowly the sound moved closer.

A boat.

I sat up and peered out of the porthole. A large boat pulled quietly up beside the *Cassandra*.

Who was it? The zoo people?

In the middle of the night?

No. It wasn't the same boat. This boat was much bigger.

As I peered out the small porthole, I saw two dark figures quietly slip on board the *Cassandra*. Then two more.

My heart began to race. *Who are these people?* I wondered. *What are they doing?*

What should I do?

Should I sneak up and spy on them? What if they see me?

Then I heard more strange noises.

A thud. A muffled cry of pain.

It came from the deck.

The deck. Where the mermaid was trapped helplessly in her tank.

Oh, no! I thought, feeling a chill of panic. *They're hurting the mermaid!*

I charged up to the deck. Sheena ran right behind me.

Stumbling over a tow rope, I grabbed the rail to steady myself. Then I darted blindly to the fish tank.

The mermaid huddled at the bottom of the tank, her arms wrapped protectively around herself.

I saw four men standing tensely near the tank. All four were dressed in black. They had black masks pulled over their faces.

One of the men held a small club in his hand.

And a body lay sprawled on the deck, face down.

Dr D!

Sheena screamed and ran to our uncle. She knelt beside him. "They hit him on the head!" she cried. "They knocked him out!"

I gasped. "Who are you?" I demanded. "What are you doing on our boat?"

The four men ignored me.

Two of them unfolded a heavy rope net and spread it over the fish tank. Then they let it fall into the tank, draping it over the mermaid.

"Stop it!" I yelled. "What are you doing?"

"Be quiet, kid," the man with the club muttered. He raised the club menacingly.

I watched helplessly as they tightened the net around the mermaid.

They were kidnapping her!

"Eeeee! EEEEEeeee!" she squealed in terror and started to thrash her arms, struggling to free herself from the heavy net.

"Stop it! Leave her alone!" I cried.

One of the men gave a low laugh. The other three still ignored me.

Sheena was bent over Dr D, frantically trying to wake him up. I ran to the hatch and shouted down into the cabin, "Alexander! Alexander! Help!"

Alexander was big and strong – maybe strong enough to stop these men.

I ran back to the tank. The mermaid was trapped in the net. All four men worked to lift her out of the tank. She squirmed and fought with all her strength.

"EEEEEE!" she screamed. The high-pitched squeal hurt my ears.

"Can't you get her to shut up?" one of the men cried angrily.

"Just load her on board," the one with the club replied sharply.

"Stop!" I yelled. "You can't do that!"

Then I totally lost it.

Without thinking, I dived towards the four of them. I don't know what I planned to do. I just knew I had to stop them.

One of them pushed me away easily with one hand. "Stay away – or you'll get hurt," he muttered.

"Let her go! Let the mermaid go!" I cried frantically.

"Forget about the mermaid," said the man. "You'll never see her again."

I grabbed the rail. My heart was pounding in my chest. I gasped for breath.

I couldn't stand the mermaid's terrified screams.

I couldn't let them take her – not without a fight.

She had saved my life once. Now it was my turn to save hers.

But what could I do?

They had lifted the mermaid out of the tank. Three men held her in the net.

She squirmed and thrashed like crazy, splashing water all over the deck.

I'll tackle them, I thought. I'll knock them over. Then I'll push the mermaid into the ocean and she can swim away to safety.

Lowering my head like a rugby player, I took a deep breath and ran right at them.

20

"Billy – stop!" Sheena screamed.

I crashed into one of the men holding the net, butting him hard in the stomach with my head.

To my dismay, the man hardly moved.

He grabbed me with his free hand, lifted me up off the deck, and heaved me into the fish tank.

I splashed into the warm water and came up, choking and sputtering.

Through the glass, I watched the men toss the mermaid aboard their boat. They were getting away!

I tried to scramble out of the tank, but it was too tall. I kept slipping down the wet glass, unable to reach the top.

I knew there was only one person who could stop the masked men now. Alexander.

Where was he? Hadn't he heard all the noise?

"ALEXANDER!" I shouted as loud as I could. But my voice was muffled by the glass walls of the tank.

Then, finally, he appeared on the deck. I saw his big blond head and muscular body moving towards me. At last!

"Alexander!" I cried, scrambling to stay afloat in the tank. "Stop them!"

I could hear the motor of the other boat begin to rumble. One by one, the masked men lowered themselves off our boat.

Three of them had left the *Cassandra*. Only one remained on deck.

Through the glass I watched Alexander run up to him and grab his shoulder.

Yes! I thought. *Get him, Alexander! Get him!*

I'd never seen Alexander hit anyone before. But I knew he could do it if he had to.

But Alexander didn't hit the masked man. Instead, he asked, "Is the mermaid safely on board?"

The masked man nodded.

"Good," Alexander replied. "And have you got the money for me?"

"Got it."

"All right," Alexander murmured. "Let's get out of here!"

I nearly choked on a mouthful of water.

I just couldn't *believe* that Alexander was working with the masked men. He had seemed like such a good guy.

But I knew now that he had arranged the whole thing. He had to be the one who had told them the mermaid was on board our boat.

"Alexander," I cried, "how could you?"

He stared at me through the glass. "Hey, Billy, it's just business," he said with a shrug. "The zoo was going to pay a million dollars for the mermaid. But my new bosses will pay *twenty* million!" A thin smile crossed his face. "You know arithmetic, Billy. Which would you choose?"

"You rat!" I shouted. I wanted to punch him. I struggled to get out of the tank. All I managed to do was splash a lot and get water up my nose.

Alexander followed the masked man to his boat. I pounded helplessly on the glass tank.

Then I saw Sheena stand up. Lowering my gaze to the deck, I saw that Dr D was moving.

Alexander didn't seem to notice. He stepped over Dr D's body. He didn't even care that Dr D could have been hurt badly.

I watched my uncle reach up and grab Alexander by the ankle.

"Whoa!" Alexander tripped and fell hard on to his elbows and his knees.

Sheena screamed and backed up to the rail.

Maybe there's still hope, I thought, my heart beating faster. Maybe they won't get away after all.

Alexander sat up, dazed, rubbing one elbow.

"Get them!" he shouted down to the masked men.

Two of the men climbed back aboard the *Cassandra* and grabbed Dr D. Sheena ran at them, flailing at them with her puny little fists.

Of course that didn't do any good. The third masked man grabbed her arms and pinned them behind her back.

"Kick him, Sheena!" I yelled through the glass.

She tried to kick the man who held her, but he just tightened his grip. She couldn't move.

"Let them go!" I screamed desperately.

"What should we do with them?" asked one of the men.

"Whatever you do, do it quickly," said Alexander. "We've got to get out of here."

The man who held Sheena glanced in at me. I was frantically treading water, trying to stay above the surface.

"They might call the island police or the Coast Guard," he said, frowning. "We'd better kill them."

"Throw them all in the tank!" suggested one of his partners.

22

"Alexander!" Dr D shouted. "I know you're not a cruel man. Don't let them do this."

Alexander avoided my uncle's hard stare. "Sorry, Dr D," he muttered. "I can't stop them. If I try to, they'll kill me, too."

Without another word, he lowered himself on to the other boat.

What a creep, I thought angrily.

Two of the masked men lifted Dr D up high and dropped him into the tank. He landed beside me with a splash.

"Are you OK?" I asked him.

He rubbed the back of his head and nodded.

Sheena was next. They tossed her in easily. She flew through the air, flailing her arms and legs. Then she plopped into the water.

The men replaced the screen lid. They clamped it shut.

I stared out at them, realizing in horror that we had no way to escape.

The water in the tank was about two metres deep. We all kicked and paddled, trying to stay above the surface. There was barely enough room for the three of us.

"All right," said one of the men. "Let's go."

"Wait!" Dr D shouted. "You can't just leave us here!"

The three men exchanged glances. "You're right. We can't," said one.

They stepped towards us.

So they aren't heartless monsters after all, I thought. They weren't going to leave us.

But what were they going to do?

The first man signalled the other two. They raised their hands to one side of the tank.

"One, two, three—" the first man called out.

On three, they pushed the tank over the side of the deck.

We were thrown together. Then our bodies slammed against the side of the tank as it dropped into the ocean.

Ocean water seeped into the tank.

"The tank – it's sinking!" cried Dr D.

We watched the kidnappers' boat as it roared away. Our tank rocked in its wake. Then it started to sink.

"We're going under!" Sheena screamed. "We're going to drown!"

All three of us desperately pushed against the screen. I beat my fists against it. Dr D tried to get his shoulder against it.

But the tank tilted in the water, and we were all tossed back.

The screen was made of heavy steel mesh and clamped on to the top of the tank. We couldn't reach the clamps from inside, so we had to try to break through it.

We pushed with all our strength. It wouldn't budge.

The tank slowly sank deeper below the surface of the dark, rolling water. The moon disappeared behind a blanket of clouds, leaving us in total darkness.

We had only a minute or two before the tank dropped completely below the surface.

Sheena started to cry. "I'm so afraid!" she shrieked. "I'm so afraid!"

Dr D pounded his fists against the glass tank wall, trying to break through.

I ran my hands all along the top of the tank, looking for a weak spot in the screen.

Then I hit something.

A tiny latch.

"Look!" I cried, pointing to the latch.

I fumbled with it, trying to open it. "It's stuck!"

"Let me try." Dr D tore at the latch with his fingers. "It's jammed shut," he said.

Sheena took a red clip from her hair. "Maybe we can loosen it with this," she said.

Dr D took the clip and scraped hard around the latch.

"It's working!" he said.

Maybe there's hope, I thought. *Maybe we'll get out of here!*

Dr D stopped scraping and tugged at the latch.

It moved!

It opened!

"We're free!" cried Sheena.

We all pushed at the screen. We pushed again.

"Come on, kids, push harder," urged Dr D.

We pushed again. The screen didn't move. The latch hadn't opened it after all. Two other latches held the screen in place.

Two latches we couldn't reach.

241

We all grew silent. The only sounds now were Sheena's soft, frightened sobs and the steady wash of the waves.

The water had risen nearly to the top of the tank. Soon it would come rushing in on us.

Suddenly, the ocean darkened. The waters grew choppy, and the tank rocked a little faster.

"What's that noise?" Sheena asked.

I listened.

Through the churning of the water, I heard a strange sound. It was very faint, as if coming from far away.

A shrill, high-pitched whistle.

"It sounds like a siren," Dr D murmured. "Lots of sirens."

The eerie wails rose and fell over the water.

Louder. Closer.

The sound – as shrill as the screech of metal – surrounded us.

Suddenly, dark, shadowy forms swirled around the tank.

We pressed our faces to the glass.

"That sound. I've never heard anything like it. What can it be?" asked Dr D.

"It – it's coming from all around!" I stammered.

The dark water tossed, churned by the shadowy forms. I peered through the foam, straining to see.

Suddenly, out of the murky water, a face appeared. It pressed itself against the glass, right in front of my face!

I gasped and pulled back.

Then I saw more faces. We were surrounded by small, girlish faces. Their wide eyes peered in at us menacingly.

"Mermaids!" I shrieked.

"Dozens of them!" Dr D murmured in hushed amazement.

They churned the water with their long tails.

Their hair, dark tangles in the black water, floated around their faces. The tank rocked harder and harder.

"What do they want?" cried Sheena, her voice shrill and trembling.

"They look angry," Dr D whispered.

I stared out at the mermaids, swirling around us like ghosts. They reached out their hands and began clutching at the tank. They smacked their tails on the water. The dark waters tossed and churned.

Suddenly, I knew. I knew what they wanted.

"Revenge," I murmured. "They've come for revenge. We took their friend. And now they're going to pay us back."

Shadowy hands pressed against the glass.

"They're pulling us under!" Dr D cried.

I gasped in terror, staring out at the hands, black outlines against the glass.

Then, suddenly, the tank began to rise. Up out of the water, higher and higher.

"Huh? What's happening?" asked Sheena.

"They – they're pushing us back up!" I cried happily.

"The mermaids aren't taking revenge – they're saving us!" Dr D exclaimed.

The tank brushed up against the *Cassandra*. I could see the mermaids' tiny hands working above us.

The clamps popped open. The screen was pulled off.

With a happy groan, Dr D boosted Sheena up. She scrambled on board the boat.

Then I climbed aboard, and we both helped pull Dr D out of the tank.

We were drenched, shivering from the cold. But we were safe.

The mermaids swarmed around the boat, their pale eyes peering up at us.

"Thank you," Dr D called down to them. "Thank you for saving our lives."

I realized this was the second time a mermaid had saved my life. I owed them more than ever now.

"We've got to get the kidnapped mermaid back," I said. "Who knows what Alexander and those creeps will do to her!"

"Yeah," cried Sheena. "Look what they tried to do to us!"

"I wish we could rescue her," Dr D murmured, shaking his head. "But I don't see how we can. How will we find the kidnappers' boat in the dark? They're long gone by now."

But I knew there had to be a way. I leaned over the rail, peering down at the mermaids floating beside us, chattering and cooing in the moonlight.

"Help us!" I pleaded with them. "We want to find your friend. Please – can you take us to her?"

I held my breath and waited. Would the mermaids understand me? Would they be able to help us – somehow?

The mermaids chattered and whistled to one another. Then one of them – a dark-haired mermaid with an extra-long tail – moved to the head of the group.

She began whistling and clicking to the other mermaids. She seemed to be giving orders.

The three of us stared in amazement as the mermaids began to form a long line, one mermaid after the other, stretching far out to sea.

"Do you think they're going to lead us to the kidnappers?" I asked.

"Maybe," Dr D replied thoughtfully. "But how will the mermaids find the boat?" He rubbed his chin. "I know. I'll bet they'll use their sonar. I wish I had time to really listen to those sounds they're making—"

"Look, Dr D!" Sheena interrupted. "The mermaids are swimming away!"

We watched the dark figures slide away through the rolling black waters.

"Quick!" I cried. "We've got to follow them."

"Too dangerous," Dr D replied, sighing. "We can't fight Alexander and four big masked men by ourselves!"

He paced back and forth on the narrow deck. "We should call the island police," he said finally. "But what would we say? That we're chasing after a kidnapped mermaid? No one would believe us."

"Dr D, we have to follow them. Please!" I pleaded. "The mermaids are swimming out of sight!"

He stared at me for a long moment. "OK. Let's get going," he said finally.

I hurried to the stern to untie the dinghy. Dr D dropped it into the water and jumped in. Sheena and I followed. Dr D started the motor – and we raced after the shimmering line of mermaids.

The mermaids glided so quickly through the rolling waters, it was hard for the small boat to keep up with them.

About fifteen or twenty minutes later, we found ourselves in a small deserted cove. The moon drifted out of the clouds. It cast pale light on a dark boat anchored near the shore.

Dr D cut the motor so the kidnappers wouldn't hear us approaching.

"They must be asleep," he whispered.

"How can Alexander sleep after what he did to us?" said Sheena. "He left us to drown!"

"Money can make people do terrible things," Dr D replied sadly. "But it's good they think we're dead. They won't be expecting us."

"But where's the mermaid?" I whispered, staring at the dark boat, bobbing gently under the misty moonlight.

We drifted silently towards the darkened boat.

Well, we've found the kidnappers, I thought, holding on to the side of the dinghy as we drew near.

There's just one problem.

What do we do next?

The air became very still. The kidnappers' boat sat gently on the calm, glassy waters of the cove.

"What happened to all the mermaids?" Sheena whispered.

I shrugged. There was no sign of them. I imagined them swimming way down below the surface, hiding.

Suddenly, at the side of the kidnappers' boat, I saw ripples in the water.

Slowly, silently, our dinghy glided towards the boat. I stared at the ripples, trying to see what was making them. Then I saw a flash of blonde hair in the moonlight.

"The mermaid!" I whispered. "There she is!"

She was floating in the water, tied to the back of the kidnappers' boat.

"They must not have a tank to keep her in," Dr D whispered excitedly. "Lucky for us."

Suddenly, we saw other figures rippling the

248

water. Mermaids arched up, circling the captured mermaid. I saw tail fins raised like giant fans. I saw hands reach around the mermaid, hands tugging at the rope that held her.

The waters tossed quietly as the figures worked.

"The mermaids are setting her free," I whispered.

"What are we going to do?" Sheena asked.

"We'll just make sure she gets away safely," Dr D replied. "Then we'll slip away. The kidnappers will never know we were here."

We watched the mermaids struggle with the rope as our dinghy washed up against the kidnappers' boat.

"Come on, mermaids!" Sheena urged under her breath. "Hurry!"

"Maybe they need some help," I said.

Dr D began to steer towards the mermaids.

I gasped as a light flared on the kidnappers' boat. A match set flame to a torch.

An angry voice boomed, "What do you think you're doing?"

I ducked away as the flaming torch was thrust in my face.

Behind the torch, I could see the kidnapper glaring down at me. He had quickly pulled on his black mask. It covered only the top of his face.

I heard a clambering sound, cries of surprise. Alexander and the other three kidnappers appeared on the deck.

"How did you get here?" demanded the man with the torch. "Why aren't you dead?"

"We've come for the mermaid," Dr D called up to him. "You can't keep her here!"

The torch swung past my head. I stood up in the dinghy and took a swipe at it, trying to knock it into the water.

"Billy, no!" cried Dr D.

The kidnapper pulled the torch away. I fell forward in the dinghy, toppling over on Sheena.

"Give us back the mermaid!" Dr D demanded.

"Finders, keepers," the kidnapper muttered. "You've made a long trip for nothing. And now look – your boat is on fire."

He lowered the torch to the dinghy and set it aflame.

The flames flared up, bright orange and yellow against the blue-black sky. They spread quickly across the front of the dinghy.

Sheena uttered a terrified scream and tried to back away from the flames.

In a panic, she started to leap into the water – but Dr D pulled her back. "Don't leave the boat! You'll drown!"

The fire crackled. The bright flames shot higher.

Dr D grabbed a yellow life jacket from the bottom of the dinghy and started frantically beating out the fire.

"Billy – get a life jacket!" he yelled. "Sheena – find the bucket. Throw water on the flames – hurry!"

I found a life jacket and beat at the flames. Sheena dumped seawater on them as fast as she could.

Over the crackling flames, I heard Alexander shout, "Get the mermaid aboard. Let's get out of here!"

"Dr D!" I cried. "They're getting away!"

Then I heard the kidnappers yelling. "The mermaid! Where's the mermaid?"

I turned to the side of the boat. The mermaid was gone. Her friends had freed her.

One of the kidnappers reached down from his boat and grabbed me. "What did you do with the mermaid?" he demanded.

"Let him go!" shouted Dr D.

I tried to squirm away from the kidnapper. He held me tight. Then I saw another kidnapper swing a club at Dr D's head.

Dr D dodged the club. The kidnapper tried to hit him in the stomach. Dr D dodged again.

I kicked and squirmed. Sheena tugged at the kidnapper's hands, trying to help me escape.

The third kidnapper picked her up by the wrists and threw her to the floor of the dinghy.

"Let go of the kids!" pleaded Dr D. "Alexander! Help us!"

Alexander didn't move from his spot on the deck. He stood with his brawny arms crossed in front of him, calmly watching the fight.

The flames had nearly been quenched, but they suddenly flared up again.

"Sheena – the fire!" I cried. "Put out the fire!"

She grabbed the bucket and poured seawater everywhere.

One of the kidnappers kicked the bucket from her hands. It landed in the water with a splash.

Sheena picked up a life jacket and beat the last of the flames out.

"Drop down into their boat and toss them in the water!" I heard a kidnapper shout up above.

A man started to lower himself into our dinghy. But suddenly he lurched forward, his arms flailing. He let out a cry of surprise as his boat began to rock violently to the left. It looked as if it had been slammed by a huge wave.

The kidnappers cried out as their boat began to rock back and forth. Slowly at first. Then violently. Gripping the sides of the dinghy, I watched them clinging to the rail, screaming in confusion and surprise.

Dr D slowly stood up, trying to see what was happening.

The boat tossed violently, as if bucking tall waves.

The mermaids. I could see them now.

They had surrounded the kidnappers' ship and were rocking it hard.

Hard. Harder. The kidnappers hung on helplessly.

"Mission accomplished!" Dr D cried happily. He started up the motor and we roared off.

Turning back, I could see the boat tilting and rocking in the water. And I could see our mermaid swimming free, behind the other mermaids in the shimmering waves.

"She got away!" I cried. "She's free!"

"I hope she'll be all right," said Sheena.

"We'll look for her tomorrow," said Dr D as he steered us back to the sea lab. "We know where to find her now."

Sheena glanced at me. I glanced back.

Oh, no, I thought. *After all this, it can't be true.*

Is Dr D going to catch the mermaid again – and give her to the zoo?

Sheena and I met in the galley the next morning. Since Alexander was gone, we had to fix our own breakfasts.

"Do you think the mermaid went back to the lagoon?" asked Sheena.

"Probably," I replied. "That's where she lives."

She spooned some cereal into her mouth and chewed with a thoughtful look on her face.

"Sheena," I said, "if someone gave you a million dollars, would you show them where the mermaid lives?"

"No," Sheena replied. "Not if they wanted to capture her."

"Me, neither," I said. "That's what I don't get. Dr D is a great guy. I just can't believe he'd—"

I stopped. I heard a noise. The sound of a motor.

Sheena listened. She heard it, too.

We dropped our spoons and ran up on deck.

Dr D was standing on the deck, staring out to sea.

A boat was approaching. A white boat with MARINA ZOO stencilled on the side in large letters.

"The zoo people!" I said to Sheena. "They're here!"

What would our uncle do? I wondered with growing dread. Would he tell them where the mermaid was? Would he accept the million dollars?

Sheena and I ducked behind the cockpit. We watched the Marina Zoo boat tie up beside the *Cassandra*. I recognized Mr Showalter and Ms Wickman.

Mr Showalter tossed a rope to Dr D. Ms Wickman jumped aboard.

The zoo people smiled and shook Dr D's hand. He nodded at them solemnly.

"We had word from the fishermen on Santa Anita that you found the mermaid," Mr Showalter said. "We're ready to take her with us now."

Ms Wickman opened her briefcase and pulled out a slender envelope. "Here is a cheque for one million dollars, Dr Deep," she said, smiling. "We've made it out to you and the *Cassandra* Research Lab."

She held out the cheque to my uncle.

I peered out from behind the cockpit. *Please don't take it, Dr D*, I pleaded silently. *Please don't take the cheque.*

"Thank you very much," my uncle said. He reached out a hand and took the cheque from her.

"A million dollars means a great deal to me and my work," Dr D said. "Your zoo has been very generous. That's why I'm sorry I have to do this."

He raised the envelope and tore it in half.

The two zoo people gasped in surprise.

"I can't take the money," Dr D said.

"Just what are you saying, Dr Deep?" Mr Showalter demanded.

"You sent me on a wild goose chase," my uncle replied. "I have searched these waters thoroughly ever since you left. With my equipment, I searched every inch of the lagoon and all the surrounding waters. I am now more convinced than ever before that mermaids do not exist."

Yaaaay! I screamed to myself. I wanted to jump up and down and cheer my head off – but I stayed hidden with Sheena behind the cockpit.

"But what about the fishermen's stories?" Ms Wickman protested.

"The local fishermen have told mermaid stories for years," Dr D told her. "I think they believe they've really seen mermaids rising through the mist on foggy days. But what they have seen are only fish, or dolphins, or manatees, or even swimmers. Because mermaids don't exist. They're fantasy creatures."

Mr Showalter and Ms Wickman both sighed in disappointment.

"Are you sure about this?" Mr Showalter asked.

"Completely sure," my uncle replied firmly. "My equipment is very sensitive. It can pick up the tiniest minnow."

"We respect your opinion, Dr Deep," Mr Showalter said with some sadness. "You're the leading expert on exotic sea creatures. That's why we came to you in the first place."

"Thank you," said Dr D. "Then I hope you'll take my advice and drop your hunt for a mermaid."

"I guess we'll have to," said Ms Wickman. "Thank you for trying, Dr Deep."

They all shook hands. Then the zoo people got back on their boat and motored away.

The coast was clear. Sheena and I came bursting out of our hiding place.

"Dr D!" cried Sheena, throwing her arms around him. "You're the greatest!"

A wide grin spread over Dr D's face. "Thanks, guys," he said. "From now on, none of us will say anything to anyone about mermaids. Is it a deal?"

"It's a deal," Sheena instantly agreed.

"Deal," I said. We all shook hands.

The mermaid was our secret.

I swore I'd never mention the mermaid to anyone. But I wanted to see her one last time. I wanted to say goodbye.

After lunch, Sheena and Dr D went to their cabins to nap. We had been up for most of the night, after all. I pretended to take a nap, too.

But once they were asleep, I sneaked out of my cabin and slipped into the bright blue water.

I swam over to the lagoon to search for the mermaid.

The sun was high in a pale blue sky. It glowed down on the still lagoon waters, making them glitter as if covered in gold.

Mermaid? Where are you? I wondered.

I was just past the reef when I felt a playful tug on my leg.

Sheena? I thought. Had she followed me *again*?

I spun around to catch her.

No one there.

Seaweed, probably, I thought. I kept swimming.

A few seconds later, I felt the tug again. Harder this time.

Hey – it must be the mermaid! I told myself.

I turned once again to search for her.

The water rippled.

"Mermaid?" I called.

A head popped out of the water.

A gigantic, slimy, dark green head.

With one enormous eye.

And a mouthful of jagged teeth.

"The sea monster!" I shrieked. "The sea monster!"

Would they believe me this time?

BEHIND THE SCREAMS

DEEP TROUBLE

CONTENTS

Bonus material
written and compiled
by Matthew D. Payne

Q & A with R.L. Stine

What's the scariest moment you've ever experienced in the water?

R.L. Stine (RLS): *I'm pretty much always fearful in the water. But one Caribbean snorkelling trip was really scary: a big fish came up and bit me! I was terrified. But later, when a friend showed me a picture he took of the "huge biting fish" I saw it was about the size of a goldfish!*

Billy Deep has a wild imagination and a thirst for adventure. Were you a lot like Billy when you were a kid?

RLS: *Not at all. I never left my room. I was always writing stories and drawing comics. I made up a superhero called Super Stooge. He wasn't smart enough to have any scary adventures!*

What advice do you have for readers who hope to write their own books some day?

RLS: *My advice is to read as much as you can, and to try and write something,* anything, *every day. Think of it this way – when you write, you are a writer!*

If you had become an undersea explorer instead of an author, which creatures would you pursue?

RLS: *Tuna fish – on toast! Actually, I've always been fascinated by stingrays. I saw a lot of them on a trip I took to Australia.*

In Goosebumps HorrorLand 2: *Creep from the Deep*, Billy and Sheena face off against some very "spirited" villains! Is the worst behind them? Or will future books bring even deeper trouble?

RLS: Creep from the Deep *is a day at the beach compared to what's waiting for the brother and sister in HorrorLand. Here's one hint: nobody will be able to recognize Sheena after her adventure in HorrorLand.*

There's Something Fishy About Mermaids

Mermaids certainly lent a helping hand (and fin) to Billy, Sheena and Dr D. But you should always approach these mythical creatures with caution. Mermaids can be found all around the world, and some aren't that friendly!

Many European cultures tell stories of mermaids that lure victims with their beauty and magical singing, only to eat them or hold them prisoner underwater! In Japan, seafarers tell tales of horrific mermaids that are nearly all-fish: Only their head is human. These creepy, eel-like creatures are thought to be the messengers of a serpent princess.

AM I PART MERMAID?

Many families in Ireland and France insist they have mermaid ancestors. If you've ever felt like a fish out of water, maybe you're part mermaid, too!

Friendlier mermaids come up on land to visit humans. Irish mermaids, while walking on their tails, must have endless patience to slowly shuffle from place to place when visiting land! In ancient Egypt, mermaids were thought to have webbed feet. It made quick visits on land a whole lot easier.

MERMAID AHOY!

Famous explorers Christopher Columbus and Henry Hudson sighted mermaids on their voyages.

SINK YOUR TEETH INTO
SOME SHARK FACTS!

The whale shark is the largest shark and the largest fish in the ocean. Scientists think whale sharks can grow up to twenty metres long – the length of one and a half school buses.

At twenty-five centimetres long, the spined pygmy shark is the smallest shark in the ocean. Despite its small size, it packs a BIG surprise: the spined pygmy shark glows in the dark.

Sharks can detect the invisible electric fields emitted by all living things. This means that even fish hiding under the sand can end up on a lunch menu!

Certain sharks can smell a single drop of blood from almost ninety metres away – the length of an American football field.

Sharks keep the tooth fairy busy. They constantly lose and regrow their teeth. Some sharks lose up to thirty thousand teeth in a lifetime.

Scientists are not sure if sharks actually sleep. Sharks at "rest" will still follow divers with their eyes.

Don't start a staring contest with a shark! Although they have eyelids, sharks don't blink.

Sharks have been on earth for around four hundred million years. They were here before the dinosaurs!

TALES OF HORROR: WHEN SHARKS ATTACK

1916 During one horrific summer, five people were attacked by sharks in the waters near Matewan, New Jersey – only one person survived.

1960 A shark lifted a small Australian dinghy out of the water. All three passengers held tight, and the shark swam away.

2007 A cargo ship tipped over in heavy seas off the coast of the Philippines. Some people survived the shipwreck only to be eaten by sharks, according to witnesses.

2007 A surfer in California is lucky to be alive after a shark missed his lunch and bit the surfer's board instead.

HOW TO SURVIVE A SHARK ATTACK

A person is more likely to be attacked by a pig than by a shark. However, if you ever find yourself staring down a shark, here are a few things that you can do to defend yourself:

1) Don't panic! Sharks are attracted to splashing. You even have to FEEL calm. Sharks can sense fear.

2) Poking and punching is good, but aim for the eyes and gills. The nose is too close to the mouth – your hand could quickly become an appetizer.

3) Make the shark work for his meal. Don't give up or play dead. As long as you fight, there's a chance the shark will give up and look for an easier meal.

An Undersea Adventure – Starring YOU!

Want to be like Billy Deep? Finish the following statements to make up your own undersea adventure.

I am an intrepid undersea adventurer, scouring the deep sea for . . .
> . . . treasure.
> . . . mysterious creatures.
> . . . a tasty tuna.

I am swimming . . .
> . . . into an underwater cave.
> . . . through a fire coral reef.
> . . . through a sunken pirate ship.

I am carrying . . .
> . . . an underwater camera.
> . . . a spear.
> . . . a light.

Suddenly, I run into . . .
> . . . a mermaid.
> . . . a disgusting sea creature with a huge eye and gross, slimy tentacles.
> . . . a great white shark.

What happens next? Write down anything that comes to mind and have fun crafting your tale. Remember what R.L. Stine says: "When you write, you're a writer!"

Goosebumps®

MONSTER BLOOD

"I don't want to stay here. Please don't leave me here."

Evan Ross tugged his mother's hand, trying to pull her away from the front porch of the small grey-shingled house. Mrs Ross turned to him, an impatient frown on her face.

"Evan – you're twelve years old. Don't act like an infant," she said, freeing her hand from his grasp.

"I *hate* when you say that!" Evan exclaimed angrily, crossing his arms in front of his chest.

Softening her expression, she reached out and ran her hand tenderly through Evan's curly carrot-coloured hair. "And I *hate* when you do that!" he cried, backing away from her, nearly stumbling over a broken flagstone in the walk. "Don't touch my hair. I hate it!"

"OK, so you hate me," his mother said with a shrug. She climbed up the two steps and knocked on the front door. "You still have to stay here till I get back."

"Why can't I come with you?" Evan demanded, keeping his arms crossed. "Just give me one good reason."

"Your trainer is untied," his mother replied.

"So?" Evan replied unhappily. "I like 'em untied."

"You'll trip," she warned.

"Mom," Evan said, rolling his eyes in exasperation, "have you ever seen *anyone* trip over his trainers because they were untied?"

"Well, no," his mother admitted, a smile slowly forming on her pretty face.

"You just want to change the subject," Evan said, not smiling back. "You're going to leave me here for weeks with a horrible old woman and—"

"Evan – that's *enough*!" Mrs Ross snapped, tossing back her straight blonde hair. "Kathryn is not a horrible old woman. She's your father's aunt. Your great-aunt. And she's—"

"She's a total stranger," Evan cried. He knew he was losing control, but he didn't care. How could his mother do this to him? How could she leave him with some old lady he hadn't seen since he was two? What was he supposed to do here all by himself until his mother got back?

"Evan, we've discussed this a thousand times,"

274

his mother said impatiently, pounding on his aunt's front door again. "This is a family emergency. I really expect you to cooperate a little better."

Her next words were drowned out by Trigger, Evan's cocker spaniel, who stuck his tan head out of the back window of the rented car and began barking and howling.

"Now *he's* giving me a hard time, too!" Mrs Ross exclaimed.

"Can I let him out?" Evan asked eagerly.

"I guess you'd better," his mother replied. "Trigger's so old, we don't want him to have a heart attack in there. I just hope he doesn't terrify Kathryn."

"I'm coming, Trigger!" Evan called.

He jogged to the gravel driveway and pulled open the car door. With an excited yip, Trigger leaped out and began running in wide circles around Kathryn's small rectangular front garden.

"He doesn't *look* like he's twelve," Evan said, watching the dog run and smiling for the first time that day.

"See. You'll have Trigger for company," Mrs Ross said, turning back to the front door. "I'll be back from Atlanta in no time. A couple of weeks at the most. I'm sure your dad and I can find a house in that time. And then we'll be back before you even notice we're gone."

"Yeah. Sure," Evan said sarcastically.

The sun dipped behind a large cloud. A shadow fell over the small front garden.

Trigger wore himself out quickly and came panting up the walk, his tongue hanging nearly to the ground. Evan bent down and petted the dog's back.

He looked up at the grey house as his mother knocked on the front door again. It looked dark and uninviting. There were curtains drawn over the upstairs windows. One of the shutters had come loose and was resting at an odd angle.

"Mom – why are you knocking?" he asked, shoving his hands into his jeans pockets. "You said Aunt Kathryn was totally deaf."

"Oh." His mother's face reddened. "You got me so upset, Evan, with all your complaining, I completely forgot. Of *course* she can't hear us."

How am I going to spend two weeks with a strange old lady who can't even hear me? Evan wondered glumly.

He remembered eavesdropping on his parents two weeks earlier when they had made the plan. They were seated across from each other at the kitchen table. They thought Evan was out in the garden. But he was in the hallway, his back pressed against the wall, listening.

His father, he learned, was reluctant to leave Evan with Kathryn. "She's a very stubborn old woman," Mr Ross had said. "Look at her. Deaf for twenty years, and she's refused to learn sign language or to lip-read. How's she going to take care of Evan?"

"She took good care of you when *you* were a boy," Mrs Ross had argued.

"That was thirty years ago," Mr Ross protested.

"Well, we have no choice," Evan heard his mother say. "There's no one else to leave him with. Everyone else is away on holiday. You know, August is just the worst month for you to be transferred to Atlanta."

"Well, excuuuuse me!" Mr Ross said, sarcastically. "OK, OK. Discussion closed. You're absolutely right, dear. We have no choice. Kathryn it is. You'll drive Evan there and then fly down to Atlanta."

"It'll be a good experience for him," Evan heard his mother say. "He needs to learn how to get along under difficult circumstances. You know, moving to Atlanta, leaving all his friends behind – that isn't going to be easy on Evan either."

"OK. I said OK," Mr Ross said impatiently. "It's settled. Evan will be fine. Kathryn is a bit weird, but she's perfectly harmless."

Evan heard the kitchen chairs scraping across the linoleum, indicating that his parents were getting up, their discussion ended.

His fate was sealed. Silently, he had made his

way out the front door and around to the garden to think about what he had just overheard.

He leaned against the trunk of the big maple tree, which hid him from the house. It was his favourite place to think.

Why didn't his parents ever include him *in their discussions?* he wondered. If they were going to discuss leaving him with some old aunt he'd never seen before, shouldn't he at least have a say? He learned all the big family news by eavesdropping from the hallway. It just wasn't right.

Evan pulled a small twig off the ground and tapped it against the broad tree trunk.

Aunt Kathryn was weird. That's what his dad had said. She was so weird, his father didn't want to leave Evan with her.

But they had no choice. No choice.

Maybe they'll change their minds and take me to Atlanta with them, Evan thought. *Maybe they'll realize they can't* do *this to me.*

But now, two weeks later, he was standing in front of Aunt Kathryn's grey house, feeling very nervous, staring at the brown suitcase filled with his belongings, which stood beside his mother on the porch.

There's nothing to be scared of, he assured himself.

It's only for two weeks. Maybe less.

But then the words popped out before he'd even

278

had a chance to think about them: "Mom – what if Aunt Kathryn is mean?"

"Huh?" The question caught his mother by surprise. "Mean? Why would she be mean, Evan?"

And as she said this, facing Evan with her back to the house, the front door was pulled open, and Aunt Kathryn, a large woman with startling black hair, filled the doorway.

Staring past his mother, Evan saw the knife in Kathryn's hand. And he saw that the blade of the knife was dripping with blood.

Trigger raised his head and began to bark, hopping backwards on his hind legs with each bark.

Startled, Evan's mother spun around, nearly stumbling off the small porch.

Evan gaped in silent horror at the knife.

A smile formed on Kathryn's face, and she pushed open the screen door with her free hand.

She wasn't anything like Evan had pictured. He had pictured a small, frail-looking, white-haired old lady. But Kathryn was a large woman, very robust, broad-shouldered and tall.

She wore a peach-coloured dress and had straight black hair, pulled back and tied behind her head in a long ponytail that flowed down the back of the dress. She wore no make-up, and her pale face seemed to disappear under the striking black hair, except for her eyes, which were large and round and steely blue.

"I was slicing beef," she said in a surprisingly

deep voice, waving the blood-stained kitchen knife. She stared at Evan. "You like beef?"

"Uh . . . yeah," he managed to reply, his chest still fluttery from the shock of seeing her appear with the raised knife.

Kathryn held open the screen door, but neither Evan nor his mother made any move to go inside. "He's big," Kathryn said to Mrs Ross. "A big boy. Not like his father. I used to call his father Chicken. Because he was no bigger than a chicken." She laughed as if she had cracked a funny joke.

Mrs Ross, picking up Evan's suitcase, glanced uncomfortably back at him. "Yeah . . . he's big," she said.

Actually, Evan was one of the shortest kids in his class. And no matter how much he ate, he remained "as skinny as a spaghetti noodle", as his dad liked to say.

"You don't have to answer me," Kathryn said, stepping aside so that Mrs Ross could get inside the house with the suitcase. "I can't hear you." Her voice was deep, as deep as a man's, and she spoke clearly, without the indistinct pronunciation that some deaf people have.

Evan followed his mother into the front hallway, Trigger yapping at his heels. "Can't you get that dog quiet?" his mother snapped.

"It doesn't matter. She can't hear it," Evan replied, gesturing towards his aunt, who was heading to the kitchen to put down the knife.

Kathryn returned a few seconds later, her blue eyes locked on Evan, her lips pursed, as if she were studying him. "So, you like beef?" she repeated.

He nodded.

"Good," she said, her expression still serious. "I always fixed beef for your father. But he only wanted pie."

"What kind of pie?" Evan asked, and then blushed when he remembered Kathryn couldn't hear him.

"So he's a good boy? Not a troublemaker?" Kathryn asked Evan's mother.

Mrs Ross nodded, looking at Evan. "Where shall we put his suitcase?" she asked.

"I can tell by looking he's a good boy," Kathryn said. She reached out and grabbed Evan's face, her big hand holding him under the chin, her eyes examining him closely. "Good-looking boy," she said, giving his chin a hard squeeze. "He likes the girls?"

Still holding his chin, she lowered her face to his. "You've got a girlfriend?" she asked, her pale face right above his, so close he could smell her breath, which was sour.

Evan took a step back, an embarrassed grin crossing his face. "No. Not really."

"Yes?" Kathryn cried, bellowing in his ear. "Yes? I *knew* it!" She laughed heartily, turning her gaze to Evan's mother.

"The suitcase?" Mrs Ross asked, picking up the bag.

"He likes the girls, huh?" Kathryn repeated, still chuckling. "I could tell. Just like his father. His father always liked the girls."

Evan turned desperately to his mother. "Mom, I can't stay here," he said, whispering even though he knew Kathryn couldn't hear. "Please – don't make me."

"Hush," his mother replied, also whispering. "She'll leave you alone. I promise. She's just trying to be friendly."

"He likes the girls," Kathryn repeated, leering at him with her cold blue eyes, again lowering her face close to Evan's.

"Mom – her breath smells like Trigger's!" Evan exclaimed miserably.

"Evan!" Mrs Ross shouted angrily. "Stop it! I expect you to cooperate."

"I'm going to bake you a pie," Kathryn said, tugging at her black ponytail with one of her huge hands. "Would you like to roll out the dough? I'll bet you would. What did your father tell you about me, Evan?" She winked at Mrs Ross. "Did he tell you I was a scary old witch?"

"No," Evan protested, looking at his mother.

"Well, I am!" Kathryn declared, and once again burst into her deep-throated laugh.

Trigger took this moment to begin barking ferociously and jumping on Evan's great-aunt.

She glared down at the dog, her eyes narrowing, her expression becoming stern. "Look out or we'll put *you* in the pie, doggie!" she exclaimed.

Trigger barked even harder, darting boldly towards the tall, hovering woman, then quickly retreating, his stub of a tail whipping back and forth in a frenzy.

"We'll put him in the pie, won't we, Evan?" Kathryn repeated, putting a big hand on Evan's shoulder and squeezing it till Evan flinched in pain.

"Mom—" he pleaded when his aunt finally let go and, smiling, made her way to the kitchen. "Mom – please."

"It's just her sense of humour, Evan," Mrs Ross said uncertainly. "She means well. Really. She's going to bake you a pie."

"But I don't want pie!" Evan wailed. "I don't like it here, Mom! She hurt me. She squeezed my shoulder so hard—"

"Evan, I'm sure she didn't mean to. She's just trying to joke with you. She wants you to like her. Give her a chance – OK?"

Evan started to protest but thought better of it.

"I'm counting on you," his mother continued, turning her eyes to the kitchen. They could both see Kathryn at the counter, her broad back to them, hacking away at something with the big kitchen knife.

"But she's . . . weird!" Evan protested.

"Listen, Evan, I understand how you're feeling," his mother said. "But you won't have to spend all your time with her. There are a lot of kids in the neighbourhood. Take Trigger for a walk. I'll bet you'll make some friends your age. She's an old woman, Evan. She won't want you hanging around all the time."

"I guess," Evan muttered.

His mother bent down suddenly and gave him a hug, pressing her cheek against his. The hug, he knew, was supposed to cheer him up. But it only made him feel worse.

"I'm counting on you," his mother repeated in his ear.

Evan decided to try and be braver about this. "I'll help you carry the suitcase up to my room," he said.

They carried it up the narrow staircase. His room was actually a study. The walls were lined with bookshelves filled with old hardcover books. A large mahogany desk stood in the centre of the room. A narrow cot had been made up under the single, curtained window.

The window faced out on to the back garden, a long green rectangle with the grey-shingled garage to the left, a tall picket fence to the right. A small fenced-in area stretched across the back of the garden. It looked like some sort of dog run.

The room smelled musty. The sharp aroma of mothballs invaded Evan's nose.

Trigger sneezed. He rolled on to his back, his legs racing in the air.

Trigger can't stand this place either, Evan thought. But he kept his thought to himself, smiling bravely at his mother, who quickly unpacked his suitcase, nervously checking her watch.

"I'm late. Don't want to miss my plane," she said. She gave him another hug, longer this time. Then she took a ten-dollar bill from her purse and stuffed it into his shirt pocket. "Buy yourself a treat. Be good. I'll hurry back as fast as I can."

"OK. Bye," he said, his chest feeling fluttery, his throat as dry as cotton. The smell of her perfume momentarily drowned out the mothballs.

He didn't want her to leave. He had such a bad feeling.

You're just scared, he scolded himself.

"I'll call you from Atlanta," she shouted as she disappeared down the stairs to say goodbye to Kathryn.

Her perfume disappeared.

The mothballs returned.

Trigger uttered a low, sad howl, as if he knew what was happening, as if he knew they were being abandoned here in this strange house with the strange old woman.

Evan picked Trigger up and nose-kissed his cold black nose. Putting the dog back down on the worn carpet, he made his way to the window.

He stood there for a long while, one hand holding the curtains aside, staring down at the small green garden, trying to calm the fluttering in his chest. After a few minutes, he heard his mother's car back down the gravel drive. Then he heard it roll away.

When he could no longer hear it, he sighed and plopped down on the cot. "It's just you and me now, Trigger," he said glumly.

Trigger was busily sniffing behind the door.

Evan stared up at the walls of old books.

What am I going to do here all day? he asked himself, propping his head in his hands. No Nintendo. No computer. He hadn't even seen a TV in his great-aunt's small living room. *What am I going to do?*

Sighing again, he picked himself up and walked along the bookshelves, his eyes scanning the titles. There were lots of science books and textbooks, he saw. Books on biology and astronomy, ancient Egypt, chemistry texts, and medical books. Several shelves were filled with dusty, yellowed books. Maybe Kathryn's husband, Evan's great-uncle, had been some sort of scientist.

Nothing here for me to read, he thought glumly.

He pulled open the closet door.

"Oh!"

He cried out as something leaped out at him.

"Help! Please – help!"

Everything went black.

"Help! I can't see!" Evan screamed.

Evan staggered back in fear as the warm blackness crept over him.

It took him a few seconds to realize what it was. His heart still thudding in his chest, he reached up and pulled the screeching black cat off his face.

The cat dropped silently to the ground and padded to the doorway. Evan turned and saw Kathryn standing there, an amused grin on her face.

How long had she been standing there? he wondered.

"Sarabeth, how did you get in there?" she asked in a playfully scolding tone, bending down to speak to the cat. "You must have given the boy a fright."

The cat mewed and rubbed against Kathryn's bare leg.

"Did Sarabeth scare you?" Kathryn asked Evan, still smiling. "That cat has a strange sense of humour. She's evil. Pure evil." She chuckled as if she'd said something funny.

"I'm OK," Evan said uncertainly.

"Watch out for Sarabeth. She's evil," Kathryn repeated, bending down and picking up the cat by the scruff of the neck, holding her up in the air in front of her. "Evil, evil, evil."

Seeing the cat suspended in the air, Trigger uttered an unhappy howl. His stubby tail went into motion, and he leaped up at the cat, barking and yipping, missed, and leaped again, snapping at Sarabeth's tail.

"Down, Trigger! Get down!" Evan cried.

Struggling to get out of Kathryn's arms, the cat swiped a clawed black paw at her, screeching in anger and fear. Trigger barked and howled as Evan struggled to pull the excited cocker spaniel away.

Evan grabbed hold of Trigger as the cat swung to the floor and disappeared out the door. "Bad dog. Bad dog," Evan whispered. But he didn't really mean it. He was glad Trigger had scared the cat away.

He looked up to see Kathryn still filling the doorway, staring down at him sternly. "Bring the dog," she said in a low voice, her eyes narrowed, her pale lips pursed tightly.

"Huh?" Evan gripped Trigger in a tight hug.

"Bring the dog," Kathryn repeated coldly. "We can't have animals fighting in this house."

"But, Aunt Kathryn—" Evan started to plead, then remembered she couldn't hear him.

"Sarabeth is a bad one," Kathryn said, not softening her expression. "We can't get her riled, can we?" She turned and started down the stairs. "Bring the dog, Evan."

Holding Trigger tightly by the shoulders with both hands, Evan hesitated.

"I have to take care of the dog," Kathryn said sternly. "Come."

Evan was suddenly filled with dread. What did she mean, *take care* of the dog?

A picture flashed into his mind of Kathryn standing at the doorway with the bloody kitchen knife in her hand.

"Bring the dog," Kathryn insisted.

Evan gasped. What was she going to *do* to Trigger?

"I will take care of you, doggie," Kathryn repeated, frowning at Trigger. The dog whimpered in reply.

"Come, Evan. Follow me," she said impatiently.

Seeing that he had no choice, Evan obediently carried Trigger down the stairs and followed his aunt to the back garden. "I'm prepared," she said, turning to make sure he was following.

Despite her age – she was at least eighty – she walked with long, steady strides. "I knew you were bringing a dog, so I made sure I was prepared."

Trigger licked Evan's hand as they walked across the garden to the long fenced-in area at the back. "It's a special place for your dog," Kathryn said, reaching up to grab one end of the rope that stretched across the run. "Attach this to the collar, Evan. Your dog will have fun here." She frowned disapprovingly at Trigger. "And there will be no problems with Sarabeth."

Evan felt very relieved that this was all Kathryn wanted to do to Trigger. But he didn't want to leave Trigger tied up in this prison in the back of the garden. Trigger was a house dog. He wouldn't be happy by himself out here.

But Evan knew he had no way of arguing with his aunt. *Kathryn is smart in a way,* he thought bitterly as he hooked Trigger's collar to the rope. *Since she won't learn sign language and won't lip-read, it means she gets to do whatever she wants, and no one can tell her no.*

He bent down and gave Trigger's warm head a pat and looked up at the old woman. She had her arms crossed in front of her chest, her blue eyes glowing brightly in the sunlight, a cold smile of triumph on her face.

"That's a good boy," she said, waiting for Evan to get up before starting back to the house. "I knew when I looked at you. Come to the house, Evan. I have cookies and milk. You'll enjoy them." Her words were kind, but her voice was hard and cold.

Trigger sent up an unhappy howl as Evan followed Kathryn to the house. Evan turned, intending to go back and comfort the dog. But Kathryn grabbed his hand in an iron grip and, staring straight ahead, led him to the kitchen door.

The kitchen was small and cluttered and very warm. Kathryn motioned for him to sit at a small table against the wall. The table was covered with a plastic chequered tablecloth. She frowned, her eyes studying him, as she brought over his snack.

He downed the oatmeal raisin cookies and milk, listening to Trigger howl in the garden. Oatmeal raisin wasn't his favourite, but he was surprised to find that he was hungry. As he gobbled them down, Kathryn stood at the doorway, staring intently at him, a stern expression on her face.

"I'm going to take Trigger for a walk," he announced, wiping the milk moustache off his upper lip with the paper napkin she had given him.

Kathryn shrugged and wrinkled up her face.

Oh. Right. She can't hear me, Evan thought. Standing at the kitchen window, he pointed to Trigger, then made a walking motion with two fingers. Kathryn nodded.

Whew, he thought. *This is going to be hard.*

He waved goodbye and hurried to free Trigger from his garden prison.

A few minutes later, Trigger was tugging at the leash, sniffing the flowers along the kerb as Evan made his way up the street. The other houses on the street were about the same size as Kathryn's, he saw. And they all had small, neatly trimmed, square front gardens.

He saw some little kids chasing each other around a birch tree. And he saw a middle-aged man in bright orange swimming trunks washing his car with a garden hose in his driveway. But he didn't see any kids his age.

Trigger barked at a squirrel and tugged the leash out of Evan's hand. "Hey – come back!" Evan called. Trigger, disobedient as always, took off after the squirrel.

The squirrel wisely climbed a tree. But Trigger, his eyesight not what it once was, continued the chase.

Running at full speed, calling the dog's name, Evan followed him around a corner and halfway down the street before Trigger finally realized he had lost the race.

Breathing hard, Evan grabbed the leash handle. "Gotcha," he said. He gave the leash a tug, trying to lead the panting dog back to Kathryn's street.

Trigger, sniffing around a dark tree trunk, pulled the other way. Evan was about to pick up the stubborn dog when he was startled by a hand grabbing his shoulder.

"Hey – who are *you*?" a voice demanded.

Evan spun around to find a girl standing behind him, staring at him with dark brown eyes. "Why'd you grab my shoulder like that?" he asked, his heart still pounding.

"To scare you," she said simply.

"Yeah. Well. . ." Evan shrugged. Trigger gave a hard tug at the leash and nearly pulled him over.

The girl laughed.

She's pretty, he thought. She had short, wavy brown hair, almost black, and flashing brown eyes, and a playful, teasing smile. She was wearing an oversized yellow T-shirt over black spandex leggings and bright yellow Nikes.

"So who *are* you?" she demanded again.

She's not the shy type, he decided. "I'm me," he said, letting Trigger lead him around the tree.

"Did you move into the Winterhalter house?" she asked, following him.

He shook his head. "No. I'm just visiting."

She frowned in disappointment.

"For a couple of weeks," Evan added. "I'm staying with my aunt. Actually, she's my great-aunt."

"What's so great about her?" the girl cracked.

"Nothing," Evan replied without laughing. "For sure."

Trigger sniffed at a bug on a fat brown leaf.

"Is that your bike?" Evan asked, pointing to the red BMX bike lying on the grass behind her.

"Yeah," she replied.

"It's cool," he said. "I have one like it."

"I like your dog," she said, eyeing Trigger. "He looks real stupid. I like stupid dogs."

"Me, too. I guess." Evan laughed.

"What's his name? Does he have a stupid name?" She bent down and tried to pet Trigger's back, but he moved away.

"His name's Trigger," Evan said, and waited for her reaction.

"Yeah. That's pretty stupid," she said thoughtfully. "Especially for a cocker spaniel."

"Thanks," Evan said uncertainly.

Trigger turned to sniff the girl's hands, his tail wagging furiously, his tongue hanging down to the ground.

"I have a stupid name, too," the girl admitted. She waited for Evan to ask.

"What is it?" he said finally.

"Andrea," she said.

"That's not a stupid name."

"I hate it," she said, pulling a blade of grass off her leggings. "Annndreeea." She stretched the name out in a deep, cultured voice. "It sounds so stuck-up, like I should be wearing a corduroy jumper with a prim white blouse, walking a toy poodle. So I make everyone call me Andy."

"Hi, Andy," Evan said, petting Trigger. "My name is—"

"Don't tell me!" she interrupted, clamping a hot hand over his mouth.

She certainly isn't shy, he thought again.

"Let me guess," she said. "Is it a stupid name, too?"

"Yeah," he nodded. "It's Evan. Evan Stupid."

She laughed. "That's *really* a stupid name."

He felt glad that he made her laugh. She was cheering him up, he realized. A lot of the girls back home didn't appreciate his sense of humour. They thought he was silly.

"What are you doing?" she asked.

"Walking Trigger. You know. Exploring the neighbourhood."

"It's pretty boring," she said. "Just a lot of houses. Want to go into town? It's only a few streets away." She pointed down the street.

Evan hesitated. He hadn't told his aunt he was going into town. *But, what the heck*, he thought. *She wouldn't care.*

Besides, what could possibly happen?

"OK," Evan said. "Let's check out the town."

"I have to go to a toy store and look for a present for my cousin," Andy said, hoisting her bike up by the handlebars.

"How old are you?" Evan asked, tugging Trigger towards the street.

"Twelve."

"Me, too," he said. "Can I try your bike?"

She shook her head as she climbed on to the narrow seat. "No, but I'll let you run alongside." She laughed.

"You're a riot," he said sarcastically, hurrying to keep up as she began to pedal.

"And you're stupid," she called back playfully.

"Hey, *Annnndreeeea* – wait up!" he called, stretching the name out to annoy her.

A few streets later, the houses ended and they entered town, a stretch of low two-storey shops and offices. Evan saw a small brick post office, a barbershop with an old-fashioned barber pole out front, a grocery store, a drive-through bank and a hardware store with a large sign in the window proclaiming a sale on birdseed.

"The toy store is on the next street," Andy said, walking her bike along the pavement. Evan tugged Trigger's leash, encouraging him to keep up the pace. "Actually, there are two toy stores, an old one and a new one. I like the old one best."

"Let's check it out," Evan said, examining the cluttered window display of the video store on the corner.

I wonder if Aunt Kathryn has a VCR, he thought. He quickly dismissed the idea. *No way...*

The toy store was in an old clapboard building that hadn't been painted in many years. A small hand-painted sign in the dust-smeared window proclaimed: WAGNER'S NOVELTIES & SUNDRIES. There were no toys on display.

Andy leaned her bike against the front of the building. "Sometimes the owner can be a little mean. I don't know if he'll let you bring your dog in."

"Well, let's give it a try," Evan said, pulling open the door. Tugging hard on his leash, Trigger led the way into the store.

Evan found himself in a dark, low-ceilinged, narrow room. It took a while for his eyes to adjust to the dim light.

Wagner's looked more like a warehouse than a store. There were floor-to-ceiling shelves against both walls, jammed with boxes of toys, and a long display counter that ran through the centre of the store, leaving narrow aisles that even someone as skinny as Evan had to squeeze through.

At the front of the store, slumped on a tall stool behind an old-fashioned wooden cash register, sat a grumpy-looking man with a single tuft of white hair in the centre of a red bald head. He had a drooping white moustache that seemed to frown at Evan and Andy as they entered.

"Hi," Andy said timidly, giving the man a wave.

He grunted in reply and turned back to the newspaper he was reading.

Trigger sniffed the low shelves excitedly. Evan looked around at the stacks of toys. It appeared from the thick layer of dust that they'd been sitting there for a hundred years. Everything seemed tossed together, dolls next to building sets, art supplies mixed in with old action figures Evan didn't even recognize, a toy drum set underneath a pile of footballs.

He and Andy were the only customers in the store.

"Do they have Nintendo games?" Evan asked her, whispering, afraid to break the still silence.

"I don't think so," Andy whispered back. "I'll

ask." She shouted up to the front, "Do you have Nintendo games?"

It took a while for the man to answer. He scratched his ear. "Don't carry them," he grunted finally, sounding annoyed by the interruption.

Andy and Evan wandered towards the back of the store. "Why do you like this place?" Evan whispered, picking up an old cap pistol with a cowboy holster.

"I just think it's neat," Andy replied. "You can find some real treasures here. It's not like other toy stores."

"That's for sure," Evan said sarcastically. "Hey – look!" He picked up a lunch box with a cowboy dressed in black emblazoned on its side. "'Hopalong Cassidy'," he read. "Who's Hopalong Cassidy?"

"A cowboy with a stupid name," Andy said, taking the old lunch box from him and examining it. "Look – it's made of metal, not plastic. Wonder if my cousin would like it. He likes stupid names, too."

"It's a pretty weird present," Evan said.

"He's a pretty weird cousin," Andy cracked. "Hey, look at this." She set down the old lunch box and picked up an enormous box. "It's a magic set. 'Astound your friends. Perform one hundred amazing tricks'," she read.

"That's a lot of amazing tricks," Evan said.

He wandered further back into the dimly lit

store, Trigger leading the way, sniffing furiously. "Hey—" To Evan's surprise, a narrow doorway led into a small back room.

This room, Evan saw, was even darker and dustier. Stepping inside, he saw worn-looking stuffed animals tossed into cartons, games in faded, yellowed boxes, baseball gloves with the leather worn thin and cracked.

Who would want this junk? he thought.

He was about to leave when something caught his eye. It was a blue can, about the size of a can of soup. He picked it up, surprised by how heavy it was.

Bringing it close to his face to examine it in the dim light, he read the faded label: MONSTER BLOOD. Below that, in smaller type, it read: SURPRISING MIRACLE SUBSTANCE.

Hey, this looks cool, he thought, turning the can around in his hand.

He suddenly remembered the ten dollars his mother had stuffed into his shirt pocket.

He turned to see the store owner standing in the doorway, his dark eyes wide with anger. "What are you *doing* back here?" he bellowed.

7

Trigger yipped loudly, startled by the man's booming voice.

Evan gripped the leash, pulling Trigger close. "Uh . . . how much is this?" he asked, holding up the can of Monster Blood.

"Not for sale," the owner said, lowering his voice, his moustache seeming to frown unpleasantly with the rest of his face.

"Huh? It was on the shelf here," Evan said, pointing.

"It's too old," the man insisted. "Probably no good any more."

"Well, I'll take it, anyway," Evan said. "Can I have it for less since it's so old?"

"What is it?" Andy asked, appearing in the doorway.

"I don't know," Evan told her. "It looks cool. It's called Monster Blood."

"It's not for sale," the man insisted.

Andy pushed past him and took the can from

304

Evan's hand. "Ooh, I want one, too," she said, turning the can around in her hand.

"There's only one," Evan told her.

"You sure?" She began searching the shelves.

"It's no good, I'm telling you," the owner insisted, sounding exasperated.

"I need one, too," Andy said to Evan.

"Sorry," Evan replied, taking the can back. "I saw it first."

"I'll buy it from you," Andy said.

"Why don't you two *share* it?" the owner suggested.

"You mean you'll sell it to us?" Evan asked eagerly.

The man shrugged and scratched his ear.

"How much?" Evan asked.

"You sure you don't have another one?" Andy demanded, going back to the shelf, pushing a pile of stuffed pandas out of her way. "Or maybe two? I could keep one and give one to my cousin."

"Two dollars, I guess," the man told Evan. "But I'm telling you, it's no good. It's too old."

"I don't care," Evan said, reaching into his shirt pocket for the ten-dollar bill.

"Well, don't bring it back to me complaining," the man said grumpily, and headed towards the cash register at the front of the store.

A few minutes later, Evan walked out into the bright daylight carrying the blue can. Trigger panted excitedly, wagging his stubby tail, pleased to be out of the dark, dusty store. Andy followed them out, an unhappy expression on her face.

"You didn't buy the lunch box?" Evan asked.

"Don't change the subject," she snapped. "I'll pay you five dollars for it." She reached for the can of Monster Blood.

"No way," Evan replied. He laughed. "You really like to get your way, don't you!"

"I'm an only child," she said. "What can I tell you? I'm spoiled."

"Me, too," Evan said.

"I have an idea," Andy said, pulling her bike off the storefront wall. "Let's share it."

"Share it?" Evan said, shaking his head. "For sure. I'll share it the way you shared your bike."

"You want to ride the bike home? Here." She shoved it at him.

"No way," he said, pushing it back towards her. "I wouldn't ride your stupid bike now. It's a girl's bike, anyway."

"It is not," she insisted. "How is it a girl's bike?"

Evan ignored the question and, pulling at Trigger's leash to keep the old dog moving, started walking back towards his aunt's.

"How is it a girl's bike?" Andy repeated, walking the bike beside him.

"Tell you what," Evan said. "Let's go back to my aunt's house and open up the can. I'll let you mess with it for a while."

"Gee, swell," Andy said sarcastically. "You're a great guy, Evan."

"I know," he said, grinning.

Kathryn was seated in the big armchair in the living room when Evan and Andy arrived. *Who is she talking to?* he wondered, hearing her voice. She seemed to be arguing excitedly with someone.

Leading Andy into the room, Evan saw that it was just Sarabeth, the black cat. As Evan entered, the cat turned and haughtily walked out of the room.

Kathryn stared at Evan and Andy, a look of surprise on her face. "This is Andy," Evan said, gesturing to his new friend.

"What have you got there?" Kathryn asked, ignoring Andy and reaching a large hand out for the blue can of Monster Blood.

Evan reluctantly handed it to her. Frowning, she rolled it around in her hand, stopping to read the label, moving her lips as she read. She held the can for the longest time, seeming to study it carefully, then finally handed it back to Evan.

As Evan took it back and started to his room with Andy, he heard Kathryn say something to him in a low whisper. He couldn't quite hear what she had said. It sounded like "Be careful." But he wasn't sure.

He turned to see Sarabeth staring at him from

the doorway, her yellow eyes glowing in the dim light.

"My aunt is completely deaf," Evan explained to Andy as they climbed the stairs.

"Does that mean you can play your stereo as loud as you want?" Andy asked.

"I don't think Aunt Kathryn has a stereo," Evan said.

"That's too bad," Andy said, walking around Evan's room, pulling back the window curtains and looking down on Trigger, huddled unhappily in his pen.

"Is she really your great-aunt?" Andy asked. "She doesn't look very old."

"It's the black hair," Evan replied, setting the can of Monster Blood on the desk in the centre of the room. "It makes her look young."

"Hey – look at all these old books on magic stuff!" Andy exclaimed. "I wonder why your aunt has all these."

She pulled one of the heavy old volumes from the shelf and blew away a layer of dust from the top. "Maybe your aunt plans to come up here and cast a spell on you while you're sleeping and turn you into a newt."

"Maybe," Evan replied, grinning. "What *is* a newt, anyway?"

Andy shrugged. "Some kind of lizard, I think." She flipped through the yellowed pages of the old book. "I thought you said there was nothing to do here," she told Evan. "You could read all these cool books."

"Thrills and chills," Evan said sarcastically.

Replacing the book on the shelf, Andy came over to the desk and stood next to Evan, her eyes on the can of Monster Blood. "Open it up. It's so old. It's probably all disgusting and rotten."

"I hope so," Evan said. He picked up the can and studied it. "No instructions."

"Just pull the top off," she said impatiently.

He tugged at it. It wouldn't budge.

"Maybe you need a can opener or something," she said.

"Very helpful," he muttered, studying the label again. "Look at this. No instructions. No ingredients. Nothing."

"Of course not. It's Monster Blood!" she exclaimed, imitating Count Dracula. She grabbed Evan's neck and pretended to strangle him.

He laughed. "Stop! You're not helping."

He slammed the can down on the desktop – and the lid popped off.

"Hey – look!" he cried.

She let go of his neck, and they both peered inside the can.

The substance inside the can was bright green. It shimmered like jelly in the light from the ceiling fixture.

"Touch it," Andy said.

But before Evan had a chance, she reached a finger in and poked it. "It's cold," she said. "Touch it. It's really cold."

Evan poked it with his finger. It was cold, thicker than jelly, heavier.

He pushed his finger beneath the surface. When he pulled his finger out, it made a loud sucking noise.

"Gross," Andy said.

Evan shrugged. "I've seen worse."

"I'll bet it glows in the dark," Andy said, hurrying over to the light switch by the door. "It looks like the green that glows in the dark."

She turned off the ceiling light, but late afternoon sunlight still poured in through the window curtains. "Try the closet," she instructed excitedly.

Evan carried the can into the closet. Andy followed and closed the door. "Yuck. Mothballs," she cried. "I can't breathe."

The Monster Blood definitely glowed in the dark. A circular ray of green light seemed to shine from the can.

"Wow. That's way cool," Andy said, holding her nose to keep out the pungent aroma of the mothballs.

"I've had other stuff that did this," Evan said, more than a little disappointed. "It was called Alien Stuff or Yucky Glop, something like that."

"Well, if you don't want it, I'll take it," Andy replied.

"I didn't say I didn't want it," Evan said quickly.

"Let's get out of here," Andy begged.

Evan pushed open the door and they rushed out of the closet, slamming the door shut behind them. Both of them sucked in fresh air for a few seconds.

"Whew, I hate that smell!" Evan declared. He looked around to see that Andy had taken a handful of Monster Blood from the can.

She squeezed it in her palm. "It feels even colder outside the can," she said, grinning at him. "Look. When you squeeze it flat, it pops right back."

"Yeah. It probably bounces, too," Evan said, unimpressed. "Try bouncing it against the floor. All those things bounce like rubber."

Andy rolled the glob of Monster Blood into a ball and dropped it to the floor. It bounced back up into her hand. She bounced it a little harder. This time it rebounded against the wall and went flying out the bedroom door.

"It bounces really well," she said, chasing it out into the hall. "Let's see if it stretches." She grabbed it with both hands and pulled, stretching it into a long string. "Yep. It stretches, too."

"Big deal," Evan said. "The stuff I had before bounced and stretched really well, too. I thought this stuff was going to be different."

"It stays cold, even after it's been in your hand," Andy said, returning to the room.

Evan glanced at the wall and noticed a dark round stain by the floorboard. "Uh-oh. Look, Andy. That stuff stains."

"Let's take it outside and toss it around," she suggested.

"OK," he agreed. "We'll go out back. That way, Trigger won't be so lonely."

Evan held out the can, and Andy replaced the ball of Monster Blood. Then they headed downstairs and out to the garden, where they were greeted by Trigger, who acted as if they'd been away for at least twenty years.

The dog finally calmed down and sat in the shade of a tree, panting noisily. "Good boy," Evan said softly. "Take it easy. Take it easy, old fella."

Andy reached into the can and pulled out a green glob. Then Evan did the same. They rolled the stuff in their hands until they had two ball-shaped globs. Then they began to play catch with them.

"It's amazing how they don't lose their shape," Andy said, tossing a green ball high in the air.

Evan shielded his eyes from the late afternoon sun and caught the ball with one hand. "All this stuff is the same," he said. "It isn't so special."

"Well, I think it's cool," Andy said defensively.

Evan's next toss was too high. The green ball of gunk sailed over Andy's outstretched hands.

"Whoa!" Andy cried.

"Sorry," Evan called.

They both stared as the ball bounced once, twice, then landed right in front of Trigger.

Startled, the dog jumped to his feet and lowered his nose to sniff it.

"No, boy!" Evan called. "Leave it alone. Leave it alone, boy!"

As disobedient as ever, Trigger lowered his head and licked the glowing green ball.

"No, boy! Drop! Drop!" Evan called, alarmed.

He and Andy both lunged towards the dog.

But they were too slow.

Trigger picked up the ball of Monster Blood in his teeth and began chewing it.

"No, Trigger!" Evan shouted. "Don't swallow it. Don't swallow!"

Trigger swallowed it.

"Oh, no!" Andy cried, balling her hands into fists at her sides. "Now there isn't enough left for us to share!"

But that wasn't what was troubling Evan. He bent down and prised apart the dog's jaws. The green blob was gone. Swallowed.

"Stupid dog," Evan said softly, releasing the dog's mouth.

He shook his head as troubling thoughts poured into his mind.

What if the stuff makes Trigger sick? Evan wondered.

What if the stuff is poison?

"Are we going to bake that pie today?" Evan asked his aunt, writing the question on a pad of lined yellow paper he had found on the desk in his room.

Kathryn read the question while adjusting her black ponytail. Her face was as white as cake flour in the morning sunlight filtering through the kitchen window.

"Pie? What pie?" she replied coldly.

Evan's mouth dropped open. He decided not to remind her.

"Go play with your friends," Kathryn said, still coldly, petting Sarabeth's head as the black cat walked by the breakfast table. "Why do you want to stay inside with an old witch?"

It was three days later. Evan had tried to be friendly with his aunt. But the more he tried, the colder she had become.

She's mean. She's really mean, he thought, as he ate the last spoonful of cereal from his bowl of shredded wheat. That was the only cereal she had. Evan struggled to choke it down every morning. Even with milk, the cereal was so dry, and she wouldn't even let him put sugar on it.

"Looks like it might rain," Kathryn said, and took a long sip of the strong tea she had brewed. Her teeth clicked noisily as she drank.

Evan turned his eyes to the bright sunlight outside the window. What made her think it was going to rain?

He glanced back at her, seated across from him at the small kitchen table. For the first time, he noticed the pendant around her neck. It was cream-coloured and sort of bone-shaped.

It is *a bone*, Evan decided.

He stared hard at it, trying to decide if it was a real bone, from some animal maybe, or a bone carved out of ivory. Catching his stare, Kathryn reached up with a large hand and tucked the pendant inside her blouse.

"Go see your girlfriend. She's a pretty one," Kathryn said. She took another long sip of tea, again clicking her teeth as she swallowed.

Yes. I've got to get out of here, Evan thought. He pushed his chair back, stood up, and carried his bowl to the sink.

I can't take much more of this, Evan thought miserably. *She hates me. She really does*.

He hurried up the stairs to his room, where he brushed his curly red hair. Staring into the mirror, he thought of the call he had received from his mother the night before.

She had called right after dinner, and he could tell immediately from her voice that things weren't going well down in Atlanta.

"How's it going, Mom?" he had asked, so happy to hear her voice, even though she was nearly a thousand miles away.

"Slowly," his mother had replied hesitantly.

"What do you mean? How's Dad? Did you find a house?" The questions seemed to pour out of him like air escaping a balloon.

"Whoa. Slow down," Mrs Ross had replied. She sounded tired. "We're both fine, but it's taking a little longer to find a house than we thought. We just haven't found anything we like."

"Does that mean—" Evan started.

"We found one really nice house, very big, very pretty," his mother interrupted. "But the school you'd go to wasn't very good."

"Oh, that's OK. I don't have to go to school," Evan joked.

He could hear his father saying something in the background. His mother covered the receiver to reply.

"When are you coming to pick me up?" Evan asked eagerly.

It took his mother a while to answer. "Well . . . that's the problem," she said finally. "We may need a few more days down here than

317

we thought. How's it going up there, Evan? Are you OK?"

Hearing the bad news that he'd have to stay even longer with Kathryn had made Evan feel like screaming and kicking the wall. But he didn't want to upset his mother. He told her he was fine and that he'd made a new friend.

His father had taken the phone and offered a few encouraging words. "Hang in there," he had said just before ending the conversation.

I'm hanging in, Evan had thought glumly.

But hearing his parents' voices had made him even more homesick.

Now it was the next morning. Putting down his hairbrush, he examined himself quickly in his dresser mirror. He was wearing denim cut-offs and a red Gap T-shirt.

Downstairs, he hurried through the kitchen, where Kathryn appeared to be arguing with Sarabeth, ran out the back door, then jogged to the garden to get Trigger. "Hey, Trigger!"

But the dog was asleep, lying on his side in the centre of his run, gently snoring.

"Don't you want to go to Andy's house?" Evan asked quietly.

Trigger stirred but didn't open his eyes.

"OK. See you later," Evan said. He made sure Trigger's water bowl was filled, then headed to the front of the house.

He was halfway down the next street, walking slowly, thinking about his parents so far away in Atlanta, when a boy's voice called, "Hey – you!" And two boys stepped on to the pavement in front of him, blocking his way.

Startled, Evan stared from one boy to the other. They were twins. Identical twins. Both were big, beefy guys, with short white-blond hair and round red faces. They were both wearing dark T-shirts with the names of heavy-metal bands on the front, baggy shorts, and high-top trainers, untied, without socks. Evan guessed they were about fourteen or fifteen.

"Who are *you*?" one of them asked menacingly, narrowing his pale grey eyes, trying to act tough. Both twins moved closer, forcing Evan to take a big step back.

These guys are twice my size, Evan realized, feeling a wave of fear sweep over him.

Are they just acting tough? Or do they really mean to give me trouble?

"I – I'm staying with my aunt," he stammered, shoving his hands into his pockets and taking another step back.

The twins flashed each other quick grins. "You can't walk on this street," one of them said, hovering over Evan.

"Yeah. You're not a resident," the other added.

"That's a big word," Evan cracked, then immediately wished he hadn't said it.

Why can't I ever keep my big mouth shut? he asked himself. His eyes surveyed the neighbourhood, searching for someone who might come to his aid in case the twins decided to get rough.

But there was no one in sight. Front doors were closed. Gardens were empty. Way down the street, he could see a postman, heading the other way, too far away to shout to.

No one around. No one to help him.

And the two boys, their faces set, their eyes still menacing, began to move in on him.

10

"Where do you think you're going?" one of the twins asked. His hands were balled into fists at his sides. He stepped closer until he was just a centimetre or two from Evan, forcing Evan to take a few steps back.

"To see a friend," Evan replied uncertainly. Maybe these guys were just bluffing.

"Not allowed," the twin said quickly, grinning at his brother.

They both sniggered and moved towards Evan, forcing him to back off the kerb on to the street.

"You're not a resident," the other one repeated. He narrowed his eyes, trying to look tough.

"Hey, give me a break, guys," Evan said. He tried moving to the side, walking on the street, to get around them. But they both moved quickly to keep him from getting away.

"Maybe you could pay a toll," one of them said.

"Yeah," the other one quickly chimed in. "You could pay the non-resident toll. You know, to get temporary permission for walking on this street."

"I don't have any money," Evan said, feeling his fear grow.

He suddenly remembered he had eight dollars in his pocket. Were they going to rob him? Would they beat him up and *then* rob him?

"You have to pay the toll," one of them said, leering at him. "Let's just see what you've got."

They both moved quickly forward, making a grab for him.

He backed away. His legs felt heavy from fear.

Suddenly, a voice cried out from down the pavement. "Hey – what's going on?"

Evan raised his eyes past the two hulking boys to see Andy speeding towards them on her bike along the kerb. "Evan – hi!" she called.

The twins turned away from Evan to greet the new arrival. "Hi, Andy," one of them said in a mocking tone.

"How's it going, Andy?" the other one asked, imitating his brother.

Andy braked her bike and dropped both feet to the ground. She was wearing bright pink shorts and a yellow sleeveless undershirt top. Her face was red, her forehead beaded with perspiration from pedalling so hard.

"You two," she said, and made an unpleasant face. "Rick and Tony." She turned to Evan. "Were they getting on your case?"

"Well. . ." Evan started hesitantly.

"We were welcoming him to the neighbourhood," the one named Rick said, grinning at his brother.

Tony started to add something, but Andy interrupted. "Well, leave him alone."

"Are you his *mother*?" Tony asked, sniggering. He turned to Evan and made goo-goo baby noises.

"We'll leave him alone," Rick said, stepping towards Andy. "We'll borrow your bike and leave him alone."

"No way," Andy said heatedly.

But before Andy could move, Rick grabbed the handlebars. "Let go!" Andy cried, trying to pull the bike from his grasp.

Rick held tight. Tony shoved Andy hard.

She lost her balance and fell, and the bike toppled over on top of her.

"Ohhh."

Andy uttered a low cry as she hit her head on the concrete kerb. She lay sprawled on the kerb, her hands flailing, the bike on top of her.

Before she could get up, Tony reached down and grabbed the bike away. He swung his legs over the seat and began to pedal furiously. "Wait up!" his brother called, laughing as he ran alongside.

In seconds, the twins had disappeared around the corner with Andy's bike.

"Andy – are you OK?" Evan cried, hurrying to the kerb. "Are you OK?"

He grabbed Andy's hand and pulled her to her feet. She stood up groggily, rubbing the back of her head. "I hate those creeps," she said. She brushed the dirt and grass off her shorts and legs. "Ow. That hurt."

"Who *are* they?" Evan asked.

"The Beymer twins," she answered, making a disgusted face. "Real heavy-duty dudes," she added sarcastically. She checked her leg to see if it was cut. It was just scraped. "They think they're so cool, but they're total creeps."

"What about your bike? Should we call the police or something?" Evan asked.

"No need," she said quietly, brushing back her dark hair. "I'll get it back. They've done this before. They'll leave it somewhere when they're finished."

"But shouldn't we—" Evan started.

"They just run wild," Andy interrupted. "There's no one home to check up on them. They live with their grandmother, but she's never around. Did they give you a hard time?"

Evan nodded. "I was afraid I was going to have to pound them," he joked.

Andy didn't laugh. "I'd like to pound them," she said angrily. "Just once. I'd like to pay them back. They pick on all the kids in the neighbourhood. They think they can do whatever they want because they're so big and because there are two of them."

"Your knee is cut," Evan said, pointing.

"I'd better go home and clean it up," she replied, rolling her eyes disgustedly. "See you later, OK? I have to go somewhere this afternoon, but maybe we can do something tomorrow."

She headed back to her house, rubbing the back of her head.

Evan returned to Kathryn's, walking slowly, thinking about the Beymer twins, daydreaming about fighting them, imagining himself beating them to a pulp in a fight as Andy watched, cheering him on.

Kathryn was dusting the front room as Evan entered. She didn't look up. He headed quickly up the stairs to his room.

Now what am I going to do? he wondered, pacing back and forth. The blue container of Monster Blood caught his eye. He walked over to the bookshelf and picked up the can from the middle shelf.

He pulled off the lid. The can was nearly full.

I guess Trigger didn't eat that much, he thought, feeling a little relieved.

Trigger!

He'd forgotten all about him. The poor dog must be hungry.

Putting down the Monster Blood, Evan bombed down the stairs, leaning against the banister and taking the stairs three at a time. Then, running full-out, he practically flew to the dog run at the back of the garden.

"Trigger! Hey – Trigger!" he called.

Halfway across the garden, Evan could see that something was wrong.

Trigger's eyes were bulging. His mouth was wide open, his tongue flailing rapidly from side to side, white spittle running down his chin hair on to the ground.

"Trigger!"

The dog was gasping hoarsely, each breath a desperate, difficult struggle.

He's choking! Evan realized.

As Evan reached the dog run, Trigger's eyes rolled back, and the dog's legs collapsed under him, his stomach still heaving, the air filled with his loud, hideous gasps.

"Trigger – no!"

Evan dived to his knees beside the dog and began to tug at Trigger's collar. The collar, Evan saw, had become way too tight.

The dog's chest heaved. Thick white spittle flowed from his open mouth.

"Hold on, boy. Hold on!" Evan cried.

The dog's eyes rolled wildly in his head. He didn't seem to see or hear Evan.

"Hold on, fella! Just *hold on!*"

The collar wouldn't budge. It was buried tightly under the dog's fur.

His hands shaking, Evan struggled to pull the collar over Trigger's head.

Come loose, come loose, come loose, he begged. *Yes!*

Trigger uttered a pained whimper as Evan finally managed to pull the collar away.

"Trigger – it's off! Are you OK?"

Still panting hard, the dog jumped immediately to his feet. He licked Evan's face appreciatively, covering Evan's cheek with his thick saliva, whimpering as if he understood that Evan had just saved his life.

"Easy, boy! Easy, fella!" Evan repeated, but the dog continued to lick him gratefully.

Evan hugged the excited dog. This had been a close call, he knew. If he hadn't come along just then. . .

Well, he didn't want to think about it.

When Trigger finally calmed down, Evan examined the collar. "What made this collar shrink like that, boy?" he asked Trigger.

The dog had walked over to the fence and was frantically slurping water from his bowl.

This is plain weird, Evan thought. *The collar couldn't have shrunk. It's made of leather. There was no reason for it to shrink.*

Then why did it suddenly start choking Trigger?

Evan turned to Trigger, studying him as the dog lapped greedily at the water, breathing hard. He turned and glanced back at Evan for a second, then returned to his frantic water slurping.

He's *bigger*, Evan decided.

He's definitely bigger.

But Trigger was twelve years old, eighty-four in human years. Older than Aunt Kathryn.

Trigger was too old for a late growth spurt.

It must be my eyes, Evan decided, tossing the collar to the ground. *This place must be making me see things.*

Kathryn was at the kitchen door, calling Evan to lunch. He poured out a bowl of dry food, shouted goodbye to Trigger, who didn't look up from the water dish, and hurried to the house.

The next morning, an overcast morning with an autumn chill in the air, Evan made his way to Andy's house. He found her huddled under a big maple tree in the neighbour's front garden. "What's going on?" he called.

Then he saw that she was leaning over something, her hands working quickly. "Come help me!" she cried, not looking up.

Evan came jogging over. "Whoa!" he cried out when he saw that Andy was struggling to free a cat that had been tied to the tree trunk.

The cat screeched and swiped its paw at Andy. Andy dodged the claws and continued to pull at the big knots in the rope.

"The Beymer twins did this, I know it," she said loudly, over the shrilly protesting cat. "This poor cat was probably tied up here all night."

The cat, in a panic, shrieked with amazingly human-sounding cries.

"Stand still, cat," Evan said as the terrified cat swiped its claws at Andy again. "Can I help?"

"No. I've almost got it," she replied, tugging

329

at the knot. "I'd like to tie Rick and Tony to this tree."

"Poor frightened cat," Evan said quietly.

"There," Andy said triumphantly, pulling the rope loose.

The cat gave one last cry of protest, its tail standing straight up. Then it darted away, running at full speed, and disappeared under a tall hedge without looking back.

"Not very polite," Evan muttered.

Andy stood up and sighed. She was wearing faded denim jeans and a pale green oversized T-shirt that came down nearly to her knees. She lifted the bottom of the shirt to examine a hole the cat had managed to snag in it.

"I can't believe those two creeps," she said, shaking her head.

"Maybe we should call the police or an animal shelter or something," Evan suggested.

"The twins would just deny it," Andy said glumly, shaking her head. Then she added, "And the cat's not a very good witness."

They both laughed.

Evan led the way back to his aunt's house. All the way back, they talked about how they'd like to teach the Beymer twins a lesson. But neither of them had any good ideas.

They found Kathryn concentrating on a jigsaw puzzle at the dining room table.

She looked up when they entered, squinting at them. "You like jigsaw puzzles? I like to keep my mind active, you know. That's why I like puzzles. Your mind can get flabby when you get to be my age. A hundred and twelve."

She slapped the table gleefully at her own wit. Evan and Andy both flashed her agreeable smiles. Then she returned to her puzzle without waiting for a reply.

"She's going to drive me bananas!" Evan exclaimed.

"Evan – she'll hear you!" Andy protested, cupping a hand over his mouth.

"I told you, she's completely deaf. She can't hear me. She doesn't *want* to hear anyone. She *hates* everyone."

"I think she's sweet," Andy said. "Why does she wear a bone around her neck?"

"Probably thinks it's cool," Evan cracked.

"Let's go upstairs," Andy urged, pushing him towards the stairs. "I still feel weird talking about your aunt right in front of her."

"You're a crazy old coot," Evan called to Kathryn, a big smile on his face.

Kathryn looked up from her puzzle pieces to cast a cold stare his way.

"She heard you!" Andy cried, horrified.

"Don't be dumb," Evan said, and started up the stairs, nearly tripping over Sarabeth.

Up in Evan's room, Andy paced uncomfortably. "What do you want to do?"

"Well . . . we could read some of these great books," Evan said sarcastically, pointing to the dusty old books that lined the walls. "Maybe find a spell to cast on the Beymer twins. You know. Turn them into newts."

"Forget about newts," Andy said dryly. "Hey – where's the Monster Blood?" Before Evan could answer, she spotted it on one of the shelves.

They raced across the room for it. Andy got there first and grabbed the can. "Evan – look," she said, her eyes growing wide with surprise. "What's going on?"

She held up the can. The green gunk had pushed up the lid and was flowing out of the can.

"Huh? Did the top break or something?" Evan asked.

He took the can from her and examined it. Sure enough, the lid had popped off. The gooey green substance was pushing up out of the can.

Evan pulled out a handful of the green gunk. "Weird," he exclaimed. "It's expanding," he said, squeezing it in his hand. "It's definitely growing."

"I guess so!" Andy exclaimed. "It grew right out of the can!"

"Hey – it's not cold any more," Evan said. He balled it up and tossed it to Andy.

"It's really warm," she agreed. "Weird!"

She tried to toss it back to him, but it stuck to her palm. "It's getting sticky," she reported. "Are you sure this is the same stuff?"

"Of course," Evan replied.

"But it wasn't sticky before, remember?" she said.

He pulled another warm hunk of it from the can.

"I guess it just changes after the can has been opened."

He squeezed the stuff into a ball shape and tossed it to the floor. "Look – it stuck to the floor. It didn't bounce."

"Weird!" Andy repeated.

"Maybe I should throw it in the bin," Evan said, prising the sticky glob from the floor. "I mean, what good is it if it doesn't bounce?"

"Hey – no way," Andy said. "We've got to see what it does next."

A soft mewing sound made them both turn towards the door.

Evan was surprised to see Sarabeth standing there, her head cocked, her yellow eyes staring at him.

Or was she staring at the glob of Monster Blood in his hand?

"That cat looks so intelligent," Andy said.

"It's as stupid as every other cat," Evan muttered. "Look. She wants to play ball with the Monster Blood."

"Sorry, cat," Andy said. "It doesn't bounce."

As if she understood, Sarabeth mewed unhappily, turned, and padded silently from the room.

"Now where am I going to keep this stuff?" Evan asked. "It's too big for its can."

"Here. How about this?" Andy asked. She

reached down to a low shelf and came up with an empty coffee can.

"Yeah. OK." Evan tossed his hunk into the coffee can.

Andy squeezed hers into a flat pancake. "Look. It isn't glowing the way it used to, either," she said, holding the pancake up for Evan to see. "But it sure is warm. Almost hot."

"It's *alive*!" Evan screamed playfully. "Run for your life! It's *alive*!"

Andy laughed and began to chase Evan, menacing him with the flat green pancake. "Come get your Monster Blood! Come and get it!"

He dodged away, then grabbed it from her hand. He squeezed it together, balling it up in one hand, then tossed it into the coffee can.

They both peered into the can. The green substance filled it up a little more than halfway.

"Go ahead. Taste it," Andy urged, poking the can in his face. "I dare you."

"Huh? No way. I double-dare you," Evan said, pushing the coffee can back to her.

"Double-darers have to go first," Andy insisted, grinning. "Go ahead. Taste it."

Evan made a disgusted face and shook his head. Then he grabbed a big hunk of it and heaved it at Andy. Laughing, she picked it up off the carpet and tossed it at his face. She threw high, and the green glob stuck to the wall.

Evan reached for another hunk.

They had a messy, hilarious Monster Blood battle until dinner time. Then, as they tried to clean up, they both heard Trigger through the open window. He was barking loudly out in his pen.

Evan reached the window first. The sky was still grey and overcast. Trigger was leaning on the wooden fence, standing on his hind legs, barking his head off.

"Whoa, Trigger," Evan called, "chill out!"

"Hey – what's with Trigger?" Andy asked. "Is your dog still growing? He looks so big!"

Evan's mouth dropped open and he uttered a silent gasp, realizing that Andy was right.

Trigger had nearly doubled in size.

"Trigger – come back! Come *back*!"

The big dog continued to run, its giant paws thundering against the concrete.

"Come back!" Evan screamed, running with long, desperate strides, his heart thudding, his legs aching with each step as he tried to catch up with the galloping dog.

The night was dark and starless. The street glistened as if it had recently rained.

Trigger's paws hit the pavement, each step a loud thunderclap that seemed to echo for ever. His giant ears flapped like wings, twin pennants caught on the wind. His big head bobbed up and down, but he didn't look back.

"Trigger! *Trigger!*"

Evan's voice seemed muffled by the gusting wind, pushed back in his face. He tried shouting louder, but no sound came out at all.

He knew he had to stop the dog from running away. He had to catch the dog and then get help.

Trigger was growing so fast, completely out of control. He was already the size of a pony and getting larger by the minute.

"Trigger! Trigger! Stop, boy!"

Trigger didn't seem to hear him. Evan's voice didn't seem to carry beyond the gusting, swirling wind.

And still Evan ran, his chest pounding, every muscle aching. And as he ran, he suddenly realized there were others running, too.

Two large figures in front of the stampeding dog.

Two large figures Evan recognized as they fled at full speed, trying to get away from the onrushing animal.

The Beymer twins. Rick and Tony.

Trigger was chasing them, Evan suddenly realized.

The boys turned a corner, on to an even darker street. Trigger followed, bounding after them. Evan continued to run, bringing up the rear of this dark, mysterious parade.

All was silent now, except for the steady, rhythmic thunder of Trigger's enormous padded paws.

Except for the *clapclapclap* of the Beymer twins' trainers as they darted along the glistening pavement.

Except for the gasp of Evan's breathing as he struggled to keep up.

Suddenly, as Evan watched in horror, the dog raised up on his hind legs. He tilted his head to the sky and let out an ear-piercing howl. Not the howl of a dog. A creature howl.

And then Trigger's features began to transform. His forehead burst forward and enlarged. His eyes grew wide and round before sinking under the protruding forehead. Fangs slid from his gaping mouth, and he uttered another howl to the sky, louder and more chilling than the first.

"He's a monster! A monster!" Evan cried.

And woke up.

Woke up from his frightening dream.

And realized he was in bed, in the study upstairs in Kathryn's house.

It had all been a dream, a frightening, wild chase of a dream.

A harmless dream. Except that something still wasn't right.

The bed. It felt so uncomfortable. So cramped.

Evan sat up, alert, wide awake now.

And stared down at his giant feet. His giant hands. And realized how tiny the bed seemed beneath him.

Because he was a giant now.

Because he had grown so huge, so monstrously huge.

And when he saw how big he had become, he opened his mouth wide and began to scream.

His screams woke him up.

This time he really woke up.

And realized that, the first time, he had only dreamed that he was awake. Had only dreamed that he had become a giant.

Dreams upon dreams.

Was he really awake now?

He sat up, blinked, rubbed his eyes, struggled to focus.

Dripping with sweat.

His blankets tossed to the floor.

His pyjamas damp, clinging to his prickly skin.

Nothing seemed familiar. It took a while to shake off the dream, to remember where he was. That he was in his room at Kathryn's. Awake now. His normal size.

Tossed by the wind, the curtains brushed over him, then were noisily sucked out the window.

Evan sat up and, still feeling shaky, peered out the window.

Wisps of grey clouds floated over a pale half-moon. Trees tossed and whispered in the cool night wind.

Only a dream.

A frightening dream. A dream on top of a dream.

He could see Trigger sound asleep, curled up on himself, pressed against the fence wall.

Trigger wasn't a monster. But he was definitely bigger, Evan saw.

Maybe there's something wrong with him. The troubling thought pushed its way into Evan's mind as he stared down at the sleeping dog.

Maybe it's glands or something.

Maybe he's eating too much. Or maybe. . .

Evan yawned. He realized he was too sleepy to think clearly. Maybe the next morning he'd see if there was a vet in town.

Yawning again, he started to settle back into bed. But something caught his eye.

The coffee can on the bookshelf. The can where he had stored the Monster Blood.

"Hey—" he cried aloud.

The green gunk was bubbling, quivering up over the top of the coffee can.

"Your dog seems to be quite healthy for his age."
Dr Forrest scratched Trigger gently under the
chin. "Look at all the white hairs," he said, bringing
his face down close to the dog's. "You're a good
old dog, aren't you?"

Trigger licked the doctor's hand appreciatively.

Dr Forrest grinned, pushing his black glasses
up on his narrow nose, the ceiling light reflecting
off his shiny forehead. He wiped his hand on the
front of his white lab coat.

Evan and Andy stood across from Trigger in
the small, brightly lit office. They had both been
tense during the long examination the vet had
given the dog. But now, hearing the doctor's
verdict, they had relaxed expressions on their
faces.

"So you think it's just a late growth spurt?"
Evan repeated.

Dr Forrest nodded, returning to his desk in

the corner. "Highly unusual," he said softly, leaning over the desk to write a note on a pad. "Highly unusual. We'll get a lab report in three or four days. It may tell us more. But the dog seems very healthy to me. I really wouldn't be alarmed."

"But do cocker spaniels usually get this big?" Evan asked, leaning down to scratch Trigger under the chin, the leash looped loosely in his hand.

Trigger wanted to leave. He pulled towards the door. Evan stood up and tugged hard at the leash to keep the dog in place. It took all of his strength. Trigger was not only bigger; he was much stronger than he had been a few days before.

"No. Not usually," the vet replied. "That's why I took the hormone tests and the blood and glandular samples. Maybe the lab will have an answer for us."

He finished writing and tore the sheet off the pad. "Here," he said, handing the paper to Evan. "I wrote down the name of a good dog food. Put Trigger on this and see that he cuts down on his between-meal snacks." He chuckled at his own joke.

Evan thanked the doctor and allowed Trigger to pull him out of the office. Andy jogged after them. In the waiting room outside, a tiny chihuahua cowered behind the sofa, whimpering at the sight of the big cocker spaniel.

"I'm glad to be out of there," Evan exclaimed as they stepped out to the pavement.

"Trigger got a very good report," Andy said reassuringly, petting Trigger's head. "Hey, look – his head is wider than my hand!"

"He's nearly as big as a sheepdog!" Evan said miserably. "And Dr Forrest says he's perfectly OK."

"Don't exaggerate," Andy scolded. She glanced at her watch. "Oh, no! I don't believe it. Late for my piano lesson. Again! Mom'll *kill* me!"

She waved goodbye, turned, and ran full speed down the pavement, nearly colliding with an elderly couple coming slowly out of the small grocery store on the corner.

"Let's go, boy," Evan said, thinking about what Dr Forrest had said. Tugging the leash, he headed out of the small town. Despite the vet's assurances, Evan was still plenty worried about Trigger.

He stopped outside the grocery. "Maybe an ice cream will help cheer me up." He tied Trigger's leash to the red fire hydrant across from the grocery's door. "Stay," he instructed.

Trigger, ignoring Evan, struggled to pull free.

"I'll only be a second," Evan said, and hurried into the store.

There were three or four people in the store, and it took a bit longer than Evan had expected. When he returned to the pavement ten minutes later, he discovered the Beymer twins busily untying Trigger.

"Hey – let go!" he cried angrily.

They both turned towards him, identical grins on their beefy faces. "Look what we found," one of them teased. The other one successfully untied the leash from the hydrant.

"Hand me that," Evan insisted, holding his chocolate ice cream bar in one hand, reaching for the leash handle with the other.

The Beymer twin held the leash handle out to Evan – then quickly snapped it back out of his reach. "Gotcha!"

The brothers laughed gleefully and slapped each other a high five.

"Stop fooling around," Evan insisted. "Hand me the leash."

"Finders, keepers," one of them said. "Isn't that right, Tony?"

"Yeah," Tony replied, grinning. "It's an ugly dog. But it's *our* ugly dog now."

"Get your own dog, wimp," Rick said nastily. He stepped forward and punched the ice cream bar out of Evan's hand. It landed on the pavement with a *plop*.

The brothers started to laugh, but their laughter was cut short as Trigger suddenly uttered a low, warning growl. Pulling back his lips, he bared his teeth, and his growl became a snarl.

"Hey—" Rick cried, dropping the leash.

With a loud, angry roar, Trigger reared up and pounced on Rick, forcing him to stagger backwards to the kerb.

Tony had already started to run, his trainers pounding the pavement noisily as he headed at full speed past the vet's office, past the post office, and kept going.

"Wait up! Hey, Tony – wait up!" Rick stumbled, stood up, and took off after his brother.

Evan grabbed for Trigger's leash – and missed.

"Trigger – whoa! Stop!"

The dog took off after the fleeting twins, barking angrily, his enormous paws thudding loudly on the pavement, picking up speed as he closed in on them.

No, Evan thought, finding himself frozen there on the corner in front of the grocery.

No. No. No.

This can't *be happening!*

It's my dream.

Is it coming true?

Evan shuddered, remembering the rest of his dream, remembering how he, too, grew until he was twice his size.

Would that part of the dream also come true?

That afternoon, about an hour before dinner time, Evan called Andy. "Can I come over?" he asked. "I have a small problem."

"Sounds like a big problem," Andy said.

"Yeah. OK. A big problem," Evan snapped impatiently. "I'm not in the mood to kid around, OK?"

"OK. Sorry," Andy replied quickly. "Any sign of Rick and Tony? They're not your problem, are they?"

"Not at the moment," he told her. "I told you, they were gone by the time I caught up with Trigger. Disappeared. Vanished. Trigger was still barking his head off. Somehow I dragged him home and got him in his pen."

"So what's your problem?" she asked.

"I can't tell you. I have to show you," he said. "I'll be right there. Bye."

He hung up the phone and hurried down the

347

stairs, carrying the bucket. Kathryn was in the kitchen, her back to him, chopping away at something with her big butcher knife. Evan hurried past and darted out the door.

Andy's house was a modern, redwood ranch style, with a low hedge of evergreens running along the front. Her dad, she said, was a fanatic about the lawn. It was clipped a perfect centimetre and a half above the ground, smooth as a carpet. A flower garden stretched along the front of the house, tall orange-and-yellow tiger lilies bobbing in the gentle breeze.

The front door was open. Evan knocked on the screen door.

"What's with the bucket?" was Andy's greeting as she let him in.

"Look," he said, out of breath from running all the way to her house. He held up the aluminium bucket he had taken from Kathryn's garage.

"Oh, wow," Andy exclaimed, raising her hands to her face as she stared into it wide-eyed.

"Yeah. Wow," he repeated sarcastically. "The Monster Blood. It's grown again. Look. It's almost filled this big bucket. What are we going to do?"

"What do you mean *we*?" Andy teased, leading him into the den.

"Not funny," he muttered.

"You didn't want to share it," she insisted.

"I'll share it now," he said eagerly. "In fact . . . do

348

you want it? I'll give it to you for a bargain price – free." He held the bucket towards her.

"Huh-uh." Andy shook her head, crossing her arms in front of her chest. "Put it down, will you?" She pointed to the corner behind the red leather sofa. "Put it over there. It's giving me the creeps."

"Giving *you* the creeps!?" Evan cried. "What am I going to do? Every time I turn around, it grows some more. It's growing faster than Trigger!"

"Hey!" they both cried at once.

Both had the same thought, the same frightening memory. Both suddenly remembered that Trigger had eaten a ball of the green gunk.

"Do you think. . ." Evan started.

"Maybe. . ." Andy replied, not waiting for him to finish his thought. "Maybe Trigger's growing because he ate the Monster Blood."

"What am I going to *do*?" Evan wailed, pacing the room nervously, his hands shoved into his jeans pockets. "The stuff is getting bigger and bigger, and so is poor Trigger. I'm all alone here. There's no one who can help me. No one."

"What about your aunt?" Andy suggested, staring at the bucket on the floor in the corner. "Maybe Kathryn can think of something—"

"Are you kidding? She can't hear me. She doesn't *want* to hear me. She *hates* me. She just

349

sits at her jigsaw puzzle and argues with that horrible black cat all day."

"OK. Forget the aunt," Andy said, making a dispirited face.

"Perhaps if you told Dr Forrest—"

"Oh, yeah. For sure," Evan snapped. "He'd really believe that Trigger is turning into a giant because I let him eat Monster Blood."

He threw himself down on the sofa. "I'm all alone here, Andy. There's no one to help me. No one I can even talk to about this."

"Except me?"

"Yeah," he said, locking his eyes on hers. "Except you."

She plopped down on the other end of the sofa. "Well, what can I do?" she said hesitantly.

He jumped up and carried the bucket over. "Take some of this. Let's split it up."

"Huh? Why don't we just toss it in the bin?" she asked, staring down at it. The green gunk was pushing up near the top of the bucket.

"Toss it? We can't," he said.

"Sure, we can. Come on. I'll show you." She reached for the bucket handle, but he shoved it out of her reach.

"What if it outgrows the rubbish bin?" he asked. "What if it just keeps growing?"

Andy shrugged. "I don't know."

"Also, I *have* to save it," Evan continued excitedly. "If it's really the thing that's causing

350

Trigger to grow, I'll need it as proof. You know. To show the doctors or whatever. So they can cure Trigger."

"Maybe we should call the police," Andy said thoughtfully, tugging at a strand of hair.

"Oh. Sure," Evan replied, rolling his eyes. "They'll really believe us. For sure. 'We bought this stuff in a toy store, officer, and now it's growing bigger and bigger and it's turning my dog into a giant monster.'"

"OK, OK. You're right," Andy said. "We can't call the police."

"So, are you going to help me?" Evan demanded. "Will you take some of this stuff?"

"I guess," she said reluctantly. "But just a little." She climbed to her feet, carefully stepping around the bucket. "I'll be right back."

She left the room, then quickly returned, carrying an empty coffee can. "Fill 'er up," she said, smiling.

Evan stared at the coffee can. "That's *all* you're going to take?" he complained. Then he immediately softened his tone. "OK. OK. It's a help."

Andy crouched down and dipped the coffee can into the middle of the bucket. "Hey!" she cried out. Her hands flew up and she tumbled back on to the floor.

"What's wrong?" Evan hurried over to her.

"It was pulling the coffee can in," she said, her features tight with fear and surprise. "Sucking it. Look."

Evan peered into the bucket. The coffee can had disappeared under the surface. "Huh?"

"I could feel it pulling," Andy said shakily. She regained her perch over the bucket.

"Let's see," Evan said, and plunged both hands into the middle of the Monster Blood.

"Yuck," Andy said. "This is really gross."

"It's pulling. You're right," Evan agreed. "It feels like it's pulling my hands down. Wow. It's so warm. As if it's alive."

"Don't say that!" Andy cried with a shudder. "Just get the can out, OK?"

Evan had to tug hard, but he managed to pull up the coffee can, filled to the top with the quivering green substance. "Yuck."

"You sure I have to take this?" Andy asked, not reaching for it even though he was holding it out to her.

"Just for a little while," he said. "Till we think of a better plan."

"Maybe we could feed it to the Beymer twins," Andy suggested, finally taking the can.

"Then we'd have *giant* Beymer twins," Evan joked. "No, thank you."

"Seriously, you'd better watch out for them," Andy warned. "If Trigger scared them away this morning, they'll be looking to get back at

352

you. They really think they're tough dudes, Evan. They can be vicious. They could really hurt you."

"Thanks for trying to cheer me up," Evan said glumly. He was still pulling tiny, clinging clumps of the Monster Blood off his hands and tossing them into the bucket.

"I was watching a video before you came over. The first Indiana Jones movie. Want to watch it?"

Evan shook his head. "No. I'd better go. Aunt Kathryn was busy making dinner when I left. Chopping up some kind of meat. Another great dinner, sitting there in silence, being stared at by Aunt Kathryn and her cat."

"Poor Evan," Andy said, half teasing, half sympathetic.

He picked up the bucket, now only two-thirds full, and let her walk him to the front door. "Call me later, OK?" she asked.

He nodded and stepped outside. She closed the door behind him.

He was halfway to the pavement when the Beymer twins slipped out from behind the evergreen hedge, their hands balled into red, beefy fists.

The brothers stepped out of the shadows of the hedge. Their short blond hair caught the late afternoon sunlight. They were both grinning gleefully.

Evan stood frozen in place, staring from one to the other.

No one said a word.

One of the Beymers grabbed the bucket from Evan's hand and tossed it to the ground. The bucket hit with a heavy *thud*, and its thick green contents oozed on to the grass, making disgusting sucking sounds.

"Hey—" Evan cried, breaking the tense silence.

He didn't have a chance to say more.

The other twin punched him hard in the stomach.

Evan felt the pain radiate through his body. The punch took his breath away. He gasped for air.

He didn't see the next punch. It landed on his cheek just below his right eye.

He howled in pain, and his hands flailed the air helplessly.

Both brothers were hitting him now. And then one of them gave Evan's shoulders a hard shove and he went sprawling on to the cool, damp grass.

The pain swept over him, blanketing him, followed by a wave of nausea. He closed his eyes, gasping noisily, waiting for the sharp ache in his stomach to fade.

The ground seemed to tilt. He reached out and grabbed it, and held on tightly so he wouldn't fall off.

When he finally managed to raise his head, Andy was standing over him, her eyes wide with alarm. "Evan—"

He groaned and, pushing with both hands, tried to sit up. The dizziness, the spinning, tilting grass, forced him to lie back down.

"Are they gone?" he asked, closing his eyes, willing the dizziness away.

"Rick and Tony? I saw them run away," Andy said, kneeling beside him. "Are you OK? Should I call my mom?"

He opened his eyes. "Yeah. No. I don't know."

"What *happened*?" she demanded.

He raised a hand to his cheek. "Ow!" It was already swollen, too painful to touch.

"They beat you up?"

"Either that or I was hit by a truck," he groaned.

A few minutes later – it seemed like hours – he was back on his feet, breathing normally, rubbing his swollen cheek. "I've never been in a fight before," he told Andy, shaking his head. "Never."

"It doesn't look like it was much of a fight," she said, her expression still tight with concern.

He started to laugh, but it made his stomach hurt.

"We'll pay them back," Andy said bitterly. "We'll find a way to pay them back. The creeps."

"Oh. Look. The Monster Blood." Evan hurried over to it.

The bucket lay on its side. The green gunk had oozed on to the grass, forming a wide, thick puddle.

"I'll help you get it back in the bucket," Andy said, leaning over to stand the bucket up. "Hope it doesn't kill the grass. My dad'll have a cow if his precious lawn is hurt!"

"It's so heavy," Evan said, groaning as he tried to push the glob into the bucket. "It doesn't want to move."

"Let's try picking up handfuls," Andy suggested. "Whoa. It doesn't want to come apart," Evan said in surprise. "Look. It sticks together."

356

"It's like toffee," Andy said. "Ever see them make toffee in those toffee machines? The stuff just sticks together in one big glob."

"This isn't toffee," Evan muttered. "It's disgusting."

Working together, they managed to lift the entire green ball and drop it into the bucket. The stuff made a sickening sucking sound as it filled the bucket, and both Evan and Andy had trouble pulling their hands out of it.

"It's so sticky," Andy said, making a disgusted face.

"And warm," Evan added. He finally managed to free his hands from it. "It's like it's trying to swallow my hands," he said, wiping his hands on his T-shirt. "Sucking them in."

"Take it home," Andy said. She looked up to the house to see her mother motioning to her from the front window. "Uh-oh. Dinner time. I've got to go." Her eyes stopped at his swollen cheek. "Wait till your aunt sees you."

"She probably won't even notice," Evan said glumly. He picked up the bucket by the handle. "What are we going to do with this stuff?"

"We'll take it back to the toy store tomorrow," Andy replied, taking long strides across the lawn to the house.

"Huh?"

"That's what we'll do. We'll simply take it back."

Evan didn't think it was such a hot idea. But he didn't have the strength to argue about it now. He watched Andy disappear into the house. Then he headed slowly back to Kathryn's, his head throbbing, his stomach aching.

Creeping along the wall of the house, he slipped into the garage through the side door to hide the bucket of Monster Blood. Sliding it behind an overturned wheelbarrow, he realized that the bucket was full to the top.

But I gave Andy a big hunk of it, he thought. *The bucket had been only two-thirds full.*

I'll have to find a bigger place to put it, he decided. *Tonight. Maybe there's a box or something in the basement.*

He crept into the house, determined to clean himself up before seeing Kathryn. She was still busy in the kitchen, he saw, leaning over the stove, putting the last touches on dinner. He tiptoed up the stairs and washed up. Unable to do much about his swollen red cheek, he changed into a clean pair of baggy shorts and a fresh T-shirt and carefully brushed his hair.

As they sat down at the dining room table, Kathryn's eyes fell on Evan's swollen cheek. "You been in a fight?" she asked, squinting suspiciously at him. "You're a little roughneck, aren't you? Just like your father. Chicken was always getting into scrapes, always picking on boys twice his size."

"I wasn't exactly picking on them," Evan

muttered, spearing a chunk of beef from his stew with his fork.

All through dinner, Kathryn stared at his swollen cheek. But she didn't say another word.

She doesn't care if I'm hurt or not, Evan thought miserably.

She really doesn't care.

She didn't even ask if it hurts.

In a way, he was grateful. He didn't need her getting all upset, making a fuss because he was in a fight, maybe calling his parents in Atlanta and telling them.

Well . . . she couldn't call his parents. She couldn't use the phone, since she couldn't hear.

Evan downed his big plate of beef stew. It was pretty good, except for the vegetables.

The silence seemed so *loud*. He began thinking about his problem – the Monster Blood.

Should he tell Kathryn about it?

He could write down the whole problem on the yellow pad and hand it to her to read. It would feel so good to tell someone, to have an adult take over the problem and handle it.

But not his Aunt Kathryn, he decided.

She was too weird.

She wouldn't understand.

She wouldn't know what to do.

And she wouldn't care.

Andy was right. They had to carry the stuff back to the toy store. Give it back. Just get rid of it.

But in the meantime, he had to find something to keep it in.

Evan waited in his room until he heard Kathryn go to bed, a little after ten o'clock. Then he crept down the stairs and headed out to the garage.

It was a cool, clear night. Crickets sent up a relentless curtain of noise. The black sky glittered with tiny specks of stars.

The round beam of light from the flashlight in his hand darted across the driveway, leading Evan to the dark garage. As he entered, something scuttled across the floor near the back wall.

Maybe it was just a dead leaf, blown by the wind when I opened the door, he thought hopefully.

He moved the flashlight unsteadily, beaming it on to the overturned wheelbarrow. Then the light darted across the garage ceiling as he bent down, reached behind the wheelbarrow, and pulled out the bucket of Monster Blood.

He moved the light to the centre of the bucket and gasped.

The green substance was quivering up over the top.

It's growing much faster than before, he thought.

I've got to find something bigger to hide it in – just for tonight.

The bucket was too heavy to carry with one hand. Tucking the flashlight into his armpit, he gripped the bucket handle with both hands and hoisted the bucket off the floor.

Struggling to keep from spilling it, he made his way into the dark house. He paused at the door to the basement steps, silently setting the heavy bucket down on the linoleum floor.

He clicked the light switch on the wall. Somewhere downstairs a dim light flickered on, casting a wash of pale yellow light over the concrete floor.

There's got to be something to put this stuff in down there, Evan thought. Hoisting up the bucket, he made his way slowly, carefully down the steep, dark stairway, leaning his shoulder against the wall to steady himself.

Waiting for his eyes to adjust to the pale light, he saw that the basement was one large room, low-ceilinged and damp. It was cluttered with cartons, stacks of old newspapers and magazines, and old furniture and appliances covered in stained, yellowed bed sheets.

Something brushed his face as he stepped away from the stairs.

He uttered a silent cry and, dropping the bucket, raised his hands to swipe at the thick cobwebs that seemed to reach out for him. They clung to his skin, dry and scratchy, as he frantically pulled at them.

He suddenly realized it wasn't the web that was moving against his cheek.

It was a spider.

With a sharp intake of breath, he brushed it away. But even after he saw the insect scuttle across the floor, he could still feel its prickly feet moving on his face.

Moving quickly away from the wall, his heart pounding now, his eyes searching the open wooden shelves hidden in shadow against the far wall, he stumbled over something on the floor.

"Oh!" He fell head first over it, throwing his hands forward to break his fall.

A human body!

Someone lying there under him!

No.

Calm down, Evan. Calm down, he instructed himself.

He pulled himself shakily to his feet.

It was a dressmaker's dummy he had stumbled over. Probably a model of Kathryn when she was younger.

He rolled it out of the way as his eyes searched the shadowy room for a container to store the

Monster Blood. What was that long, low object in front of the worktable?

Moving closer, he saw that it was an old bathtub, the insides stained and peeling. *It's big enough*, he realized, and quickly decided to store the green gunk inside it.

With a loud groan, he hoisted the bucket on to the side of the old tub. His stomach muscles were still sore from the punch he had taken, and the pain shot through his body.

He waited for the aching to fade, then tilted the bucket. The thick green substance rolled out of the bucket and hit the tub bottom with a sickening soft *plop*.

Evan set the bucket aside and stared down at the Monster Blood, watching it ooze, spreading thickly over the bottom of the bathtub. To his surprise, the tub appeared nearly half full.

How fast was this stuff growing?!

He was leaning over the tub, about to make his way back upstairs, when he heard the cat screech.

Startled, he let go of the side of the tub just as Sarabeth leaped on to his back. Evan didn't have time to cry out as he toppled forward, over the edge of the tub and into the thick green gunk.

Evan landed hard on his elbows, but the thick Monster Blood softened the fall. He heard the cat screech again and pad away.

He sank into the ooze, his arms and legs flailing, trying to lift himself away. But the sticky substance was sucking him down, pulling him with surprising force.

His whole body seemed to be held by it, stuck as if in cement, and now it was quivering up, bubbling silently, rising up to his face. *I'm going to suffocate*, he realized.

It's trying to choke me.

The warmth of it spread across his body, invaded his chest, his legs, his throat.

I can't move.

I'm stuck.

It's trying to choke me.

No!

He pulled his head up just as the green gunk began to cover his face.

Then he struggled to twist his body, to twist himself around in it. With great effort, panting loudly, hoarse cries escaping his open lips, he pulled himself up into a sitting position.

The green substance rose up even higher, as if it were reaching up to him, reaching to drag him back down into it.

Evan gripped the side of the tub with both hands, held on to it tightly, and began to force himself up. Up, up from the clinging, pulling ooze. Up from the strange force that seemed to be drawing him back with renewed power.

Up. Up.

"No!" he managed to scream as the warm green ooze slid over his shoulders.

"No!"

It was gripping his shoulders now, sliding around his neck, sucking him down, pulling him back into its sticky depths.

Down. Down.

It's got me, he realized.

It's got me now.

20

"No!" Evan screamed aloud as the green gunk bubbled up to his neck.

Pulling him. Pulling him down.

"No!"

Try again. Up.

Try again.

Up. Up.

Yes!

Gripping the sides of the tub, he was moving upward, pulling himself, hoisting himself, straining with all of his strength.

Yes! Yes! He was beating it.

He was stronger than it was. One more tug and he would be free.

With a relieved sigh, he dropped over the side of the tub on to the cool basement floor.

And lay there, pressed against the damp concrete, waiting to catch his breath.

When he looked up, Sarabeth stood a few metres away, her head cocked to one side, her yellow eyes peering into his, an expression of supreme satisfaction on her dark feline face.

The next morning, after a fitful, restless sleep, Evan brought the pad of yellow lined paper and a marker to the breakfast table.

"Well, well," Kathryn greeted him, placing a bowl of shredded wheat in front of him, "you certainly look like something the cat dragged in!" She laughed, shaking her head.

"Don't mention *cat* to me," Evan muttered. He shoved the bowl of cereal aside and pointed to the pad in his hand.

"Don't let your cereal get soggy," Kathryn scolded, reaching to push the bowl back to him. "You get more of the vitamins that way. And it's good roughage."

"I don't care about your stupid roughage," Evan said moodily, knowing she couldn't hear him. He pointed to the pad again and then began to write, scribbling quickly in big black letters.

His writing caught her interest. She moved around the table and stood behind him, her eyes on the pad as he wrote his desperate message.

I HAVE A PROBLEM, he wrote. I NEED YOUR HELP. THE BATHTUB DOWNSTAIRS IS OVERFLOWING WITH GREEN MONSTER BLOOD AND I CAN'T STOP IT.

He put down the marker and held the pad up close to her face.

Looking up at her from the chair, seeing her

pale face in the morning sunlight as she leaned over him in her grey flannel dressing gown, Kathryn suddenly looked very old to him. Only her eyes, those vibrant, blue eyes running quickly over his words, seemed youthful and alive.

Her lips were pursed tightly in concentration as she read what he had written. Then, as Evan stared eagerly up at her, her mouth spread into a wide smile. She tossed back her head and laughed.

Completely bewildered by her reaction, Evan slid his chair back and jumped up. She rested a hand on his shoulder and gave him a playful shove.

"Don't kid an old woman!" she exclaimed, shaking her head. She turned and headed back to her side of the table. "I thought you were serious. I guess you're not like your father at all. He never played any dumb jokes or tricks. Chicken was always such a serious boy."

"I don't care about Chicken!" Evan shouted, losing control, and tossed the pad angrily on to the breakfast table.

His aunt burst out laughing. She didn't seem to notice that Evan was glaring at her in frustration, his hands tightened into fists at his sides.

"Monster Blood! What an imagination!" She wiped tears of laughter from her eyes with her fingers. Then suddenly, her expression turned serious. She grabbed his earlobe and squeezed it.

369

"I warned you," she whispered. "I warned you to be careful."

"Ow!"

When he cried out in pain, she let go of his ear, her eyes glowing like blue jewels.

I've got to get out of here, Evan thought, rubbing his tender earlobe. He turned and strode quickly from the kitchen and up to his room.

I knew she wouldn't be any help, he thought bitterly.

She's just a crazy old lady.

I should pull her down to the basement and show her the disgusting stuff, he thought, angrily tossing the clothes he had worn yesterday on to the floor.

But what's the point? She'd probably laugh at that, too.

She isn't going to help me.

He had only one person he could rely on, he knew.

Andy.

He called her, punching in her number with trembling fingers.

"Hi. You're right," he said, not giving her a chance to say anything. "We have to take the stuff back to the store."

"*If* we can carry it," Andy replied, sounding worried. "That hunk of Monster Blood you gave me – it outgrew the coffee can. I put it in my parents' ice bucket, but it's outgrowing that."

"How about a plastic rubbish bag?" Evan suggested. "You know. One of the really big lawn bags? We can probably carry it in a couple of those."

"It's worth a try," Andy said. "This stuff is so disgusting. It's making all these sick noises, and it's really sticky."

"Tell me about it," Evan replied gloomily, remembering the night before. "I took a *swim* in it."

"Huh? You can explain later," she said impatiently. "The toy store opens at ten, I think. I can meet you on the corner in twenty minutes."

"Good deal." Evan hung up the phone and headed to the garage to get a plastic lawn bag.

Andy showed up with her plastic bag wrapped around the handlebars of her BMX bike. Once again, Evan had to go along beside her on foot. His plastic bag was bulging and so heavy he had to drag it over the pavement. He couldn't lift it.

"The tub was nearly full to the top," he told Andy, groaning as he struggled to pull the bag over the kerb. "I'm afraid it's going to burst out of this bag."

"Only two streets to go," she said, trying to sound reassuring. A car rolled by slowly. The driver, a teenager with long black hair, stuck his head out the window, grinning. "What's in the bag? A dead body?"

"Just rubbish," Evan told him.

"That's for sure," Andy muttered as the car rolled away.

Several people stopped to stare at them as they entered town. "Hi, Mrs Winslow," Andy called to a friend of her mother's.

Mrs Winslow waved, then gave Andy a curious stare and headed into the grocery store.

Andy climbed off her bike and walked it. Evan continued to drag his bulging bag behind him.

They made their way to the next street, then started to cross over to the toy store.

But they both stopped short in the middle of the street.

And gaped in shock.

The door and window of the store were boarded up. A small hand-printed sign tacked to the top of the door read: OUT OF BUSINESS.

Desperate to get rid of the disgusting contents of the rubbish bags, Evan pounded on the door anyway.

"Come on – somebody! Somebody, open up!"

No reply.

He pounded with both fists.

Silence.

Finally, Andy had to pull him away.

"The store is closed," a young woman called from across the street. "It closed a few days ago. See? It's all boarded up and everything."

"Very helpful," Evan muttered under his breath. He slammed his hand angrily against the door.

"Evan – stop. You'll hurt yourself," Andy warned.

"Now what?" Evan demanded. "Got any more fantastic ideas, Andy?"

She shrugged. "It's your turn to come up with something brilliant."

Evan sighed miserably. "Maybe I could give it to Kathryn and tell her it's beef. Then she'd chop it up with that knife she's always carrying around."

"I don't think you're thinking too clearly right now," Andy said, putting a sympathetic hand on his shoulder.

They both stared down at the rubbish bags. They appeared to be moving – expanding and contracting, as if the green globs inside were *breathing*!

"Let's go back to Kathryn's," Evan said, his voice trembling. "Maybe we'll think of something on the way."

Somehow they managed to drag the Monster Blood back to Kathryn's house. The sun was high in the sky. As they headed to the garden, Evan was drenched with sweat. His arms ached. His head throbbed.

"Now what?" he asked weakly, letting go of the bulging lawn bag.

Andy leaned her bike against the side of the garage. She pointed to the big aluminium rubbish bin next to the garage door. "How about that? It looks pretty sturdy." She walked over to it to investigate. "And look – the lid clamps down."

"OK," Evan agreed, wiping his forehead with the sleeve of his T-shirt.

Andy pulled off the lid of the big bin. Then she

dumped in the contents of her bag. It hit the bottom with a sick, squishy sound. Then she hurried to help Evan.

"It's so heavy," Evan groaned, struggling to pull the bag up.

"We can do it," Andy insisted.

Working together, they managed to slide the Monster Blood from the plastic bag. It rolled out like a tidal wave, sloshing noisily against the sides of the bin, raising up as if trying to escape.

With a loud sigh of relief, Evan slammed the metal lid down on top of it and clamped the handles down.

"Whoa!" Andy cried.

They both stared at the bin for a long moment, as if expecting it to explode or burst apart. "Now what?" Evan asked, his features tight with fear.

Before Andy could reply, they saw Kathryn step out of the kitchen door. Her eyes searched the garden until she spotted them. "Evan – good news!" she called.

Glancing back at the rubbish bin, Evan and Andy came hurrying over. Kathryn was holding a piece of paper in her hand. A letter.

"Your mother is coming to pick you up this afternoon," Kathryn said, a wide smile on her face.

I think Kathryn is glad to get rid of me, was Evan's first thought.

And then, dismissing that thought, he leaped up and whooped for joy. It was the best news he'd ever received.

"I'm outta here!" he exclaimed after his aunt had returned to the house. "I'm outta here! I can't wait!"

Andy didn't appear to share his joy. "You're leaving your aunt a nice little surprise over there," she said, pointing to the rubbish bin.

"I don't care! I'm outta here!" Evan repeated, raising his hand for Andy to slap him a high five.

She didn't cooperate. "Don't you think we have to tell someone about the Monster Blood? Or do something about it – before you leave?"

But Evan was too excited to think about that now. "Hey, Trigger!" he called, running to the dog's pen at the back of the garden. "Trigger – we're going home, boy!"

Evan pulled open the gate – and gasped.

"Trigger!"

The dog that came bounding towards him *looked* like Trigger. But the cocker spaniel was the size of a pony! He had *doubled* in size since the day before!

"No!" Evan had to hit the ground as Trigger excitedly tried to jump on him. "Hey – wait!"

Before Evan could get up, Trigger began barking ferociously. The huge dog was already past the gate and thundering across the garden towards the street.

"I don't believe it!" Andy cried, raising her hands to her face, staring in shock as the enormous creature bounded around the side of the house and out of sight. "He's so – big!"

"We've got to stop him! He might hurt someone!" Evan cried.

"Trigger! Trigger – come back!" Still off balance, Evan started to run, calling frantically. But he stumbled over Andy's bike and fell on to the rubbish bin.

"No!" Andy shrieked, looking on helplessly as the metal bin toppled over, with Evan sprawled on top of it. The bin hit the driveway with a loud *clang*.

The lid popped off and rolled away.

The green gunk poured out.

It oozed away from the bin, then stopped and appeared to stand up. Quivering, making loud sucking sounds, it righted itself, pulling itself up tall.

As the two kids stared in silent horror, the quivering green mass appeared to come to life, like a newly born creature pulling itself up, stretching, looking around.

Then, with a loud sucking sound, it arched towards Evan, who was still sprawled on the toppled bin.

"Get up, Evan!" Andy cried. "Get up! It's going to roll right over you!"

"Noooooo!"

Evan uttered an animal cry, a sound he had never made before – and rolled away as the quivering green ball bounced towards him.

"Run, Evan!" Andy screamed. She grabbed his hand and pulled him to his feet. "It's alive!" she cried. "Run!"

The Monster Blood heaved itself against the garage wall. It seemed to stick there for a brief second. Then it peeled off and came bouncing towards them with surprising speed.

"Help! Help!"

"Somebody – please – *help*!"

Screaming at the top of their lungs, Evan and Andy took off. Scrambling as fast as he could, his legs weak and rubbery from fear, Evan followed Andy down the driveway towards the front garden.

"Help! Oh, please! Help us!"

Evan's voice was hoarse from screaming. His heart thudded in his chest. His temples throbbed.

He turned and saw that the Monster Blood was right behind them, picking up speed as it bounced across the garden, making disgusting squishing noises with each bounce.

Plop. Plop. Plop.

A robin, pulling at a worm in the grass, didn't look up in time. The trembling green mass rolled over it.

"Oh!" Evan moaned, turning back to see the bird sucked into the green ball. Its wings flapping frantically, the bird uttered a final cry, then disappeared inside.

Plop. Plop. Plop.

The Monster Blood changed direction, still bouncing and quivering and leaving white stains on the grass like enormous round footsteps.

"It's alive!" Andy screamed, her hands pressed against her cheeks. "Oh, my God – it's *alive!*"

"What can we do? What can we do?" Evan didn't recognize his own terrified voice.

"It's catching up!" Andy screamed, pulling him by the hand. "Run!"

Gasping loudly, they made their way to the front of the house.

"Hey – what's happening?" a voice called.

"Huh?"

Startled by the voice, Evan stopped short. He

looked to the pavement to see the Beymer twins, matching grins on their beefy faces.

"My favourite punching bag," one of them said to Evan. He raised his fist menacingly.

They took a few steps towards Evan and Andy. Then their grins faded and their mouths dropped open in horror as the gigantic green mass appeared, heading down the drive, rolling as fast as a bicycle.

"Look out!" Evan screamed.

"Run!" Andy cried.

But the two brothers were too startled to move.

Their eyes bulging with fear, they threw their hands up as if trying to shield themselves.

Plop. Plop. Plop.

The enormous ball of Monster Blood picked up speed as it bounced forward. Evan shut his eyes as it hit the twins with a deafening *smack*.

"Ow!"

"No!"

Both brothers cried out, flailing their arms, struggling to pull themselves free.

"Help us! Please – help us!"

Their bodies twisted and writhed as they struggled.

But they were stuck tight. The green gunk oozed over them, covering them completely.

Then it pulled them inside with a loud sucking *pop*.

Andy shielded her eyes. "Sick," she muttered. "Oooh. Sick."

Evan gasped in helpless horror as the Beymer brothers finally stopped struggling.

Their arms went limp. Their faces disappeared into the quivering gunk.

The sucking sounds grew louder as the two boys were pulled deeper and deeper inside. Then the Monster Blood bounced high, turned, and started back up the drive.

Andy and Evan froze, unsure of which way to head.

"Split up!" Evan cried. "It can't go after us both!"

Andy returned his frightened stare. She opened her mouth, but no sound came out.

"Split up! Split up!" Evan repeated shrilly.

"But—" Andy started.

Before she could say anything, the front door of the house burst open, and Kathryn stepped out on to the porch.

"Hey – what are you kids doing? What's *that*?" she cried, gripping the screen door, her eyes filling with horror.

Picking up speed, the giant ball bounded towards the porch.

Kathryn tossed up her hands in fright. She stood frozen for a long moment, as if trying to make sense of what she was seeing. Then, leaving the front door wide open, she spun around and fled into the house.

Plop. Plop. Plop.

The Monster Blood hesitated at the front porch.

It bounced in place once, twice, three times, as if considering what to do next.

Evan and Andy gaped in horror from across the lawn, trying to catch their breath.

A wave of nausea swept over Evan as he saw the Beymer twins, still visible deep within the quivering glob, faceless prisoners bouncing inside it.

Then suddenly, the Monster Blood bounced high and hurtled up the stairs of the porch.

"No!" Evan screamed as it squeezed through the open doorway and disappeared into the house.

From the middle of the garden, Andy and Evan heard Kathryn's bloodcurdling scream.

"It's got Aunt Kathryn," Evan said weakly.

Evan reached the house first. He had run so fast, his lungs felt as if they were about to burst.

"What are you going to do?" Andy called, following close behind.

"I don't know," Evan replied. He grabbed on to the screen door and propelled himself into the house.

"Aunt Kathryn!" Evan screamed, bursting into the living room.

The enormous glob filled the centre of the small room. The Beymer twins were outlined in its side as it bounced and quivered, oozing over the carpet, leaving its sticky footprints in its path.

It took Evan a few seconds to see his aunt. The bouncing hunk of Monster Blood had backed her against the fireplace.

"Aunt Kathryn – run!" Evan cried.

But even he could see that she had nowhere to run.

"Get out of here, kids!" Kathryn cried, her voice shrill and trembling, suddenly sounding very old.

"But, Aunt Kathryn—"

"Get out of here – now!" the old woman insisted, her black hair wild about her head, her eyes, those blue, penetrating eyes, staring hard at the green glob as if willing it away.

Evan turned to Andy, uncertain of what to do.

Andy's hands tugged at the sides of her hair, her eyes wide with growing fear as the seething green glob made its way steadily closer to Evan's aunt.

"Get out!" Kathryn repeated shrilly. "Save your lives! I made this thing! Now I must die for it!"

Evan gasped.

Had he heard correctly?

What had his aunt just said?

The words repeated in his mind, clear now, so clear – and so frightening.

"I made this thing. Now I must die for it."

"No!"

Gaping in horror, as the sickening glob of Monster Blood pushed towards his aunt, Evan felt the room tilt and begin to spin. He gripped the back of Kathryn's armchair as pictures flooded his mind.

He saw the strange bone pendant Kathryn always wore around her neck.

The mysterious books that lined the walls of his bedroom.

Sarabeth, the black cat with the glowing yellow eyes.

The black shawl Kathryn always wrapped around her shoulders in the evening.

"I made this thing. Now I must die for it."

Evan saw it all now, and it began to come clear to him.

Evan pictured the day he and Andy brought home the can of Monster Blood from the toy store. Kathryn had insisted on seeing it.

On studying it.

On touching it.

He remembered the way she rolled the can around in her hands, examining it so carefully. Moving her lips silently as she read the label.

What had she been doing? What had she been saying?

A thought flashed into Evan's mind.

Had she been casting a spell on the can?

A spell to make the Monster Blood grow? A spell to terrify Evan?

But why? She didn't even know Evan.

Why did she want to frighten him? To . . . *kill* him?

"Be careful," she had called to him after handing the blue can back. "Be careful."

It was a real warning.

A warning against her spell.

"You did this!" Evan shouted in a voice he didn't recognize. The words burst out of him. He had no control over them.

"You did this! You cast a spell!" he repeated, pointing an accusing finger at his aunt.

He saw her blue eyes shimmer as they read the expression on his face. Then her eyes filled with tears, tears that overflowed on to her pale cheeks.

"No!" she cried. "No!"

"You did something to the can! You did this, Aunt Kathryn!"

"No!" she cried, shouting over the sickening grunts and *plop*s of the mountainous ball that nearly hid her from view.

"No!" Kathryn cried, her back pressed tightly against the mantelpiece. "I didn't do it! *She* did!"

And she pointed an accusing finger at Andy.

26

Andy?

Was Aunt Kathryn accusing *Andy*?

Evan spun around to confront Andy.

But Andy turned, too.

And Evan realized immediately that his aunt wasn't pointing at Andy. She was pointing past Andy to Sarabeth.

Standing in the doorway to the living room, the black cat hissed and arched her back, her yellow eyes flaring at Kathryn.

"She did it! She's the one!" Kathryn declared, pointing frantically.

The enormous glob of green Monster Blood bounced back, retreated a step, as if stung by Kathryn's words. Shadows shifted inside the glob as it quivered, catching the light filtering in through the living room window.

Evan stared at the cat, then turned his eyes to Andy. She shrugged, her face frozen in horror and bewilderment.

Aunt Kathryn is crazy, Evan thought sadly.

She's totally lost it.

She isn't making any sense.

None of this makes sense.

"She's the one!" Kathryn repeated.

The cat hissed in response.

The glob bounced in place, carrying the unmoving Beymer brothers inside.

"Oh – look!" Evan cried to Andy as the black cat suddenly raised up on its hind legs.

Andy gasped and squeezed Evan's arm. Her hand was as cold as ice.

Still hissing, the cat grew like a shadow against the wall. It raised its claws, swiping the air. Its eyes closed, and it became consumed in darkness.

No one moved.

The only sounds Evan could hear were the bubbling of the green glob and the pounding of his own heart.

All eyes were on the cat as it rose up, stretched, and grew. And as it grew, it changed its shape.

Became human.

With shadowy arms and legs in the eerie darkness.

And then the shadow stepped away from the darkness.

And Sarabeth was now a young woman with fiery red hair and pale skin and yellow eyes, the same yellow cat eyes that had haunted Evan since he'd arrived. The young woman was dressed in a swirling black gown down to her ankles.

She stood blocking the doorway, staring accusingly at Kathryn.

"You see? She's the one," Kathryn said, quietly now. And the next words were intended only for Sarabeth: "Your spell over me is broken. I will do no more work for you."

Sarabeth tossed her red hair behind a black-cloaked shoulder and laughed. "I'll decide what you will do, Kathryn."

"No," Kathryn insisted. "For twenty years, you have used me, Sarabeth. For twenty years you have imprisoned me here, held me in your spell. But now I will use this Monster Blood to escape."

Sarabeth laughed again. "There is no escape, fool. All of you must die now. *All* of you."

"All of you must die," Sarabeth repeated. Her smile revealed that she enjoyed saying those words.

Kathryn turned to Evan, her eyes reflecting her fear. "Twenty years ago, I thought she was my friend. I was all alone here. I thought I could trust her. But she cast a spell on me. And then another. Her dark magic made me deaf. She refused to let me lip-read or learn to sign. That was one way she kept me her prisoner."

"But, Aunt Kathryn—" Evan started.

She raised a finger to her lips to silence him.

"Sarabeth forced me to cast the spell on the can of Monster Blood. She had warned me that I was allowed no guests, you see. I was her slave. Her personal servant for all these years. She wanted me all to herself, to do her evil bidding.

"When you arrived," Kathryn continued, her back still pressed against the fireplace mantel, "she first decided to scare you away. But that was impossible. You had nowhere to go. Then she became desperate to get you out of the way. She was terrified that you would learn her secret, that you would somehow free me of her spell. So Sarabeth decided that you had to die."

Kathryn's eyes fell. She sighed. "I'm so sorry, Evan. I had no choice, no will of my own." She turned her eyes to Sarabeth. "But no more. No more. No more. As I plunge myself into this ghastly creation, Sarabeth, I will end your spell. I will end your hold over me."

"The children will still die," Sarabeth said quietly, coldly.

"What?" Kathryn's eyes filled with fury. "I will be gone, Sarabeth. You can let the children go. You have no reason to do them harm."

"They know too much," Sarabeth replied softly, crossing her slender arms in front of her, her yellow eyes aglow.

"We've got to get out of here," Evan whispered to Andy, staring at the seething green glob.

"But how?" Andy whispered back. "Sarabeth is blocking the doorway."

Evan's eyes darted around the small room, searching for an escape route.

Nothing.

Sarabeth raised one hand and drew it towards her slowly, as if summoning the green glob.

It quivered once, twice, then moved obediently in the direction of her hand.

"No! Sarabeth – stop!" Kathryn pleaded.

Ignoring Kathryn, Sarabeth gestured with her hand again.

The green gunk bubbled and rolled forward.

"Kill the children," Sarabeth commanded.

The enormous glob picked up speed as it rolled across the carpet towards Evan and Andy.

"Let's rush the door," Evan suggested to Andy, as they backed up away from the rolling Monster Blood.

"She'll never let us past," Andy cried.

"Kill the children!" Sarabeth repeated, raising both hands high above her head.

"Maybe one of us can get by her!" Evan cried.

"It's too late!" Andy shrieked.

The bouncing, pulsating, green glob was just a few metres away.

"We – we're going to be sucked in!" Evan screamed.

"Kill the children!" Sarabeth screamed triumphantly.

The glob rolled forward.

Evan sighed, feeling all hope sink. Frozen in place, he felt as if he weighed a hundred stone.

Andy grabbed his hand.

They both closed their eyes and held their breath, and waited for the impact.

To their surprise, the Monster Blood emitted a deafening roar.

"Huh?"

Evan opened his eyes. Andy, he saw, was staring at the doorway, beyond Sarabeth.

The Monster Blood hadn't roared.

"Trigger!" Evan cried.

The huge dog bounded into the doorway, its deafening bark echoing off the low ceiling.

Sarabeth tried to get out of the dog's way. But she was too late.

Thrilled to see Evan, Trigger enthusiastically

leaped at Sarabeth – and pushed her from behind.

Under the weight of the gigantic paws, Sarabeth staggered forward . . . forward . . . forward – raising her hands as she collided with the Monster Blood.

There was a wet *smack* as Sarabeth hit the surface of the green glob.

Then loud, disgusting sucking noises.

Her hands hit first. They disappeared quickly. And then Sarabeth was in up to her elbows.

And then the glob seemed to give a hard tug, and her body hit the surface. Then her face was pulled in, covered over.

Sarabeth never uttered a sound as she was pulled inside.

Whimpering with joy, completely unaware of what he had done, the dog loped into the room and headed for Evan.

"Down, boy! Down!" Evan cried, as Trigger happily leaped at him.

And as the dog jumped, he began to shrink.

"Trigger!" Evan called in astonishment, reaching out to hold the dog.

Trigger didn't seem to notice that he was changing. He licked Evan's face as Evan held on tightly.

In seconds, Trigger was back to normal cocker spaniel size.

"Look – the glob is shrinking, too!" Andy cried, squeezing Evan's shoulder.

Evan turned to see that the green glob was rapidly growing smaller.

As it shrunk, the Beymer brothers fell to the floor.

They didn't move. They lay face down in a crumpled heap. Their open eyes stared lifelessly. They didn't appear to be breathing.

Then one blinked. The other blinked.

Their mouths opened and closed.

"Ohhh." One of them uttered a long, low groan.

Then, pulling themselves up slowly, they both looked around the room, dazed.

The trapped robin had also fallen to the floor. Chirping furiously, it flapped its wings wildly and fluttered about the room in a panic – until it found the open living room window and sailed out.

Andy held on to Evan as they stared at the Monster Blood, expecting Sarabeth to reappear, too.

But Sarabeth was gone.

Vanished.

The Monster Blood, shrunk to its original size, lay lifeless, inert, a dull green spot on the carpet, no bigger than a tennis ball.

The Beymer brothers stood up uncertainly, their eyes still reflecting terror and confusion.

They stretched as if testing their arms and legs, seeing if their muscles still worked. Then they scrambled out of the house, slamming the screen door behind them.

"It's over," Kathryn said softly, moving forward to put an arm around Evan and Andy.

"Sarabeth is gone," Evan said, holding Trigger tightly in his arms, still staring at the tiny wedge of Monster Blood on the floor.

"And I can hear!" Kathryn said jubilantly, hugging them both. "Sarabeth *and* her spells are gone for good."

But as she said this, the screen door swung open and a shadowy figure stepped into the living room doorway.

29

"Mom!" Evan cried.

He set down Trigger and hurried to greet her, throwing his arms around her in a tight hug.

"What on earth is going on here?" Mrs Ross asked. "Why did those two boys come bursting out like that? They looked scared to *death*!"

"It – it's a little hard to explain," Evan told her. "I'm so glad to see you!"

Trigger was glad, too. When he finally had finished jumping up and down and whimpering, Kathryn led Evan's mom to the kitchen. "I'll make some tea," she said. "I have a rather long story to tell you."

"I hope it isn't *too* long," Mrs Ross said, glancing back questioningly at Evan. "We have a four o'clock plane to catch."

"Mom, I think you'll find this story interesting," Evan said, flashing Andy an amused look.

The two women disappeared into the kitchen.

Andy and Evan dropped down wearily on to the sofa.

"I guess you're going for ever," Andy said. "I mean, to Atlanta and everything—"

"I'd like to . . . uh . . . write to you," Evan said, suddenly feeling awkward.

"Yeah. Good," Andy replied, brightening. "And my dad has a phone credit card. Maybe I could get the number and . . . you know . . . call you."

"Yeah. Great," Evan said.

"Could I ask one small favour?" Andy asked.

"Yeah. Sure," Evan replied, curious.

"Well, it's going to sound strange," Andy said reluctantly. "But can I . . . uh . . . can I have the little bit of Monster Blood that's left? You know. Sort of as a memento or something?"

"Sure. OK with me," Evan said.

They both turned their eyes to where it had come to rest on the carpet.

"Hey—" Andy cried in surprise.

It was gone.

BEHIND THE SCREAMS

MONSTER BLOOD

CONTENTS

Q & A with R.L. Stine

Fright Gallery: Monster Blood

Recipe for Monster Blood Punch

Can YOU Save the World
from Monster Blood?

Bonus material
written and compiled
by Matthew D. Payne

Q & A with R.L. Stine

What's the creepiest toy you had as a child? Was it creepier than Monster Blood?

R.L. Stine (RLS): *I had a toy skeleton – the kind you are supposed to put together. But I never put it together because I thought the bones were real. I found out years later that they were plastic!*

Do you think you would be tempted to eat Monster Blood?

RLS: *Only if it tasted like banana cream pie.*

If so, what would you do once you were a giant?

RLS: *Eat the world's biggest banana cream pie.*

Speaking of huge (as in huge success!), Goosebumps has sold hundreds of millions of books worldwide. When did you first know that Goosebumps was a success? How did you celebrate?

RLS: *I was in my hometown of Columbus, Ohio, driving to a bookstore for a book signing. I remember I was stuck in a huge traffic jam, and I was really worried I would be late and growing more and more annoyed at all the traffic. When we finally neared the bookstore, I realized that the traffic jam was caused by all the people who were coming to see me! I celebrated by signing hundreds of books!*

What's the weirdest fan letter you've ever received?

RLS: *It's the weirdest and also my favourite. Here goes: "Dear R.L. Stine: I have read 40 of your books, and I think they are really boring."*

Monster Blood returns in the all-new Goosebumps HorrorLand ❸: *Monster Blood for Breakfast!* Could you reveal some hints about other villains who might be returning?

RLS: *You just can't keep a Goosebumps villain down. Don't be surprised if we get another visit from a certain mask . . . you know the one I mean, right?*

Fright Gallery: Monster Blood

FIRST APPEARANCE *Monster Blood*

OTHER APPEARANCES *Monster Blood II, III* and *IV*

ORIGINS Some say Monster Blood is a harmless toy from WAGNER'S NOVELTIES AND SUNDRIES cursed by the wicked cat Sarabeth. Others say Monster Blood is a secret laboratory experiment gone bad.

SPECIAL POWERS Monster Blood grows extremely fast – doubling in size every day. Monster Blood has a strong pull – putting just one finger in this angry glob is enough to cause your doom.

ODD SIDE EFFECTS By eating Monster Blood, even the smallest fry can grow extra, extra large.

WEAKNESSES Monster Blood doesn't last for ever. Check Monster Blood cans for an expiration date!

LIVING OR DEAD? Dead

FAVOURITE PHRASE Although Monster Blood does not talk, it's known to make horrible sucking and slurping sounds.

HOBBIES & INTERESTS Collecting . . . EVERYTHING IN ITS PATH!!!

LAST SEEN Goosebumps HorrorLand ❸: *Monster Blood for Breakfast!*

SPLAT STATS

STRENGTH	●	●	●	●	●	●	●	●	●
INTELLIGENCE	●	●							
SPEED	●	●	●	●	●				
ATTACK SKILLS	●	●	●	●	●	●			
HUMOUR	●	●	●						
EVIL	●	●	●	●	●	●	●		

Recipe for Monster Blood Punch

When you're dying of thirst, nothing quite hits the spot like Monster Blood! If fresh Monster Blood isn't sold in your neighbourhood (and we hope it's not), then try this tasty substitute.

Makes 4 Servings

Ingredients:

1 Package Lime Jelly
2 Cups White Grape Juice
Green Food Colouring

Preparation:

Prepare jelly as instructed on box.

When jelly is set, take a fork and squish it into tiny pieces.

In a medium-sized punch bowl, combine jelly and grape juice and mix well.

Add a few drops of green food colouring until the mixture resembles fresh Monster Blood.

Spoon mixture into cups, slurp and enjoy.

Although Monster Blood is usually green, don't be afraid to try new colour combinations: green jelly with cranberry juice, yellow jelly with apple juice, different food colouring, etc.

Warning: If you hear strange gurgling noises coming from the punch bowl ... RUN FOR YOUR LIFE!

Can YOU Save the World From MONSTER BLOOD?

Nobody wants Monster Blood oozing around their neighbourhood, but it can strike anywhere, anytime, anyplace. Will you be ready to save your neighbourhood from a Monster Blood attack? Take this Monster Blood quiz to find out.

1 If one of your friends finds a can of Monster Blood on a dusty shelf, you tell him/her to. . .

A OPEN IT!

B LEAVE IT ALONE!

C CALL SLAPPY THE DUMMY!

2 A TV news reporter describes a bucket of Monster Blood found on a nearby farm. You immediately rush to the scene and. . .

A Feed it to the cows and chickens and then start an interspecies animal war.

B Bury it using the farmer's tractor.

C Take it home and show your neighbours.

3 Your friend gets sucked into an especially large glob of Monster Blood. You. . .

A Jump in after him/her.

B Look around for a cat that might be cursing the Monster Blood.

C Take photos for your scrapbook.

4 Your friend dares you to eat Monster Blood. You. . .

A Pull out a fork and start chowing down.

B Tell your friend to GROW UP!

C Make your friend eat it instead.

5 A vat of Monster Blood is found on a rooftop. You. . .

A Tip it over on to the street.

B Have a helicopter lift it off and drop it into the nearest volcano.

C Charge your friends a tenner apiece to take a look.

6 Your cat leaves a small vial of Monster Blood on your doorstep. You. . .

A Scratch your cat behind the ears while thanking it.

B Demand that your cat change back into its human form.

C Immediately eat the Monster Blood.

7 A 6-foot-tall glob of Monster Blood is oozing down the street. You tell your friends to. . .

A Slow down the Monster Blood so you can get your camera.

B Run as fast as they can and as far as they can.

C Get some buckets to collect samples.

8 A kooky scientist moves in next door. Late one night, you spy him mixing a large vat of Monster Blood. You. . .

A Knock on his door and ask to take a closer look.

B Report him to the authorities.

C Go back to sleep.

9 Your friend mistakenly feeds Monster Blood to his pet fish. You. . .

A Release the fish back into the wild when he outgrows his tank.

B Find the source of the Monster Blood and destroy every last drop.

C Quickly feed the fish to your cat.

10 A neighbouring town has been taken over by Monster Blood. You hear it's coming towards your town, so the best thing to do would be to. . .

A Ask your parents if you can skip school to watch it pour into your town.

B Demand that your mayor build a 20-foot-tall protective wall around your town.

C Carry a bucket over to the next town so you can collect some of your very own Monster Blood.

Give yourself 1 point for each time you answered (B). Once you've counted all of your points, read below to see how you've rated!

0 – 2 Points: Your neighbourhood doesn't stand a chance. Better hope someone else can take care of the job!

3 – 6 Points: You need to brush up on your Monster Blood facts! If you're not careful this green glob just might outsmart you!

7 – 10 Points: You have some mighty fine Monster Blood skills. We hope you never need to use them!